Grandpa Gristle has a story to tell...

Snuggle up, bedbugs, and I'll tell you how I lost my ear.

I warn you, it's not a pretty tale. Losing your favorite ear, no matter how it happens, is never pretty.

The whole story, in fact, is no tea party for teddy bears. Oh, there's beauty, too, and plenty of it. But all the foul parts, the frightening parts, your dear mother would want me to skip over those.

Lucky for us, she's not listening.

Grandpa Gristle's BEDTIME TALES

HOW I LOST MY EAR

How I Lost My Ear
Copyright © 2018 by Adam Beck

All rights reserved. No part of this publication may be reproduced in any form without written permission from the author, except for the use of brief quotations in a book review or article.

Published by Bilingual Adventures
Website: bilingualadventures.com
Twitter: @bilingualbook

First Edition, 2018

ISBN 978-4-908629-03-7

For Keimi and Kian, who heard this story first. —AB

For Jo, Molly and Hannah. XXXXXX —SF

Contents

PART ONE 1
Benjamin Boyd 3
A New Nickname 8
A Mysterious Stranger 14
Ben's Dream 19
Grandma 23
The Golden Box 30
Mayor Olympus 36
The Abernathy Pumpkin Patch 43
Old Man Fibber's Story 48
Grizzly Woods 52
The Gingerbread Boy 56
Crabapple Cliff 59
PART TWO 67
The Birthday Party 69
The Monster 74
The Monster's Eye 82
The Dying Llama 86
The Dancing Bear 90
A Heartbroken Sigh 99

The Bloody Tutu	102
The Miracle Worker	107
One Last Song	114
143 Angry Llamas	119
Old Man Fibber and Carl	124
A Whack on the Nose	129
The Drumbeat Dies	134
Crabapples	137
Grandma's Hat	143
Wet Skin and Hair	150
Born in the Air	156
The Cricket	163
Near-Death Experience	172
Just a Dream?	177
Shish Kebab	187
Wonder Boy	194
The Picnic Basket	201
The Last Shootout	206
The Sheriff and His Deputy	212
Happy Hibernation	220
Heavy Breathing	224
Bear-Killer Boyd	230
The Big Mound	236

Delirious	*240*
One Split Second	*246*
BLAM!	*253*
A Ringing Burp	*259*
Red Leather Case	*265*
River of Tears	*271*
Thunder and Lightning	*277*
The Dark Belly	*284*
Sad as the Sky	*291*
Like Father, Like Son	*298*
PART THREE	*305*
A Scrumptious Day	*307*
The Marching Moose	*316*
New Evidence	*321*
Defiant Cry	*330*
Upside Down	*336*
A Wisp of Smoke	*344*
Final Formation	*357*
A Shining Example	*365*

Part One

Benjamin Boyd

Snuggle up, bedbugs, and I'll tell you how I lost my ear.

I warn you, it's not a pretty tale. Losing your favorite ear, no matter how it happens, is never pretty.

The whole story, in fact, is no tea party for teddy bears. Oh, there's beauty, too, and plenty of it. But all the foul parts, the frightening parts, your dear mother would want me to skip over those.

Lucky for us, she's not listening.

It all started with a boy named Benjamin Boyd.

Benjamin Boyd was walking home from school, his nose in another book, when a rosy glow caught the corner of one eye. The truth is, he nearly passed right by without a glance. If he had, the whole fate of Boony Point might have turned out far different.

Your Grandpa Gristle's left ear included.

It was a sunny afternoon in June, two days before his twelfth birthday, when he stopped short in front of the big window of the Olympus Music Shop.

His eyes bugged.

Sitting in a sunbeam, glittering like a great ruby, practically pulsing all on its own—

A pair of bongos.

He stood there gazing at the gleaming bongos for the longest time, his wire-rimmed glasses pressed against the shop window. He imagined how beautiful the sound of those bongos must be—especially compared to the battered old drum he had at home.

He was pasted to the window so long that Mayor Sackbutt, who ran the shop, finally noticed the small boy and poked out his big friendly face. There was a high tinkle from the bell over the door then the mayor was booming, "Butterfingers! Admiring my Giant Heart bongos? That marvelous instrument arrived from Bloat City just this morning!"

Mayor Sackbutt was loud in every way.

Startled, Ben dropped his book with a *thump*.

"What's that you're reading now, Butterfingers?"

Ben stooped for the book. His heavy school bag slid off his shoulder, nearly crunching his toes.

"*King Grub*," he said faintly, hoisting his things. His eyes were drawn right back to the ruby-red drum.

Mayor Sackbutt chuckled. "That's how I felt when I first laid eyes on them! They're the finest bongos made in this state!"

The jolly mayor stepped out on the sidewalk. He was dressed in an old lemon-colored suit three sizes too small and on the bow tie choking his throat was a drip of blueberry jam. But as always, his silver hair was gooped perfectly in place.

"Say, how's the tuba? I hope you're still practicing hard for the tryouts! They're just three weeks away, you know!"

Ben turned slowly. "Yes, well, about the tuba…"

"Butterfingers, what happened to your head?" Mayor Sackbutt had spied a big band-aid on Ben's forehead, peeking through his wild mop of blond curls.

"Oh, it's nothing… My football helmet… It got stuck on my head again."

"Yes, football can be a rough game."

Ben hated to fib, but he was too ashamed to tell Mayor Sackbutt the truth. It wasn't the football helmet that got stuck on his head, not this time. It was the tuba. And ever since his father pried it off, he had been afraid to go anywhere near it. It was now lurking in the locked cellar.

"Anyway," he added quickly, "I don't think the tuba is the best instrument for me."

"Oh, that's too bad," said Mayor Sackbutt. "We could use a new tuba player. Gusto is graduating, you know." He pulled a handkerchief from his breast pocket and wiped the sweat from his chins.

Ben's eyes stole back to the drum. "Actually, I have some bongos. Well, they're not really mine, they're my father's. But he said I could play them."

"The bongos, huh? We don't have any bongos in the Marching Moose."

Ben looked up at the mayor and made a hopeful smile. "Maybe then I'll have a better chance. I mean, since you don't already have any."

"We've never had any bongos, as far as I know. Ever since Mayor Olympus—" He stopped and swallowed hard. "Ever since Mayor Olympus founded the Marching Moose seventy-eight years ago."

The boy's smile dimmed. "Oh," he said. He turned for a last look at the Giant Heart bongos. "I guess I better be heading home."

"That doesn't mean we *can't* have any bongos in the band," the mayor added with a grin. "Mayor Olympus set the rule, and I've stuck by it ever since I took up the baton myself: All instruments have an equal opportunity to wear the antlers."

Ben beamed.

The mayor put a pudgy pink hand on Ben's shoulder. "Would you like to play them? They sound even more scrumptious than they look."

"Really?"

"Sure, son, come inside."

And just like that, the door tinkled open—to the most terrifying summer of our lives.

A New Nickname

BEN FOLLOWED MAYOR SACKBUTT into the Olympus Music Shop, the wooden floor creaking like old bones under their feet. The shop smelled of band music and children's spit. Hundreds of children had taken music lessons in this shop over the years, first from Mayor Olympus himself, then his nephew Mayor Lofty, then his grand nephew Mayor Cheeks, and finally his great-grand nephew Mayor Sackbutt.

Ben peered past Mayor Sackbutt's wide behind. For as far back as he could remember, the dim, musty shop had never changed. Except for the shiny new instruments, everything in the place looked ancient, like it had petrified from the time Mayor Olympus first opened it.

Mayor Sackbutt reached into the window. "Yes, they're a beauty!" he boomed. As he leaned in to take the leather strap of the gleaming drum, he caught sight of his face in the bell of a baritone. He eyed his hair with pleasure, then smoothed his silver sideburns.

Ben held his breath as the mayor turned back with the Giant Heart bongos.

"Why don't you sit over there, Butterfingers," said Mayor Sackbutt. "In one of those chairs under the picture."

Ben gazed up at the portrait on the wall—a huge portrait of Mayor Olympus, frozen forever at the age of twenty-eight. Held in a heavy gold frame, the black and white photograph showed the strapping legend of Boony Point in his Marching Moose uniform, from his glossy black boots to the tall rounded hat with the antlers sticking out the sides. His dark eyes sparkled kindly at the world from his handsome, chiseled face. His toothy grin beamed with courage and might. Even his hair, wavy as the sea, fell strongly to his shoulders.

Standing by his side was a moose, giving the same toothy grin. The moose had just three legs.

One of the mayor's hands was curled over the moose's neck; the other was holding a long white bone.

Every time he stepped into the shop, Ben would stare at the portrait in wonder: it was like a Greek god, and his crippled moose, had once walked Boony Point.

But then he shuddered, thinking how the picture had been taken only the day before Mayor Olympus—

"Have a seat, son."

Ben blinked, then set his things on the floor beside a wobbly wooden chair. He sat down, his legs dangling. Mayor Sackbutt squeezed into the other chair. It groaned under his weight.

"Here you go! Let's hear you play!"

Mayor Sackbutt smiled and gave the bongos to Ben. The silvery drum heads shimmered in the dull light. The polished red wood felt smooth and warm in his hands. They were heavier than his father's old birch bongos.

He spread his knees, then pinched the drum between them. His face lit up as he brought his hands in the air. The Giant Heart bongos began beating with life on the first strike, sounding out with a splendid *boom*—quickly followed by the jarring *crash* of the drum hitting the floor as it slipped between his knees.

Ben gasped.

"Don't you worry, Butterfingers," said the mayor, his thin lips in a tight smile. "These bongos are made of diamond mahogany. I don't expect a little tumble to the floor will do any damage."

He leaned over in his chair to retrieve the drum. The chair groaned again.

"Mayor Sackbutt, I'm so sorry—"

The mayor's chunky fingers were set to curl around the drum strap…when the front leg of his chair broke off like an old tooth. He pitched forward onto the floor.

"Mayor Sackbutt!" Ben jumped to his feet and gaped down at the beached mayor. "Mayor Sackbutt, are you all right?"

"I'm fine, Butterfingers," Mayor Sackbutt murmured. "I knew it was about time we got a few new chairs."

"Mayor Sackbutt, take my hand."

Ben was hardly strong enough to pull the plump mayor off the floor, but Mayor Sackbutt took the boy's small hand. "You're a good boy, Butterfingers," he said, grunting to his feet. "Why don't you see about the bongos? I'll get another chair."

The mayor rubbed his knee and limped to a desk in the corner. He settled gingerly in the chair by the desk, then took up a hand mirror and comb. After fussing a long while with his hair, he carried the chair over to Ben. Ben had already picked up the bongos from the floor, cleared away the broken chair, and read several pages in *King Grub*.

Mayor Sackbutt eased into the new chair. "Let's try it again," he breathed.

The good news is that this time Ben was careful to slip the drum strap over his head before putting the bongos between his knees.

The bad news is that a blind baboon could have played better.

Benjamin Boyd was a wonder of clumsiness: his hands flopped like fish tails; only one pinky showed signs of rhythm; even his poor eyes got crossed up. It's lucky he didn't sprain his wrist or break a thumb.

Still, the sound of the Giant Heart bongos was thrilling. It filled the small shop with a booming power that Ben imagined might lift the sagging roof right into the sky.

The sound was so marvelous, in fact, that Ben was convinced he could claim a spot in the marching band if he auditioned with the Giant Heart bongos. And once he was in the state champion Marching Moose, the town's pride and joy, he would be virtually guaranteed a new nickname—a name people would respect...a name people would admire, even...

Like Fire Hands! thought Ben, as his hands slapped at the drum. *Hello, Fire Hands! How are you, Fire Hands? Fire Hands, you look sharp in those antlers! Play the Giant Heart bongos for us, Fire—*

Then suddenly Ben paled at another thought, an awful thought. If some other kid bought these bongos first, he'd have no chance at all! Compared to the Giant Heart bongos, his father's bongos sounded like rusty bait buckets. He would be shown up in front of the whole town at the tryouts! He had to get them right away!

Ben quickly thanked Mayor Sackbutt and flew from the shop. He practically ran the whole way home to the Boyd Llama Farm. He begged his parents to buy the bongos, but they wavered. They had already paid good money for a tuba now stewing in the cellar. Ben pleaded, near tears, but his parents would only agree to think it over.

And the very next day, when Ben raced to the Olympus Music Shop after school to see the Giant Heart bongos in the shop window, his heart plunged to his penny loafers.

In the middle there, where the ruby-red bongos had been, was a mousy-brown bassoon.

The Giant Heart bongos were gone.

A Mysterious Stranger

NOW I KNOW YOU'RE ANXIOUS to hear what happened to those Giant Heart bongos. But before I can carry on with the story, you need to stop snickering every time I mention Mayor Sackbutt's name. Because it's not what you think. The mayor's nickname had nothing to do with his big saggy backside. He earned his nickname years before, when his far end was nowhere near the size it finally became.

In fact, the sackbutt is a musical instrument, an early sort of trombone. (Ask your mother if you don't believe me.) From the time he was a boy, Mayor Sackbutt was a sackbutt prodigy. By age thirteen, he was hailed the finest, not to mention the loudest, sackbutt player in the whole state. He even gave a recital that year at the governor's mansion in Bloat City.

So just stop that snickering.

Back then, everybody in Boony Point got a nickname, sooner or later. The town itself even had a nickname: "Nickname City." The tradition went back a long way, even before Mayor Olympus. Some people didn't much like the nicknames they were saddled with, like Butterfingers Boyd, and that's one reason Mayor Olympus was so revered. Changing a name was no easy matter, but Mayor Olympus stood as the shining example of that feat. And that's why the toes of his bronze statue out on Olympus Field began to gleam, from all the rubbing folks did as they whispered hopeful prayers for new nicknames of their own.

Ben rubbed those toes a lot too.

So you can imagine Ben's shock when he saw that the Giant Heart bongos had disappeared from the window of the

Olympus Music Shop, one of the buildings ringing Olympus Field in the heart of town. He had been waiting years for his twelfth birthday, when he would finally have the chance to try out for the Marching Moose. In those years he survived marching mishaps with other instruments before he made his attempt at the tuba. The worst of it, until then, was when he poked himself in the eye with an oboe. But after his father had to pull the tuba off his head, he was ready to give up and resign himself to being called Butterfingers. That's when his father dug out the old birch bongos, as a last resort, and Ben regained a bud of hope. And that hope had suddenly bloomed when he played the wonderful ruby-red drum...

Ben stood gaping at the spot where the Giant Heart bongos had glittered the day before. Desperate to think it was all his imagination, he blinked behind his glasses, hoping when he opened his eyes again the bassoon would be gone and the bongos would be back—

But no. That horrible bassoon was still there.

Ben wilted. Some other kid must have bought the Giant Heart bongos! He couldn't try out for the Marching Moose now! He would be the laughingstock of Boony Point!

He was set to head home, set to be Butterfingers forever, when his mind groped for one last scrap of hope...

When they fell to the floor yesterday, they got a little dusty, right? Mayor Sackbutt is probably just polishing them up! I bet he's sitting there at his desk right now with his handkerchief in one hand and the Giant Heart bongos in the other!

His heart thumping, Ben creaked open the door. The bell tinkled overhead as he stepped inside.

Yes, there was Mayor Sackbutt at his desk! With the handkerchief in one hand! And in the other hand he had... a jelly doughnut.

"Butterfingers! It's good to see you again so soon!" he boomed, his lime green suit glowing in the dim light. He waved Ben over with the doughnut. "How about a bite?"

"No, thank you, Mayor Sackbutt."

"It's still warm!"

"I'm not very hungry."

"Are you sure?"

Ben nodded.

Mayor Sackbutt shrugged and chomped. "It's blueberry, my favorite," he said, chewing and smacking. "The Olympus Bakery still uses the same recipe devised by Mayor Olympus, you know. Our tastebuds are blessed to have young Pudge over there, upholding the tradition of this remarkable doughnut."

He daintily wiped his mouth with the handkerchief, then sharked another bite.

Ben gulped a breath. "Mayor Sackbutt, about the bongos—"

"Yes, the Giant Heart bongos!" the mayor said, puffing powdered sugar. "What a gorgeous instrument! And the tone"—he shook his doughnut for emphasis—"the tone is *scrumptious*, wouldn't you agree?"

A blob of blueberry jam plopped onto the mayor's lap. He scooped at his pants with the handkerchief.

"Is it...I mean, are they...still here?" Ben asked in a small voice.

"What's that?" Mayor Sackbutt said.

"The Giant Heart bongos... I didn't see them in the window."

Mayor Sackbutt sucked thoughtfully on his handkerchief. "It's a puzzling thing," he said. "Only an hour ago a *mysterious stranger* came into the shop. I'd never seen him before, not in my entire life. I suppose that means he isn't from these parts."

Ben held his breath. A fly buzzed by.

"As it turns out," the mayor went on, shooing the fly with his handkerchief, "that *mysterious stranger* is a collector of fine bongos. Naturally, when he saw the Giant Heart bongos, he knew they were an exquisite instrument and would make an important addition to his collection."

Ben gave a shuddering sigh.

"Are you sure I can't interest you in a bite?" Mayor Sackbutt said. "It's very tasty."

"No, thank you, Mayor Sackbutt."

Ben turned. As he did, the portrait of Mayor Olympus caught his eye. Mayor Olympus was gazing straight at him. And suddenly, like a bolt of lightning in a dark sky, he was lit with the thought: *Maybe I can't play the Giant Heart bongos at the tryouts, but nobody else will be playing them, either. I still have three weeks. If I practice hard, maybe I have a chance after all...*

Then he plodded out the door and opened *King Grub* for the long walk home.

Ben's Dream

THE NEXT DAY WAS BEN'S BIRTHDAY. June eighth is your Grandpa Gristle's birthday too. (Don't you forget next time.) I was born on the very day that Benjamin Boyd turned twelve. I probably would have been born the night before, on June seventh, but Doc Sprinkle had trouble turning me loose. He was at our house half the night, and they say I nearly died before I saw the dawn. But Doc Sprinkle, that man was a miracle worker, and he finally tugged me out at daybreak.

It was my ears that had me stuck. Two big healthy ears on the sides of my head, sticking out like hub caps.

June eighth was also the first day of summer vacation for the children of Boony Point. Normally, Ben had to wake up pretty early for school, since the Boyd Llama Farm was some distance from town, but he was still happily asleep that morning.

King Grub was open and sprawled across his glasses, and one hand held a dying flashlight. He wore Marching Moose pajamas, with short sleeves, and was snuggled to his waist in a Marching Moose blanket. Besides the band-aid on his forehead, he had band-aids on both elbows and another peeking out across his belly button.

Of course, all children are clumsy little creatures when they're small and just starting to move through the world; they often stumble and drop things. Most children, though, slowly outgrow these clumsy ways. But Benjamin Boyd did not. And when he continued to stumble and drop things, long past the time other children had gone on to greater childhood embarrassments, he became branded with the nickname Butterfingers.

I suppose that's one reason he took to books like he did.

He was always absent in a book, lost in imaginary worlds where his ears wouldn't hear that name. In fact, he spent so much time reading, his family began to fret that he lived more in his imagination than he did in the real world.

And that's exactly where he was that morning: lost in imagination, lost in a dream…

He was striding across Olympus Field in a tall hat with moose antlers flaring from the sides. He had on a glittering brown jacket, matching pants with a stubby tail, and shiny black boots.

He was high-stepping in formation, a member of the Marching Moose. He was there in the back row with the other percussion, the gleaming ruby-red bongos around his neck. His hands were thumping smartly on the drum, booming along as the band blared the Boony Point anthem.

Leading the band was Mayor Sackbutt, jiggling in his tight uniform and moose hat. In one hand he pumped a silver baton; in the other he gripped a jelly doughnut.

The band marched past the steel water tower that loomed over the grassy-green field. The big head of a moose puffing on a trombone—the band's mascot—was painted on the side. By the water tower was the bronze statue of Mayor Olympus, shining in the sun.

Mayor Sackbutt blew on the silver whistle clenched between his teeth and the band instantly pulled up. They marched in place, knees high, playing for the figure of Mayor Olympus and the baby moose draped over his shoulders like an enormous scarf.

The music rose to a rousing end and the marching stopped cold. The final blast of the town anthem echoed in the air above Olympus Field.

Silence lingered…then Ben heard a sound. Low cries, like llamas bleating.

He saw Mayor Sackbutt waving him to the front with his baton. As the low cries continued, Ben went marching from the rear to join the mayor. His whole body tingled with excitement. He knew the mayor would now bestow his new nickname.

He saw Mayor Sackbutt's sweaty face. He saw the dark blueberry stains on his uniform. His heart thumped eagerly as the mayor spit the whistle from his mouth and grinned down at him.

"How about a bite?" Mayor Sackbutt boomed.

"Butterfingers!"

Ben stared at the doughnut in the mayor's hand.

"Butterfingers! Wake up, young man!"

It was half-eaten and dripping blueberry jam.

"Butterfingers! It's almost seven o'clock!"

He reached for the doughnut...

BANG-BANG-BANG!

The pounding on his door finally jarred Ben awake. He bolted up in bed. *King Grub* dropped into his lap. For a second he thought it was the doughnut.

Crabapples, Butterfingers! Crabapples!"

BANG-BANG-BANG!

Ben groaned, still groggy. He blinked behind his glasses, then gave a puzzled glance to the open window. Outside was a chorus of low cries.

"Butterfingers, I need my crabapples!"

BANG-BANG-BANG!

Ben swung his legs out for the floor. His feet got tangled in the blanket and he tumbled to his knees. The flashlight clattered across the room. The book cartwheeled toward the door.

He grunted, "I'm coming, Grandma."

Grandma

BEN KICKED AWAY THE BLANKET and wobbled to his feet. When he stooped to pick up *King Grub*, his nose wrinkled. A faint sour odor was drifting beneath the door.

"Butterfingers, what in the name of Johnny Appleseed are you doing in there?"

Ben opened the door and blinked down at his grandmother. Her bright green eyes blazed behind her thick glasses.

"How many times do I have to tell you? *While the dew is on the fruit!* That's when they're juicy gems! You dillydally away the morning and those sparkling drops of dew will be dried up by the time—"

Ben saw that Grandma's eyes had flashed to the book in his hand.

"I should have known!" she cried. "Lazing in your bed with a book! Lost again in your imagination! I've been warning your mother—imagination turns the mind to mush! The only thing that separates us from the beasts of this world is a firm mind with a hard grip on reality! A head full of porridge, young man, is at the mercy of brainless instinct!"

She went on without a breath.

"At this rate, you'll end up no better than Old Man Fibber. It was an overcooked imagination that led to his downfall, you know. And now his only friend in the world is that hideous Carl! I hear the two of them even take baths together!"

Ben gazed down at Grandma as she carried on about Old Man Fibber and Carl splashing around in a big white bathtub in their barn. Though Ben was short for his age, he was growing some lately and he was now a head taller than her. Grandma's small bony frame was wrapped in her yellow bathrobe; on her feet were her yellow slippers. In her left hand (with that mangled stub of a pinky finger) was the brown wicker picnic basket; in her right was the rolling pin that had pounded on his bedroom door. Her puckered mouth, working hard as ever on her lined face, glistened with pink gums; her false teeth bulged in the pocket of her bathrobe.

And on her head was the most beautiful set of bouncy blond curls this side of Bo Peep.

"What is it this time, Butterfingers? Another book about ogres?"

"No, Grandma."

"*Beastly Butts*, wasn't it?"

"Grandma, that was *Beastly Brutes*."

The old woman snorted.

Ben flourished the new book, eyes twinkling through his round glasses. "This one is called *King Grub!*"

"King *what*?"

"*King Grub*," he said more loudly. Grandma claimed to be hard of hearing, but Ben had come to suspect she only listened at her convenience. She could hear a compliment about her hair from miles away. "Grandma, it's an amazing story! You really should read it! It all starts with an old farmer who's plowing up his field when he spots something glittering in the ground. He looks closer and sees a little white grub, wriggling there in the dirt, with a tiny golden crown on its head—"

"Frankly, I'd prefer an amazing story about a grubby boy picking crabapples for his grandmother." As Grandma said this, her hand with the picnic basket went flashing out like a viper. Ben flinched and clunked the back of his head on the door frame. His grandmother seemed impossibly old, but he was always surprised at how fast she could move when she got the gumption.

"I'm not going to bite you, boy," Grandma said with a chuckle. She tapped the lump in her pocket with the rolling pin and made a gummy grin. "I don't have my teeth in yet."

Ben rubbed the back of his head.

"Anyway, a bite of boy would hardly be good for my hair. I need my crabapples for that."

Ben reached for the handle of the basket. It used to be that Grandma picked her own crabapples year round. After a mug of hot crabapple cider, she would change from her bathrobe into her yellow rain suit and charge out to Crabapple Cliff with the picnic basket in her hand. And until his legs turned to spaghetti, old Alf was there trotting by her side—though the little pug had always been skittish about stepping onto the cliff.

But now it was Ben's job to pick the crabapples in summer. The year before, Grandma had finally persuaded Ben's mother that he could do it during summer vacation. Aging grandmothers, she argued, shouldn't have to tromp miles in the summer heat to collect a basket of crabapples when there was a perfectly healthy grandson loitering in the house.

"Look at my curls!" Grandma rattled on, fluffing her hair and stirring up that sour odor. "Look how they shine! Your curls would shine too, if you had enough sense to eat crabapple pie. It's nearly a crime against nature what you and your mother do with the gorgeous blond hair I gave you. Just look at that shabby haystack on your head!"

Ben's tongue shuddered at the thought of Grandma's crabapple pie. He had tried it once, just once, when he was five, and the sour taste (not a speck of sugar in the whole thing) had stuck to him like a tick until he was almost six.

"You know what happens if you don't keep a healthy head of hair? Your hair falls out, that's what, just like those busybodies in the school cafeteria. When I had the misfortune of working there, Snooty Potts was shedding black hair like a Scottish terrier! That hair was everywhere! Hair in the meatloaf! Hair in the green beans! Hair in the banana cream pudding! Lordy, that was the hairiest pudding ever seen on this earth! The poor children were shaving it off with their butter knives! It was because of that pudding I quit, you know. Principal Prim told us all to start wearing hairnets. *Hairnets!*" She spat out the word like a bug. "How could I wear a hairnet? How could someone with curls like these even consider such a thing? It would be suicide for my scalp!"

Grandma gave her hair another fluff, bouncing the curls and gassing Ben.

As much as he hated to admit it, it was true, Ben thought. His grandmother had the most beautiful blond curls he'd ever seen, even gleaming golder than any princess in his books. But those ribbons... Why were those same faded yellow ribbons always tied in her hair?

"Snooty Potts wears a wig now, you know. I saw her at the Olympus Market last month. It wouldn't surprise me if she was bald as a watermelon, like your father. That's what comes from delinquent hair care."

Ben flashed on the black and white photo his father had shown him after the old bongos were retrieved from the attic. His father was a lean, happy-go-lucky student at Bloat City University back then. He had dark hair down to his shoulders, and the birch bongos were dangling around his neck.

"I warned your mother when she first brought him home to the farm. Oh, he had a fancy head of hair at the time. But he quickly turned up his nose at the piece of crabapple pie I offered. I warned her that day: 'Lorelai,' I said, 'he has a fancy head of hair now, but he'll be bald as a watermelon by the age of twenty-seven.'"

Ben did a fast calculation and winced at the thought of being bald as a watermelon in just fifteen years.

Grandma frowned. "Now stop lollygagging and get your boots on! I want the best fruit on that tree, Butterfingers! The kind *sweating* dew! But be on your guard for the wormy ones! If there's a hole, even a pinprick, err on the side of caution, young man. Remember, eighty-six for the pie and eleven for my cider! That's ninety-seven crabapples!"

"Grandma, I need to change."

"Then why are you still dawdling in the hallway?"

With that, she shuffled off toward the stairs.

Ben stood at the door, suddenly aware of the llamas again now that Grandma had stopped gabbing.

"Grandma..."

The old woman whirled. "I hear dew drying, Butterfingers!"

"The llamas... They sound upset today."

"It's Henry the Eighth," said Grandma. "It seems His Highness is sick. Your folks drove him into town to see Doc Sprinkle."

"Oh."

Grandma shook the rolling pin. "Now get your rear in top gear!" She turned and marched down the stairs.

Ben listened to the llamas' worried cries, wondering what was wrong with Henry the Eighth. He'd never been sick a day in his life.

When he stepped back into his room, his eyes boggled.

He now saw it across the room, across the stacks of books that rose waist-high from the floor. It was perched in the corner, on top of the small bookcase that had overflowed long ago. It was glowing in a ray of sunlight, like a treasure chest in a sunken ship.

It was a box, wrapped in gold paper and tied with a big red bow.

The Golden Box

HIS EYES FIXED ON THE GOLDEN BOX, Ben weaved past the tipsy piles of books. When he reached the corner, he set the picnic basket and *King Grub* on the bookcase.

On top of the box was a square white envelope with his name on it. Below his name his mother had written in a hurried hand:

> *Ben, Henry is sick. Went to see Doc Sprinkle. Will be back soon.*
> *Love,*
> *Mom*

Ben tore open the envelope, wincing when the flap nicked his finger. He sucked on the red paper cut for a moment, then pulled free a birthday card.

On the front was the face of the Marching Moose mascot, puffing on his trombone. The words being blown from the bell declared: YOU'RE 12 YEARS OLD TODAY! (The Olympus Gift Shop was the only store in the state that sold birthday cards like these.)

Ben made a small gasp. He looked back at the golden box. Could it be? But Mayor Sackbutt had told him that "a mysterious stranger" bought the Giant Heart bongos! Was the mayor just playing along with his parents' surprise? Had his parents gotten him the bongos after all?

He quickly opened the card to find a herd of moose in marching band uniforms, playing instruments and high-stepping in unison. The message from the front continued: TIME TO TOOT YOUR OWN HORN!

Below that his mother had written in her lovely cursive:

Happy Birthday, Ben! Practice hard for the tryouts!
We love you,
Mom, Dad, and Grandma

Ben's heart soared. He set the card by the box and tugged off the red ribbon. Without even the worry of another paper cut, he tore away the gold wrapping. He opened the box and dug through some white tissue paper.

The Giant Heart bongos! The beautiful Giant Heart—

He froze, eyes goggling. He blinked behind his glasses. The joy drained right from him, like a bathtub slurping dry.

These…these weren't the gleaming mahogany bongos from the Olympus Music Shop. They were his father's birch bongos, still the color of curdled cream, still pitted with tooth marks where a rat once gnawed at the wood.

"Butterfingers!" came a shout from downstairs. "Are you dressed?"

Ben stood there staring, dumbfounded.

"Butterfingers, can you hear me?"

"Coming, Grandma!"

Ben leaned in to inspect the old bongos more closely. He tapped them with a finger and heard the same dull, familiar sound.

"Your pants go on your legs!"

"I know, Grandma!"

He gaped at the old bongos for another moment, his mind a blank. Then he heaved a sigh heavier than any birthday boy on record and hurried to change into a pair of cut-off jeans and his favorite Mayor Olympus T-shirt. By the time he was knotting his boots, he heard a soft tapping sound from downstairs. He paused and listened as the noise grew louder.

What? Wait! That sounds like...like *bongos!*

Ben grabbed the picnic basket and bolted into the hall.

The drumming sound filled the house as he dashed toward the stairs.

Then he heard a burst of whooping laughter too.

Ben froze at the top step. Grandma was dancing there at the bottom of the staircase, drumming away and braying with delight.

Around her neck, dangling from the leather strap, were the Giant Heart bongos.

Ben's mouth worked hard, but no words came out.

"Happy birthday, Butterfingers!" Grandma sang, giving the bongos one last thump.

"But what...? Ben sputtered, pointing back toward his room. "But how...?"

"That was my gift to you," Grandma said, grinning with glee. "The prettiest humdinger of a practical joke yet. Last night, while you were all sound asleep, I tiptoed into your

parents' bedroom. The box was already wrapped, but it was easy enough to razor open to give you a sweet birthday switcheroo." She broke into more laughter. "The beauty of this one will be hard to beat, but don't underestimate my powers for mind-boggling pranks!"

"Grandma…" Ben growled under his breath. He started down the stairs. He was overjoyed that the Giant Heart bongos were his, but Grandma's latest practical joke made him simmer inside. Why couldn't she be a kindhearted old woman like other grandmothers? Why did she have to act like an obnoxious older (much older) sister?

"Give me my bongos, Grandma," he said.

Grandma slipped the drum strap carefully over her blond curls and held the bongos out to Ben. Her laughter trailed off and her eye suddenly had a tear. "Practice hard for those tryouts," she said.

Ben snatched the strap and pulled the drum from her hands. As he slid the strap over his head, a thrilling tingle went through him. He brushed past Grandma and headed to the front door with the picnic basket in his hand.

"Butterfingers, wait!" Grandma croaked. She disappeared through the kitchen door and returned with a silver canteen and something wrapped in a white napkin. Ben caught a tempting smell from across the room.

Grandma wrinkled her nose. "It's a gingerbread boy," she said, slipping the plump napkin and canteen into the picnic basket. "Your mother suffered another baking fit last night."

"Thanks, Grandma," Ben mumbled. Then he quickly pushed through the screen door and marched past Alf, sprawled there under the porch swing in his little Marching Moose sweater. Grandma's ancient pug looked up at Ben with one watery eye. The other eye continued peering down at a waddling green caterpillar.

"While the dew is on the fruit!" Grandma called after him, holding the screen door wide. "Don't you dillydally, Butter-fingers!"

Ben hurried down the dirt driveway for Route Z.

"And no wormy ones, you hear me! No wormy ones!"

Mayor Olympus

"Grandma," Ben continued to growl as he started up dusty Route Z for Crabapple Cliff. He grit his teeth at the thought of other practical jokes his grandmother had played on him over the years...

Like the time he was settling down in bed to read, but his flashlight wouldn't work. When he unscrewed the bottom to look inside, a frog leaped out and bounced off his forehead. He then made a mess of his room trying to catch it and put it outside.

Or the time he had that dream about treasure beneath the willow tree. Of course, most folks wouldn't start digging up their backyard just because of a dream. But Ben wanted to believe it so badly, he couldn't stop himself from grabbing a shovel. And it was only after he dug a deep hole that Grandma cheerfully confessed she had been whispering in his ear for over an hour while he slept: "treasure under the willow tree...treasure under the willow tree..."

"Someday," Ben vowed to himself, "I'll get Grandma back! I'll come up with the biggest humdinger of a practical joke yet! Something that will leave her sputtering! No, something that will leave her *speechless!* She'll stand there, her mouth wide open, but totally mute! No more gabbing! No more whooping! Just mute as a mushroom!"

Ben grinned, picturing his grandmother as a two-legged toadstool. His mood lifted, right along with the warm sun climbing in the sky. He didn't know how he would do it, but today he was twelve, and he was feeling older and stronger than yesterday.

With the picnic basket in his left hand, he began thumping the Giant Heart bongos with his right. He lifted his knees higher and imagined himself in a Marching Moose uniform, strutting across Olympus Field.

It was a long walk from the Boyd Llama Farm to Crabapple Cliff. But Route Z was too rocky to ride a bicycle. And a car could only make it as far as the edge of Grizzly Woods. From there, the forest had to be hiked to finally reach the cliff.

Ben smiled at the sound of the Giant Heart bongos ringing out across the countryside. The tall sunflowers by his side,

growing in long rows, nodded their heads to the rhythm. The gleaming seeds from these sunflowers (the rare supernova variety) were the secret behind the Boyd Llama Farm's generations of state-champion llamas.

Route Z snaked along the edge of the llama farm. Whenever a car or truck sped down the dirt road, a cloud of dust swirled in the air. Not many vehicles traveled Route Z, though, so Ben was all alone for the first part of his march to the cliff.

As he thumped the bongos, Ben daydreamed about Mayor Olympus. It was a habit from his long walks to school. The story of Mayor Olympus gave him the courage to endure each school day as Butterfingers Boyd.

Like all human beings, it was hope that kept Ben going. In his case the hope that one day he would gain a new nickname, as Mayor Olympus once did.

Ben had never seen a picture of Mayor Olympus as a child, but he tried hard to imagine what he must have looked like: a small sickly boy with horrible boils all over his face, his shoulders, his back, his thighs, even his rear end. Angry red boils that oozed with sticky, foul-smelling pus.

Pus. That became his nickname.

But as Pus grew older, he bloomed big and strong. The boils disappeared and the face that emerged was said to be the most handsome in the whole state. What's more, it turned out there was nothing the gifted Pus couldn't do, and do better than anyone for miles around. It got to the point where Mayor Cowlick was heard to exclaim: "That young man, he's like all them Greek gods rolled up into one."

And soon after, on the day Pus unseated Mayor Cowlick as mayor of Boony Point at the age of nineteen, the town dubbed him…Olympus.

Ben continued marching up Route Z, his right hand thumping away on the Giant Heart bongos. He was approaching a fork in the road: Route Z curved to the left; straight ahead was the paved blacktop, Olympus Drive. Olympus Drive was the fastest way into town—this was the way he walked to school each day.

It was also the way to Leech Lake. Ben thought happily of the trip he and his father would take that afternoon to go fishing and swimming.

But this morning he followed the bend in the dirt road, the sunflowers nodding their goodbyes. As he came to the fields of goldenrod that waved on both sides, he caught their sweet scent and his mind drifted on with the story of Mayor Olympus…

Ben pictured the new mayor walking through Grizzly Woods, all those years ago. It was a fine summer day and he was searching through the dim forest for rare roots and berries. He was eager to save a deathly ill little girl named Giggles by brewing up a special remedy. (Don't you worry, Giggles lived.) But in the deepest, darkest part of the forest, he came upon a horrific scene.

A huge grizzly bear, claws long as sickles, was mauling at a moose. The moose was on the ground, grunting its last breaths of life. Standing by the big moose's side was a baby moose. The baby was in shock, its spindly legs quivering, its round eyes gaping at Mayor Olympus. But before Mayor Olympus could act, the bear slashed at the baby moose with its claws, raking the flesh from one front leg.

Mayor Olympus gave a great shout and the bear turned. It reared up on its back legs and roared like the devil himself. Then it charged at Mayor Olympus with its fangs bared and its claws held high.

Mayor Olympus was a big man, but the grizzly bear was a monster. Still, Mayor Olympus didn't move a muscle. He didn't run; he didn't climb a tree; he didn't drop to the ground like a possum and play dead. He just stood there with his

pouch of roots and berries, waiting patiently for the ferocious bear to attack.

A heartbeat later it was towering over him, arms raised high and ready to shred that unblemished skin right off his face. But before the claws could come down, Mayor Olympus dropped the pouch and shot out his hand, jabbing a finger deep into its left armpit. The finger drilled at the bear's poptic artery, temporarily pinching off the blood pumping to its brain.

The savage beast instantly collapsed into Mayor Olympus's arms; he set the limp bear gently on the ground.

Mayor Olympus rushed over to the baby moose. It was now lying beside its dead mother and whimpering in pain. He ripped his shirt into strips and wrapped the wound on the moose's leg. Then hoisting the bawling creature onto his broad, bare shoulders, its legs dangling down around his neck, he carried it back to town. He fought bravely to save its injured leg, but the wound was too severe. In the end, the leg had to be amputated.

After that, the orphaned moose took to hobbling after Mayor Olympus wherever he went. Mayor Olympus named him Norman.

Ben pictured the portrait of Mayor Olympus and Norman as he made his way up dusty Route Z. He smiled at the thought of their two big grins.

Then he remembered the bone.

Legend holds that Norman's leg bone was the inspiration for the Marching Moose. After amputating Norman's leg, Mayor Olympus gazed at the streak of long white bone shining through the gash made by the grizzly bear's claws. He then cleaned off the flesh, buffed the bone to a pure white sheen, and scratched Norman's name in one end.

It would be his baton.

Mayor Olympus gathered a group of children from Boony

Point, brought them to his new music shop to teach them to play musical instruments, and began leading them in band practice every day after school on the grassy town square across the street. Norman always stood nearby, balanced on three legs, in the very spot where the bronze statue would later be raised. He loved watching Mayor Olympus toss the bone-baton high into the air and catch it behind his back.

Eleven months later, Mayor Olympus and the Marching Moose were crowned the finest youth marching band in the whole state. Though small in numbers back then, they held that title for the next nine years, becoming the pride of Boony Point.

A warm breeze crossed Route Z, now running straight as a corn stalk, but Ben shuddered. It had happened on a day like today, on a quiet summer afternoon during band practice.

Just one day after their grinning portrait was taken, Mayor Olympus and Norman, along with all eighteen members of the Marching Moose and their instruments, vanished from the face of the earth.

The Abernathy Pumpkin Patch

THE BOYD LLAMA FARM had the biggest herd of llamas in the whole state. Whenever something passed by on Route Z, whatever it might be, all 144 curious creatures would stop grazing on the goldenrod and rush to the road.

And today, as you know, the llamas were feeling especially edgy.

So when Ben finally reached the timber fences, 143 llamas came stampeding up to him on both sides. They stood there straining at the fences, the fluffiest, most colorful llamas around, in shades of ivory, cinnamon, apricot, auburn, chestnut, rust, pearl gray, and charcoal. Their large eyes were round with fear and hope, praying (in a llama way) that the wonderful thumping sound they heard somehow heralded good news about Henry.

Henry was the 144th llama at the Boyd Llama Farm, but he wasn't just one of the herd. He was Henry the Eighth, the latest, and the greatest, in a long line of state champion llamas that stretched back to Henry the First. Henry the Eighth was the biggest, most beautiful llama the Boyd Llama Farm had ever had: his coat was a gleaming harvest gold; his limbs and neck were long and regal; his large head, always held like a prince, sported tall proud ears and cool amber eyes. He had won the blue ribbon at the state fair six years in a row, and the next fair was just a month away.

But that morning, when Ben's father went to give Henry his platter of roasted (and lightly salted) sunflower seeds, the prize-winning llama was sprawled out on the hay in his stall. His legs were rigid as iron pipes and his fine white teeth were clenched in a crazy grimace. He was wheezing a mile a minute through his big nostrils and his eyes were glazed and gaping helplessly at Ben's father. So Ben's parents frantically hauled him into the trailer and floored the old Rambler pickup truck into town to see Doc Sprinkle.

The 143 llamas eyed Ben as they chewed quietly on mouthfuls of goldenrod. Ben marched in place for a moment, then stopped smartly and placed the picnic basket down on the road.

"I can't dillydally," he told the llamas, "but I don't think Grandma will starve if I play for you for just a minute." He knew they were worried about Henry and maybe a short performance on the Giant Heart bongos would help take their minds off their troubles.

Now with both hands, Ben began to play. His drumming was clumsy, but the llamas were hardly music critics and they quickly fell under the spell of the booming bongos. They stopped chewing and stared in wonder. They started swaying their necks and humming softly with delight.

When Grandma was on the road, the llamas were far less charmed.

Ben finished his performance with a loud flourish. He bowed to both sides of the road as the llamas snorted for an encore. Then he reached for the picnic basket, catching the scent of the gingerbread cookie. He lifted the lid of the basket and peeked inside the napkin: the big gingerbread boy was trimmed with white icing. Ben grinned at its smiling face. His mouth watered.

"I'll just eat one leg," he told himself. "And I'll save the rest for Crabapple Cliff." He broke off the left leg and popped it into his mouth.

Chewing happily on the spicy gingerbread, Ben slapped the lid shut and picked up the basket. Then, thumping the drum again with one hand, he launched into a high-stepping march. He continued up Route Z, a perky yellow butterfly now flitting alongside him. The 143 llamas followed as far as they could, up to the edge of the Boyd Llama Farm. They jostled there at the fences, staring at Ben's back and bleating with worry again.

The butterfly hovered there, leaving Ben on his own as he entered the Abernathy Pumpkin Patch.

* * *

He hadn't been as far as the Abernathy Pumpkin Patch in almost a year—not since the last day of summer vacation the year before. Because he always walked Olympus Drive to get to school, he only had to come this way when he picked crabapples for Grandma. And he hadn't been looking forward to it.

The sun was glowing warm up ahead, but Ben shivered. His hands fell silent on the drum heads. His heart thumped instead.

There weren't any pumpkins in the Abernathy Pumpkin Patch. The last pumpkins had shriveled on the vine years ago and rotted right in the fields. But everyone still called it that: the Abernathy Pumpkin Patch.

It just goes to show how the people of Boony Point hold fast to a name.

The Abernathy Pumpkin Patch may sound like a small plot of land, but it was a sprawling farm that rolled across Route Z. A gray and barren place, like the lonely moon, Ben always got a sad, creepy feeling when he had to tread through it.

He tiptoed up the road. His eyes darted from side to side. Nothing moved. A breeze whistled off-key through the old vines that still strangled the ground. There was the smell of ruin in the air.

It's hard to believe, but the hills of the Abernathy Pumpkin Patch once boasted the grandest pumpkins in the whole state. People near and far would come to cut them off the vine to make jack-o'-lanterns for Halloween. Everyone in town even turned out on Halloween night for the liveliest party around: they wore flashy costumes, jiggled on hayrack rides, bobbed for juicy apples. It was Boony Point's biggest affair of the year.

But everything changed when Arnold Abernathy—now known to all as Old Man Fibber—inherited the farm.

Ben thought of the story his father had told him about Old Man Fibber. His father said it was all in the old man's head, but Ben couldn't help feeling frightened by the tale—and fascinated too.

He was trying to picture Old Man Fibber as a boy, hiding behind a leg of the water tower on Olympus Field, when he came to the foot of a tall rise in the road. He sucked a breath and puffed his way to the peak. The sight of the crumbling farmhouse and barn below, surrounded by mountains of scrapped machines and metal, like some huge junk yard, was always a small shock. But this time his whole body froze. His breath caught in his throat. His heart skipped a beat.

There by the road, in front of the Abernathy farmhouse, was a towering dark figure.

Old Man Fibber's Story

BEN SQUINTED INTO THE SUN. He put a hand above his glasses, but saw only a silhouette, tall as a silo.

Of course, most small boys with a large imagination, surprised by a gigantic dark figure on the Abernathy Pumpkin Patch, would probably have the good sense to turn tail and run home. And most days Ben would already have bolted, even though he knew Grandma would give him a tart tongue-lashing if he brought back an empty picnic basket.

But the story of Old Man Fibber was now stirring in his head. He had to look. He had to see what was looming there by the roadside.

Ben took a small step down the long, dusty slope. He paused, squinting and listening. He heard his own heart pounding.

The figure didn't move, didn't make a sound.

He took a second step. He paused.

Then another step. Another pause.

One more step…and suddenly his foot slid in the dust. He was now tumbling head over heels down the hill, the bongos swinging wildly around his neck and clunking him in the chin.

He sat up at the bottom, caked in Route Z. He spit the grit from his mouth and glanced up through grimy glasses. He couldn't see anything, but he now heard a sound—a soft, creaky groan. He blew the dust from his glasses and looked back. From this angle, with the figure now blocking the sun, he could see it clearly.

It was fifty feet tall, with heavy legs and feet; its belly was bulging. The thick right arm hung to its knee, the left arm was raised to its face. Its head was huge, its ears big and dangling;

the lower jaw jutted from a massive mouth. And the eyes... the right eye was gray and glaring, but the left eye was hidden, covered by the left hand.

It was a monster.

And it was made of junk.

Ben slowly rose from the ground. He edged closer to the junk monster.

The groan came again and he paused, holding his breath. He realized the breeze was justling at the joints, making the metal creak.

When he reached the wide shadow falling across the road, he stopped. He studied the rusty figure, how it had been welded together from the scrapped machines and pieces of metal that were heaped in hills around the house and barn: tractor sides, car doors, truck fenders, bicycles and tricycles, refrigerators, pop-bottle machines, stoves, toasters, barbecue grills, bed frames, radiators, ladders, gutters, tin roofing, garbage cans, milking pails, mailboxes, guard rails, street signs, poles and pipes, chicken wire, barbed wire, basketball hoops, hub caps, dustpans, shovel heads, pitchfork prongs— even a fancy birdcage for an earlobe.

Ben stared at the great gray eye, fashioned from a steel kitchen sink. "It's like Old Man Fibber's story," he whispered with a shiver.

Just then he was jarred by a fierce roar...which quickly died away.

His eyes goggled behind his glasses. He looked past the junk monster to the old farmhouse where Old Man Fibber lived. The whole house was wilting to one side and the roof was nearly peeled clean of shingles. The ground around the house was frosted white, like a light snowfall, from all the paint that had flaked off the walls.

But the house was still. The only sounds were Ben's hard breathing and the soft groaning of the junk monster.

Moments later another roar ripped the air…and again died to silence.

His eyes flicked beyond the farmhouse. *It's coming from the barn.*

Like the house, the barn looked like it would topple right to the ground if the breeze picked up. The pale red boards were slowly rotting away, leaving gouges and gaps in the wood.

Ben peered at a big gash in the side of the barn, but he was too far off to see anything but a black hole.

He heard a third roar, louder and longer…but that died away too.

Then a gruff voice erupted from inside the barn. His spine went stiff at a burst of muffled cursing. As the rant went on, raw as a slaughterhouse, he also caught the sound of splashing, like something was thrashing about in a bathtub.

His ears burning, his heart banging, Ben turned and hurried up Route Z toward Grizzly Woods.

Grizzly Woods

BEN HAD A SIDE ACHE by the time he reached Grizzly Woods. He had run all the way from the Abernathy Pumpkin Patch and was now bent over and breathing hard, his hands on his knees. The Giant Heart bongos were still dangling from his neck, but the picnic basket was sitting in the dust of Route Z.

When his side ache faded, he looked up at Grizzly Woods, a stone's throw off the right side of the road.

The name Grizzly Woods didn't suit it much anymore, but people still called it that. I suppose long ago, when the first settlers of Boony Point gave the name, the trees were smaller. But now the bigsap maples and ragbark oaks were giants, towering up to the sky and blocking the sunlight.

It was more forest than woods.

And there weren't any grizzly bears in it, either. There used to be, of course, when Mayor Olympus was in town. But after he and Norman and the Marching Moose disappeared, the people of Boony Point hunted down every last grizzly bear. It was the grizzlies, they said, that stole away the mayor and their children.

In fact, the only grizzly for miles around now was Stanley, Doc Sprinkle's dancing bear.

Ben shuddered. He knew there weren't any grizzly bears left in Grizzly Woods, but he couldn't help feeling frightened when it was looming before him.

He picked up the picnic basket and waded into the patch of overgrown goatsbeard that rose between Route Z and Grizzly Woods. When he reached the treeline, he paused and looked down: Grandma had worn a narrow path into the ground from years of marching through the forest to the cliff.

The summer before, Ben discovered that walking quickly

along the path brought him to Crabapple Cliff in about fifteen minutes. And the only creatures he encountered that whole summer were birds and squirrels and a possum with six babies clinging to its back.

Still, as he carefully stepped over a large root and entered the dim forest, he could barely keep his hair from uncurling and standing on end.

Grizzly Woods was always a gloomy place, but it made Ben especially skittish today after seeing the junk monster. As his feet crackled the leaves and twigs littering the path, he began to see the monster all around him in the forest: its legs in tree trunks; its arms in branches; its ears in old round stumps.

And its eye! Up ahead, above the path, was a gray glow!

Ben stopped, goosebumps breaking on his skin. He pushed his glasses into place and peered through the murk. He took a step forward, straining to see—

Wait, it was more of a whitish glow...

Step by step, Ben crept up the path. Slowly, he could make out a dark cutleaf elm...a branch reaching over the path...and perched there, a very large owl.

A great frosty owl!

The owl stared silently at Ben with orange eyes. Ben breathed with relief and put down the picnic basket.

"Listen to this," he said to the owl. He raised his hands above the bongos and began fumbling a loud beat.

But the great frosty owl is a bad-tempered bird and less forgiving than a llama. It hooted crossly then spread its big wings and flapped off the branch. It sailed toward Ben and gave his hair a sharp tug with its talons—*"Ouch!"*—before disappearing into the darkness.

His hands rose to rub his head.

And that's when Ben heard the footsteps. They were lumbering up from behind. He heard a low snuffling sound too. His heart hammered as he flashed on the story of Mayor Olympus and the grizzly bear.

A grizzly bear! There are still grizzly bears in the forest after all!

He grabbed the basket and ran up the path toward Crabapple Cliff. But the footsteps and snuffling sound followed, louder each second.

He was running for his life when his foot caught a root. He flew to the ground hard, the picnic basket landing with a clatter. His glasses tumbled off his nose.

The lumbering footsteps stopped behind him on the path.

Ben whirled around. He squinted through the gloom, but without his glasses he could only see a blurry form.

He patted the earth frantically, finally touching the wire frames. He jammed them on and turned to look—

There it was, huge and hairy, staring with big dark eyes—and snuffling at him.

The Gingerbread Boy

IT WAS A MOOSE.

Although the grizzly bears had been hunted from Grizzly Woods long ago, the forest was still home to a glut of moose. After Mayor Olympus and Norman disappeared, the town of Boony Point passed a new law in their honor, popularly known as "The Moose Taboo." As the law declared: "It shall henceforth be forbidden to render harm or mistreatment of any manner upon the moose inhabitants of Grizzly Woods." This law even protected the bolder ones that sometimes would stroll right into town and snuffle peppermint drops from the hands of unsuspecting children. And so, over the next sixty-nine years, as a result of "The Moose Taboo," as well as the fact they no longer had grizzly bears to fear, there was an outburst of moose in the forest.

With all those moose in Grizzly Woods, it's surprising, really, that Benjamin Boyd hadn't already come nose-to-snout with a moose the summer before. But he had never carried fresh gingerbread through the forest until that morning. And the tantalizing scent had lured the lumbering animal to Grandma's path, where it was now grunting for a bite.

Moose, of course, are giant creatures that can use their antlers and hooves to turn small children into waffle batter. Fortunately, they aren't very aggressive; as a rule, they'd rather hide from human beings. That is, until they sniff out some kind of fragrant treat with their big snouts, like a peppermint drop or a gingerbread boy. In that case, it would be wise to remember that they're also moody beasts and you don't want to get on their bad side. And this moose, parked there on the path not twenty steps from Ben, was now scowling and snorting and stamping at the earth.

Ben quaked. He thought of the time he was walking home from school after a Christmas party. He was reading *Santa Claus and the Alien Invasion* and licking a candy cane when a moose suddenly appeared on the outskirts of town and followed him halfway home. The moose didn't end its pursuit until he threw his candy cane at it. Then it stopped and snuffled up the shattered pieces from the road.

He didn't want to surrender his snack this time.

"Go away!" Ben called out, his voice cracking.

But the moose bellowed at Ben, shaking its antlers and stomping its hooves.

Ben scrambled back to the picnic basket. His hand shook as he reached inside. When the moose spotted the big cookie, its eyes bulged and its nostrils flared. It snuffled with excitement.

Ben leaped to his feet. He sighed at the smiling face of the gingerbread boy, then hurled it over the moose's head. When the moose turned, he grabbed the picnic basket and dashed up the path toward Crabapple Cliff.

As he ran through the dim forest, Ben fixed his eyes on the ground to keep from tripping again. He clutched the picnic basket in his left hand and cradled the bongos with his right so they wouldn't bounce at his chest. He could feel his heart drumming against the mahogany.

Ben wondered if he could ever be as brave as Mayor Olympus. "Mayor Olympus didn't turn and run when that grizzly bear attacked!" he scolded himself. "He stood his ground. And he showed that bear who was boss! He never would have abandoned his breakfast like that!"

He was replaying this encounter with the moose in his head, picturing himself jabbing his finger into its armpit, when he saw a glint of light in the distance. At last, he was approaching Crabapple Cliff.

He stopped to catch his breath. He listened for footsteps, but heard only his own heavy breathing. His stomach rumbled. He pushed his glasses into place and began walking. The light ahead turned bigger and brighter with each step, like he was reaching the end of a long tunnel. After getting used to the gloom of the forest, he was now squinting at the growing ball of light.

Finally, he stepped from Grizzly Woods and into the sunshine of Crabapple Cliff.

Crabapple Cliff

BEN BLINKED UNDER THE BRIGHT SUN, still climbing in the sky. A shiver shot through him as a crash came from the sea, slamming the boulders at the foot of the high cliff.

Raising a hand to his eyes, Ben peered at the huge old crabapple tree. It towered there in the middle of the rocky bluff, like a mirage in the desert, but it was solid as iron, with roots that dug deep. He listened to the wind whistle softly through the branches, heavy with small red fruit, and wrinkled his nose at the faint sour odor.

It smelled like Grandma.

It was odd enough that a crabapple tree was even growing in such a lonely spot, but this tree—a Queen Tartelicious—was a hardy giant. It was nearly a hundred feet tall, with stout limbs that always seemed to have ripe crabapples hanging from them, no matter the season.

Ben trudged through the waist-high horsetail at the edge of Grizzly Woods. The horsetail thinned into patches of prickleweed as he approached the barren cliff. He flinched at a jumping cricket.

Grandma had warned him not to dillydally, but he was tired and hot and needed a rest. He made his way across the rusty-red ground for the shade of the crabapple tree.

"I'll sit here for just a minute," he told himself. "Then I'll pick Grandma's crabapples."

He set the picnic basket on the ground and plopped down beside it. Then he leaned back against the scaly trunk and squinted out at the sea. The Giant Heart bongos, still draped around his neck, were cradled in his hands.

He closed his eyes and let out a heavy breath. He listened to the sounds of the crashing waves and the whistling

wind—and his rumbling stomach.

He thought of the moose and the lost cookie. His mouth watered—then he realized how thirsty he was.

Sitting up, he fished the battered canteen from the picnic basket. The cap, fixed to the side with a short chain, went *clunk* against the gray metal when he unscrewed it. He took big gulps of milk, now lukewarm, to quiet his hunger as much as his thirst. Then he propped the canteen by his side, the cap still unscrewed.

Ben looked down at the bongos and smiled. "The Giant Heart bongos," he whispered, as if reciting a prayer in church. He ran his fingers over the warm maroon wood. He caressed the yak skin stretched over the tops of the twin drum heads. Then he crossed his legs and squeezed the bongos between his knees.

He began to play.

The Giant Heart bongos boomed to life. The sound throbbed in the air, filling the wide cliff.

He tried different tones, different rhythms. It was all clumsy noise, of course, but the mighty ring of the drum lifted the boy's heart higher than the curious, squawking seagull flying past.

"I just need a little practice," he told himself. "And I'll be sure to get a spot in the Marching Moose."

Ben pounded away happily on the Giant Heart bongos.

"Hey, Fire Hands!" he called out. "Don't play that drum in Grizzly Woods! You'll start a forest fire!"

He chuckled, then wondered aloud, "Forest Fire Hands... No, that's too long..."

Ben went on like this for a while, thumping the drum and dreaming of big fiery nicknames.

"Maybe Wildfire Hands... Or Firebolt Hands... Or even Lightning Hands..."

Then his whole body froze. *"Dragon Hands!"* he cried.

"I can be *Dragon Hands!*"

It was right after that cry that he heard a sound, or thought he did.

What was that?

Ben swung around, expecting to see the snuffling moose at the edge of Grizzly Woods, back for another gingerbread boy. But there was just the wall of silent trees.

He scanned the bluff from side to side. Nothing.

He listened hard, but heard only the waves and the wind.

He gazed up at the bobbing branches of the crabapple tree. "It must be the breeze," he mumbled.

Ben went back to the bongos. He drummed more quietly at first, then thumped away again.

"Dragon Hands," he said with a grin. "I'm going to be Dragon—"

There it is.

He stopped short, his hands in the air. He held his breath and listened hard, but the sound had quit. He peered out at the cliff, his eyes wide as windows. The sound seemed to be coming from somewhere beyond it, somewhere below it.

There it is again.

It was a low sound, a groan.

The hair on his neck prickled.

Ben rose to his feet, knocking over the canteen. The milk spilled out, but he was too alarmed by the groaning sound to even notice.

He stood there under the tree, his mind racing. He cocked his head toward the cliff and listened, but the sound had stopped.

A moment later, his eyes narrowed. He was recalling what his grandmother had said: "*The beauty of this one will be hard to beat, but don't underestimate my powers for mind-boggling pranks!*"

Of course, most grandmothers wouldn't dare crawl down

the side of a steep cliff to pull a practical joke on their grandsons—even if they wanted to. But Grandma, as you've already guessed, was no ordinary grandmother.

Ben imagined the old woman slinking past him on his way out to the cliff and then digging into the rock face with those thorny fingernails—

No, that's ridiculous. She might be a good climber, and loony as lugnuts, but even Grandma wouldn't go that far to play a prank on me...

Or would she?

His eyes narrowed again. *That's just what she wants me to think! She tricks me into thinking she would never go this far to pull a practical joke and I wind up getting fooled twice!*

"Grandma!" he called. "I'm not falling for another practical joke today!"

Ben had never been to the edge of Crabapple Cliff before. His parents had warned him to keep away from the edge and he had gladly obeyed: he was terrified of heights. Even as a baby, he would only eat while held in their laps at the kitchen table. He refused to sit in a high chair.

With his hands gripping the sides of the bongos, he took a step forward.

There was another deep groan.

"Grandma?" he said. "Grandma, I know it's you!"

Step by step, the small boy crept forward, all ears. The groans went on, each one longer, louder.

When he neared the edge of the cliff, he slipped the drum strap from his neck and set the bongos safely on the ground. Then he got down on his belly and inched his way ahead.

"Nice try, Grandma! But you didn't fool me this time!"

He crept even with the edge, then stretched his neck to peer over the side...

But Grandma wasn't there. No one was there. He saw only scraggly roots from the crabapple tree poking out from cracks in the cliff…and a petrifying drop down—far, far down—to the sea and boulders below.

His eyes fluttered; he felt dizzy. Still on his belly, he pushed back from the cliff. He lay there at the edge, breathing hard.

At that moment a great bellow burst the air.

Ben's whole body turned to ice. He listened to the heavy grunts of something stirring below him. He heard clattering and clumping and scraping.

"That's definitely not Grandma," he squeaked.

And then he was on his feet, grabbing the bongos by the strap, racing toward the crabapple tree. Behind him the grunts grew louder and the scraping sounds echoed off the side of the cliff, like fingernails raking on a chalkboard.

At the foot of the Queen Tartelicious, Ben looked up. He gulped. He wasn't much good at climbing the tree in the first place. Last summer he would only pick crabapples from the lowest branches—and even getting up there was no cinch. The thought of climbing higher than that made him woozy.

He glanced back toward the cliff; the grunting and scraping were getting louder. He slung the bongos around his neck and grit his teeth. Then he leaped for the lowest branch. He missed. The Giant Heart bongos were weighing him down. And the hard mahogany thumped him in the knee as he dropped to a squat. He grimaced and looked back; the grunting and scraping now throbbed in his ears.

He took several steps back, made a running leap for the branch—and caught it!

But then he dangled there, as he did every time in gym class when they had to do chin-ups. He struggled and kicked and almost pulled himself onto the branch…but then lost his grip and fell. He landed on his tail, the bongos clunking him in the head.

As Ben turned toward the cliff, a massive hand, hairy as a spider, came scrabbling over the edge, digging fast into the rock with its fingernails.

At this point I think your average boy would have screamed himself silly. But Benjamin Boyd just sat there. He sat there gaping behind his glasses, his mouth so wide you could practically see his heart rattling against his ribs.

Part Two

The Birthday Party

BENJAMIN BOYD WASN'T THE ONLY ONE celebrating a birthday that day. Governor Gus Glutty's daughter was turning twelve too.

Governor Glutty's daughter, Mary-Margaret, was having a much larger party than Ben, though. This year, in fact, would be her biggest birthday party yet, with a thousand children expected at the governor's whopping mansion in Bloat City.

A first glance at the hulking, angry Mary-Margaret Glutty might lead you to believe she would rather brain a kitten than cuddle it. But she had a soft side too: she loved animals with all the passion she hated human beings. And like every year, her guests would come bearing furry gifts for the enormous petting zoo behind the mansion.

After the children spent several hours petting the smaller animals and trying to ride the larger ones, they would return to the mansion for the birthday cake. Of course, you need a pretty big cake to feed one thousand hungry children. So the cake prepared for this year's party was colossal: the size and shape of a humpback whale. (It could even spout cream soda from its blowhole.)

But the highlight of the party each year was the entertainment. Once the cake was wolfed down, the sugar-happy children stampeded into the auditorium to shriek with delight at an amazing animal act. In the past, these animal acts had included a trio of singing parrots, a pair of chimpanzees who juggled balls and clubs and meat cleavers, and a kangaroo that could jump rope like a third-grade girl—even with an actual third-grade girl bouncing along gleefully in its pouch.

For this year's record-setting party, Governor Glutty's secretary had booked the most popular animal act in the whole state: a family of otters that performed breathtaking tricks on a high wire and trapeze (without a net).

Unfortunately, the otters had woken up that morning with terrible stomach cramps after eating a bowl of bad clams the night before. They were in no condition to perform somersaults on the trapeze or even ride a bicycle across the high wire. The governor's secretary tried frantically to find another big-name animal act on short notice—she would have even settled for a gorilla who was all thumbs on the harp—but as you might expect, everyone was booked on the first day of summer vacation. (And sadly, the kangaroo was still in a neck brace after a jump roping trick that went terribly wrong.)

That, you see, is how Doc Sprinkle received the early morning telephone call from the governor's secretary, asking if Stanley could perform at Mary-Margaret Glutty's birthday party.

Stanley, of course, was Doc Sprinkle's grizzly bear. Now it's true that the people of Boony Point hunted down all the grizzly bears in Grizzly Woods after Mayor Olympus disappeared. But it's also true that, a week later, Doc Sprinkle (who was just a boy at the time) heard a yipping sound coming from his backyard and found a hungry bear cub. He gave it a bowl of jello and named it Stanley. It was the only survivor of the bloody bear hunt.

Some folks in town were bent on killing it, but the new mayor, Mayor Lofty, who later raised the bronze statue of Mayor Olympus and Norman on Olympus Field, put his foot down. The slaughter had to stop, he said.

So Doc Sprinkle reared Stanley from the time he was a cub, and as the bear grew, trained him to dance.

As it turned out, that grizzly bear loved to dance, and he took pride in it too. But truth be told, he was never much of a dancer. Oh, the big handsome bear looked impressive indeed when he stepped onto a stage in his frilly lavender tutu. But he was always pretty clumsy, wobbling around up there on his back legs, blundering through his trademark dance, a happy Irish jig. And he was getting on in years now, just like Doc Sprinkle, so he didn't do much leaping about anymore, if he could help it. Still, Stanley was the only dancing bear in the whole state, so when someone needed a dancing bear, Doc Sprinkle was the lone name in the phone book.

The call from the governor's mansion came less than fifteen minutes before Ben's parents rolled up to Doc Sprinkle's place, right by the Olympus Music Shop, with Ben's father gripping the wheel of the pickup and Ben's mother trying to comfort poor Henry the Eighth in the trailer. They found this note thumbtacked to the door:

GOVERNOR GLUTTY CALLED! HE WANTS
STANLEY TO DANCE AT HIS DAUGHTER'S
BIRTHDAY PARTY AT THE GOVERNOR'S MANSION!
WISH US LUCK! WE'LL BE BACK TONIGHT!

Doc Sprinkle, as you can tell, was puffed up with excitement. He wouldn't admit it, but he had long been disappointed that Stanley was always passed over for these birthday parties. Year after year, ever since his daughter was born, the governor had invited other animals to perform—even that ridiculous burping panda!—but the call for Stanley had never come.

Until that morning.

Ben's parents quickly climbed back into the truck and sped toward Bloat City, more than three hours away. Henry's nostrils were starting to foam and they were frantic to find Doc Sprinkle. They were terrified at the thought of losing their state champion llama. Henry the Eighth hadn't even produced a son yet, an heir. Without a Henry the Ninth, their long line of state champions would come to an end.

But Ben's father was unable to catch Doc Sprinkle. As he was speeding out of town, he was stopped by Sheriff Silver. Ben's father appealed to the sheriff to let them go, for Henry the Eighth's sake.

Sheriff Silver took his sweet time writing up a speeding ticket.

The Monster

BACK IN BOONY POINT, Ben was watching a second massive hand rise over the edge of Crabapple Cliff and dig into the rock. Then, with a thunderous grunt, the rest of it came pulling up over the side. It rose to its feet in the bright sunlight. It stood there, fifty feet tall, one eye blinking down at Ben.

It was a monster.

And this time it was real.

Oh, I know what you're thinking: monsters aren't real. But people only say that because they've never seen one. If you stop and think about it, there are all kinds of monstrous things you haven't seen with your own eyes that are still real. Like the enormous elephant seal, for one. You've never seen an elephant seal in person, but they're real, aren't they? And what about the giant squid? Seen any giant squid lately? But they're real too, every twenty-foot tentacle.

The truth is, there are more monsters in this world than you can shake a stick at—even the sort of monsters grown-ups try to pretend don't exist at all, for fear of scaring the little ones. Things like red-eyed demons and ghouls with dripping skin, green toothy goblins and those hungry creatures with the terrible termite faces I once saw skulking in your bedroom closet.

Not to mention huge, hairy ogres.

Benjamin Boyd didn't realize he was face to face with an ogre. Even if he could have kept his wits, sitting there on his backside beneath the Queen Tartelicious, the ogre looming before him was so much bigger, so much hairier than the ogres in *Beastly Brutes*.

Its feet were the size of rowboats; its legs were tree trunks, gnarled with muscle; its belly blubbered like a whale. The chest and shoulders were slumped, but dangling down were thick arms that hung to its knees—one hand was scratching at its thigh with a ragged fingernail. It had no neck; instead, its giant head rose from the shoulders and the big ears had fleshy lobes. Its mouth was enormous, the jaw jutting out, the bottom lip bulging and drooling. Above the squashed nose, with its huffing nostrils, were the deep-set eyes: one cold and gray and blinking; the other, a dark empty socket.

And everywhere was the hair, brown and dirty and tangled as weeds grown wild.

Ben was staring at the eye socket when the ogre's mouth dropped open like a cave. The creature made a tremendous yawn.

At the sound of the yawning roar, Ben yelped and leaped to his feet. The ogre's good eye narrowed. Then it took a thundering step toward the crabapple tree.

The ogre's strides were long, but each step was stiff and slow. As it grunted across the quaking cliff, Ben heard another sound too: a strange rattling sound that seemed to be coming from the monster's jiggling belly.

Ben quickly backed away from the crabapple tree to take another running leap for the lowest branch. Though stripping off the bongos first might have been wise, he was far too frazzled to think clearly. His heart raced as he rushed toward the tree and jumped—

And caught the branch!

The mighty Queen Tartelicious trembled from the ogre's heavy steps. Ripe red crabapples dropped from above, peppering him in the head. The small boy struggled, his feet kicking in the air…

It's remarkable the things a person can accomplish when danger is drawing near—like a gigantic ogre, for instance. No one in Boony Point would ever have thought that Butterfingers Boyd, as clumsy and scared of heights as he was, could have done what he did next.

With all the strength in his slender arms, Ben pulled himself onto the limb. Then he grabbed another branch, and another. Higher and higher he climbed, scampering up the crabapple tree like a spider monkey, the bongos bobbing around his neck.

By the time the ogre bellied up to the tree, Ben had nearly reached the top. He felt the shaking stop and he turned; it made him dizzy to find the ground so far below.

The ogre stood blinking up at him. Then it erupted in another yawn.

Ben peered into the black pit of the ogre's mouth. Like a great frosty owl, it had no teeth at all. There was only a wide, wet tongue that led down the dark tunnel to its belly.

A ray of sunlight glinted off something deep in its gut.

If Ben had known more about ogres right then, the fact that it had no teeth might have been a dead giveaway. You see, ogres live a long time, much longer than human beings, and they go on growing throughout their lives—even past the point all their teeth have finally rotted from their heads. And the bigger an ogre grows, the more brutal and bloodthirsty it becomes. At the same time, it gets slower in every way: its brain is slow; its body is slow; even its digestion is slow.

A split second after Ben saw the glint in its gut, there came a cloud of foul breath, like a blast of poison gas. Ben choked and coughed and nearly lost his balance. With his eyes stinging behind his glasses, he sank into the crook of two limbs and clung to them with both hands. The cloud lifted as a breeze blew through the tree. He freed one hand to rub quickly at his eyes.

When Ben could focus again on the ogre, he found its hairy arm reaching up toward him. But even on tiptoe, it could only grasp a branch ten feet below where he sat.

The ogre scowled and tore the thick branch off the tree with an explosive snap. Grumbling to itself, it hurled the branch to the ground. Then it turned back and gripped the trunk, halfway up, with its long fingers.

Ben's blood froze. *It's going to rip the tree right out of the ground!*

Tugging on the trunk, the ogre grunted with one hand; it groaned with the other; it growled with both. The Queen Tartelicious swayed in the air, but it was fixed firmly to the earth, its roots spreading deep and wide.

The ogre paused, its hands wrapped around the tree trunk. The tree had stopped swaying, but Ben's body still quivered.

Then the ogre bellowed and began shaking the tree violently.

The trunk rocked. Branches rattled. Crabapples hailed down. Ben hung on with all his might, but he was finally jarred from his perch. He was left clinging to the two tree limbs, his body flailing in the air, the bongos bounding around his neck. When the drum clunked him in the jaw, he started to scream.

The ogre roared in reply and shook the tree even harder. Ben was whipped back and forth, high above the ground. He shut his eyes and continued to shriek. It was like a carnival ride: a crazy, out-of-control, never-ending nightmare of a carnival ride.

Ben held on, eyes tight, wailing until his voice was gone. He knew that any second he would lose his grip too. He saw himself plunging to the ground, or even right into the monster's waiting mouth…

And suddenly the shaking stopped. Ben heard the ogre give a disgusted grunt. He opened his eyes and saw it release the tree trunk.

Ben hung there from the branches, his head spinning, his throat raw from screaming. He watched as the ogre turned away from the tree. He hoped desperately it would give up and lumber away to wherever it had come from.

But the ogre snorted and stomped over to the broken limb. It reached down, snatched up the branch, then turned back toward Ben.

Ben paled as he pictured the monster swatting him from the tree.

He kicked his legs in the air, trying to pull himself back up to his perch. He saw the monster raise the ragged branch high, like a club—and then the branch came crashing his way.

Ben gave a grunting heave and managed to hoist himself up. Wedged again in the crook of the two limbs, he lifted his legs a heartbeat before the ogre's branch thrashed through the air, right where his body had been.

He glanced up, frantic to climb higher. But he was nearly at the top already, and he knew the branches above would be too thin to hold his weight. It seemed there was nothing he could do to prevent the monster from finally knocking him from the tree with its branch. And then what? Even if the fall didn't break his leg, or his neck, the monster would quickly be upon him.

The ogre bellowed at Ben. Ben saw it was gripping the limb like a sword this time, ready to thrust the thorny end at him.

He opened his mouth to scream, but could only croak like a toad.

Then he saw the branch snaking up through the crabapple tree…

Ben had no time to think, but it was clear there was no escape. The next thing he knew he was beating wildly on the bongos with his right hand, his eyes squeezed tight.

He didn't expect anyone could hear him—like he knew no one had heard him scream. But he didn't want to see the branch coming. He didn't want to hear it knifing through the tree. He didn't want the last memory of his life to be the monster's cold, gray eye glaring up at him.

He just wanted to drown it all out with the beautiful boom of the Giant Heart bongos.

The Monster's Eye

HIGH IN THE QUEEN TARTELICIOUS, Ben clung to the tree with his left hand and pounded on the bongos with his right. The rest of his small body was coiled tight, his eyes squeezed shut, waiting for the jolt from the ogre's branch.

But that jolt didn't come.

Still thumping the drum, Ben opened one eye—the ragged end of the branch was right in front of his glasses. He gasped at the sight, then saw that the branch wasn't moving: it had stopped cold in the air, quivering inches from his head.

Ben looked down with both eyes. The ogre's good eye had gone dark, like the empty socket. It took a second for him to realize that the eye was closed...

Now I wish I had a good explanation for what happened next, but there are some things in this world that no one can really explain, not even your dear mother. The truth is, sometimes even the brainiest among us can only sit in dumb wonder at the great goings-on of the universe. Oh, grown-ups may pretend to know all the answers, but sometimes (probably most of the time) grown-ups are no wiser than tots when it comes to the mysteries that surround us.

And this, you'll see, is one of those times.

Ben now watched as the ogre's huge head rocked gently from side to side. Then its hand with the torn branch fell slowly to its knee, the branch slashing down through the tree limbs as it retreated. The long fingers opened and the branch dropped to the ground with a harmless *thud*.

The ogre began grunting softly to the beat of the bongos. The rhythm in its head seeped to its shoulders and the shoulders started to sway, then the chest, then the belly. When the big belly shook, Ben heard the rattling sound again. Before long, the creature's whole body was stirring to the sound of the drum.

Ben watched, hypnotized by the sight, until the swaying finally tapered off...and the monster stood there, still as the Queen Tartelicious...

Seconds later, its eye snapped open. Ben was so surprised that he lurched backward, nearly toppling from the tree.

But as he held on, thumping the drum, he saw a change in the monster's eye. Though it was aimed his way, Ben had the feeling it wasn't really seeing him at all. It was now glassy like a mirror, and looked more silver than gray—

Then the ogre exploded in a leap and began to dance. Whatever was rattling in its belly was surely weighing it down, but the monster moved with impossible grace as it went gliding back and forth across Crabapple Cliff. It was so light on its huge, hairy feet that it hardly made a tremor.

Of course, when the ogre started dancing, Ben couldn't help finally thinking that all this was just his imagination. He must have fallen asleep under the crabapple tree, and that's where he really was right now, dreaming up this whole monster business.

He even tried prodding himself awake. He had heard the thing to do, when you're having a bad dream, is give yourself a hard pinch. So he wiggled his body firmly into the crook of the two branches, freed his other hand, and pinched his ear—

And pinched it again—

And pinched it once more—

But nothing happened. (Except for a smarting left ear.) He was still in the tree, still thumping the drum...and the monster was still there too, dancing over the rocky-red bluff.

If there was any bright side to this bad news, at least the creature wasn't thrashing him with the tree limb. But now Ben could only pray that his drumming would finally tire the monster out and it would retreat, far, far away.

He let go of his ear and began playing the bongos with both hands. With two hands on the drum, the rhythm changed: it became bouncier, livelier. To the boy's surprise, the monster followed, its movement becoming bouncier, livelier too.

Ben tried another rhythm—slower and softer this time—and again the ogre obeyed. It drew closer to the tree and moved with slower, softer steps.

He changed the rhythm once more, then over and over, stunned by the sight of the monster following him so nimbly each time…

But by and by he felt his hands begin to tingle. How long could he keep playing? As the question came, a cold shiver shot down his spine.

What if I'm the one that tires out first?

The Dying Llama

IT WAS MID-MORNING BY THE TIME Ben's parents rumbled into Bloat City. They quickly got lost in the maze of gray skyscrapers and smoky-black factories, but eventually sputtered up to the golden gates of Governor Glutty's huge white mansion. They parked the Rambler truck by the curb and rushed over to the large guard marching back and forth inside the tall, spiky gates. He had a rifle propped on his shoulder.

"Excuse me, sir," called Ben's father. His name was Walter Boyd, a middle-aged man still clinging to his youth. But the bald head under his lucky fishing hat, and a growing pot belly, were making it hard to hold out much longer. "We need to speak with Doc Sprinkle. He's here from Boony Point, for the birthday party."

"It's an emergency," added Ben's mother, Lorelai Boyd, in a trembling voice. She had left the house so suddenly that morning her wavy hair was sticking out like modern art and just three fingernails had polish.

The guard stopped crisply and turned. He had a square head and a stern face.

"The birthday party commenced at oh-nine-hundred hours," he said, barking out each word like a German Shepherd through the shiny bars of the gates. "I'm under strict orders not to let anyone in or out until the party has concluded at fifteen-hundred hours. I can only accept birthday presents for Miss Mary-Margaret Glutty."

"We have a sick llama, sir," Ben's father said, pointing to the trailer. He removed the pale green hat and ran his fingers through his hairless head, a nervous habit from the days his hair was long and lush.

"He's very sick," Ben's mother said. "We're afraid he

might…he might be…" She faltered and began sobbing softly into a handkerchief.

"He might be dying," Ben's father said quietly. He pulled his hat back on and put his arm around Ben's mother.

The guard paused, listening to the low groans coming from the trailer. His eyes narrowed.

"What sort of cheap birthday present is that?" he barked. "Couldn't you even get the little girl a healthy animal?"

Ben's father blinked. "Sir, this llama—"

"I can see you're not exactly made of money," the guard said, nodding at the rusty old truck. "But this is Governor Gus Glutty's daughter. Governor Glutty expects healthy animals for his little girl. It's true, someone brought a camel today that had a slight cough, and one of the raccoons had a touch of diarrhea, but a *dying llama?* Good heavens, man. What were you thinking?"

Ben's father opened his mouth to speak, but the guard nodded again at the truck and carried on: "Now take your dying llama away from here before that groaning puts a damper on a little girl's birthday party. Perhaps you can get your money back and buy a healthy animal instead. There haven't been any beavers yet today. Or buffaloes, for that matter. You come back with a healthy beaver or buffalo and that will make Governor Glutty and his daughter Miss Mary-Margaret—"

"Sir, this llama is not a present!" Ben's father shouted. "His name is Henry the Eighth and he happens to be the champion llama of this whole state! He's been the champion for the past six years! Yesterday he was fit as fiddlesticks and today he's lying on his side and foaming from the nose!" Ben's father pressed his face between the bars. "We need Doc Sprinkle! We need him right away!"

The guard quickly swooped the rifle to his chest. "I told you," he snapped. "I'm under strict orders not to let anyone in or out until the party has concluded. I can only accept presents—*healthy* presents—for Miss Mary-Margaret Glutty. I'm sorry about the dying llama, but you'll just have to wait to see your Doc Sparkle."

"What about another vet?" Ben's mother jumped in. "There must be a vet nearby!"

The guard shook his square head. "I'm afraid all the vets in town are at the birthday party too. As you might imagine, it takes every available veterinarian to ensure that all the birthday presents are healthy enough to place in the petting zoo." The guard shouldered his rifle. "Now kindly move that moaning llama down the street before I have your vehicle towed." He turned smartly and resumed marching back and forth inside the golden gates.

Ben's parents stared at the governor's mansion, tears filling their eyes. Then they turned and hurried back to Henry the Eighth. After moving the truck down the street to a parking meter, they sat glumly in the trailer, waiting for Doc Sprinkle.

They each held one of Henry's hooves as he lay there whimpering in the hay.

The Dancing Bear

YOU MAY FIND THIS HARD TO BELIEVE, but back when your Grandpa Gristle was an infant, there were no newfangled gadgets like the little phones people tote around today like an extra extremity. And so, when Ben's father felt the urge to call home and let Ben know where they were, he had to leave the trailer to look for a public telephone. But when he finally found a pay phone (in a grimy pizza parlor, where the owner loudly protested his "fishy-smelling hat"), no one answered back at the Boyd Llama Farm.

Ben, as you know, was preoccupied with an ogre out on Crabapple Cliff. Grandma, for her part, was pulling a tick from Alf's rump and pretending not to hear the ring.

After the one thousand children had gorged on humpback whale cake and were so bristling with sugar they could hardly sit still, Stanley's performance began. As the music to a happy Irish jig was heard in the auditorium, the big grizzly bear came toddling out onto the stage in his lavender tutu. But the moment he took to dancing—stretching his arms high and clumping cheerfully on his hind legs—the crowd of worked-up children let out a howl of laughter.

From inside the trailer, Ben's parents heard the howling outburst—and then a shocked, angry roar. The governor's mansion quickly erupted in a great commotion of laughter and roars and startled shouts.

Ben's father and mother jumped from the trailer. They rushed back to the gates in time to see Stanley, still upright on two legs, come barreling past the fat white columns at the entrance to the mansion. The grizzly bear charged down the tall marble steps leading to the wide walkway, his furry face wet with tears.

   Behind him hobbled Doc Sprinkle, dressed in a moth-eaten tuxedo. He was a thin man with small spectacles, wispy white hair, and a bad leg. He was clutching a doctor's bag and clicking down the steps with a wooden cane. At the top of the cane was whittled a likeness of Stanley's head, in happier times.

On the doctor's heels was a tidal wave of children, hooting and pointing, led by the hulking Mary-Margaret Glutty in a sparkly pink party dress. A green boa constrictor was wrapped around her neck like a scarf. Governor Gus Glutty, his frazzled secretary, and dozens of veterinarians were chasing after them.

"Stanley! Stanley!" cried Doc Sprinkle in a high, broken voice. "Stanley, wait!"

But Stanley continued racing down the walkway toward the tall, spiky gates.

The guard planted his black boots in the middle of the walkway and whipped his rifle to his chest. "Halt!" he boomed. "The party isn't over!"

But the bear ran right past him.

Stanley then hurled his big body onto the gates with a clanging crash and started scrambling over.

The guard whirled around. "Halt!" he boomed again, raising his rifle. "Halt or I'll shoot!"

From the top of the gate, Stanley glanced back warily at the guard.

"I warn you. I'm under strict orders to shoot anyone attempting to enter or leave before the party has concluded at fifteen-hundred hours—"

Clattering up from behind, Doc Sprinkle swung his black bag and knocked the rifle barrel toward the ground. In that instant, Stanley heaved his body over the spikes at the top of the gate. But as he did, he raked his thigh on a spike and tore his lavender tutu. He dropped to the sidewalk on his hind legs, a red gash on his thigh, his eyes round and wild and flicking left and right.

A bloody scrap of the frilly tutu still clung to the spike at the top of the gate.

Ben's parents gaped at Stanley; Stanley gaped at Ben's parents. Then the grizzly bear bolted to the right, fleeing away in his torn tutu.

Doc Sprinkle eyed Stanley's back through the bars of the gate. "Stanley! Stanley!" he sobbed. But the big bear, sucking furiously on two front claws, dashed away into the distance.

Then he noticed Ben's parents standing there on the other side of the gate. He blinked in surprise. "Water Boy? Lollipop?"

Ben's father winced at the sound of his nickname. "Doc, the guard!"

The guard was scowling and striding toward Doc Sprinkle. The children were behind him, buzzing like a swarm of bees. Governor Glutty, his secretary, and the veterinarians were shouting and waving their arms in the air.

Doc Sprinkle was bony thin and he easily squeezed through the gate. But his big black bag got wedged between the bars. He tugged on the handles as the guard drew near. "Water Boy, help me!"

Ben's father rushed to Doc Sprinkle and pulled him by the waist. The gate rattled and the scrap of bloody tutu dropped off the spike and fell to the sidewalk. Just as the guard was lunging for the doctor's bag, it slipped through the gate.

"Halt!" the guard barked, pointing his rifle between the bars. "All of you!"

Doc Sprinkle and Ben's parents froze at the sight of the rifle.

"I told you to wait until the party was over, didn't I? Now drop that bag, Doc Sparkle, and all of you put your hands over your heads—"

And then the wild wave of children crashed into the gate. The guard was crushed against the bars, his cap flying off, his rifle fumbling from his hands. It fell to the sidewalk outside the mansion and discharged with a *bang*. The guard's square head was left jammed between the metal bars.

"Where is it?" the children screamed. "Where's the bear?"

They pressed their eager, cake-smeared faces through the bars and caught sight of a small brown spot. "There it is!"

"After the bear!" Mary-Margaret Glutty demanded. "Everyone after the bear!"

Then the hundreds of children started squeezing through the bars of the gates, like Doc Sprinkle. But their bellies were so bloated with cake and cream soda that they quickly became stuck, their gleeful laughter turning to frantic shrieks and sobs.

Governor Glutty and the other grown-ups bounded to the bawling children and started pulling at their arms and legs, trying to free them from the gates.

In that moment, Doc Sprinkle grabbed up the scrap of Stanley's tutu from the sidewalk and hurried away with Ben's parents. As he hobbled along with his cane, Doc Sprinkle peered back over his shoulder in the direction Stanley had fled. His eyes searched the horizon, but there was no sign of the big grizzly bear. Stanley was gone.

Doc Sprinkle hobbled on. Tears were now streaming down his worn face.

"They were laughing at him," he said, his voice shaking. "I told them not to. Before he came on stage, I told them not to laugh. Stanley may not be the most talented dancing bear in the world, but he has his pride, you know."

"Of course he does," said Ben's mother, putting her hand on Doc Sprinkle's bony shoulder.

"Doc, don't you worry. This happened at the state fair too, remember? But he made his way home that time, didn't he? I expect he'll head for home again."

"I hope you're right, Water Boy," Doc Sprinkle said with a sniffle as they reached the Rambler.

"You ride home with us, Doc," Ben's father said. "This will all blow over in a day or two and we can come back here for your truck."

Above the shrieking and shouting at the gates of the governor's mansion, a loud groan was heard from the trailer. Doc Sprinkle's wet eyes grew wide.

"It's Henry the Eighth," said Ben's mother.

"Doc, we know you're upset," said Ben's father. "But the truth is, we came all this way because of Henry. Please look at him, Doc. He's very sick."

"Henry the Eighth? What's wrong with him?"

The llama recognized Doc Sprinkle's voice and groaned

even louder.

Ben's father shook his head. "I don't know, Doc," he said with a sigh. "He was fine yesterday, but this morning I found him in the barn, stiff as roof beams."

"Please, Doc," said Ben's mother, her voice trembling. "Please help Henry."

Doc Sprinkle nodded. "I'll do everything I can, Lollipop." He took a quick glance back in the direction Stanley had fled and then followed her into the trailer. Ben's father joined them by Henry the Eighth's side.

Doc Sprinkle knelt down and laid his bag, his cane, and the bloody scrap of tutu in the straw. He stroked Henry's furry cheek. The champion llama was now jittering on the floor, his muscles cramping in spasms. His eyes were wet and wild and his teeth had begun to chatter. Whitish foam was still frothing from his nostrils.

The old doctor took one look at the llama and knew what was wrong. He had seen this once before, years ago. When Stanley was still a cub, and first learning to dance, the bear had nearly died right there in its tutu. Ever since then he kept a vial of the anti-venom in his medicine chest. But he had never needed it—until today.

"Drive!" Doc Sprinkle shouted at Ben's father. "Drive as fast as you can!"

A chill blew through Ben's father. "Doc, what is it?"

Doc Sprinkle fought back more tears as he recalled Stanley's own brave battle with death. "Henry's been bit!" he said. "And the anti-venom is back in Boony Point!"

"Bit?" Ben's mother said. "Bit by what?"

"A white widow!"

Ben's father and mother gasped.

"He's dying, Water Boy! We don't have a second to spare!"

"But Boony Point is hours from here, Doc!" Ben's father said. "There's anti-venom here in Bloat City, isn't there?"

"Bloat City's last white widow was squashed years ago. I'm afraid looking for the anti-venom around here would be a wild goose chase—"

"Halt!"

They whirled around. Charging up the sidewalk was the guard, the rifle in his hands. His square head now looked more like a rectangle.

"Halt!"

"Water Boy, go! Get us back to Boony Point! I'll do everything I can to keep Henry alive!"

Wincing again at the sound of his nickname, Ben's father leaped from the trailer and darted to the driver's seat. Ben's mother clamped the trailer gate shut.

But the truck wouldn't start.

"Halt or I'll shoot!" The guard was approaching fast.

The engine sputtered and sputtered and finally, with a

blast from the tail pipe, the Rambler roared to life. The guard raised his rifle, but the truck spewed out a cloud of black smoke, blanketing his face.

And with a squeal of bald tires, Ben's father sped off for Boony Point.

A Heartbroken Sigh

THREE HOURS AFTER HE FIRST STRUCK the Giant Heart bongos, Ben was still thumping away, high in the Queen Tartelicious tree on Crabapple Cliff. But his arms were about limp as boiled bootlaces now; his eyes were smarting from the sweat dripping down his face; his throat was dry and his stomach was empty.

Still, he pressed on, slapping at the drum heads. The monster, of course, matched his choppy rhythm, dancing in a more herky-jerky fashion. But as it punched and popped its limbs, it still showed no sign of tiring. Ben sighed as he watched it move about the cliff, its belly jiggling and rattling.

He wasn't wearing a watch, but the hot sun had climbed high in the sky so he judged it was almost noon. Grandma expected him back with her crabapples by then. He pictured her scowling at the second hand on the cuckoo clock in the living room, the cuckoo bird jabbing the air twelve times with its annoying call.

He always hated that cuckoo clock.

Grandma will be angry, he thought, wincing at an image of the old woman grinding her false teeth together.

But on the heels of that thought came a happier notion: he realized that Grandma's anger might be the very thing that could save him from the monster.

If I'm not back by noon, then Grandma will get Dad to drive her out to Grizzly Woods in the truck. And Dad will be worried about me, even worried enough to bring his shotgun. If it's almost noon, I won't have to wait much longer for help. They'll be here at the cliff in less than thirty minutes!

To nurse his strength, Ben played the bongos more slowly.

The ogre followed, moving lightly, smoothly. Like a gigantic butterfly, it stretched out its long arms and fluttered across the bluff. Each minute dragged on endlessly for Ben, but the monster moved in a trance, its silver eye twinkling in the sunlight.

The boy was no longer paying much mind to the ogre, though; he was watching Grizzly Woods for a sign of his father. Then through his sweat-streaked glasses he saw something stir at the edge of the forest. His heart gave a cry—*Dad!*

He studied the trees...but saw only branches bobbing in the wind...

Finally, when he figured it had been at least thirty minutes, probably even an hour, he made a heartbroken sigh. Tears rolled down his face and plopped onto the surface of the drum.

At that moment, when it was clear his father wasn't coming after all, the hope suddenly drained from him. And with hope gone, his strength went too.

His hands dropped limp. The bongos fell silent.

The ogre was dancing near the edge of the cliff. When the booming drum quit, it stopped in its tracks. Ben watched it turn toward the crabapple tree, its eye blinking up at him, again cold and gray—and then narrowing on the ragged branch there on the ground.

Ben gulped.

They say time stops when you're about to die. And in that instant your whole life flashes before your eyes. Your Grandpa Gristle, of course, can attest to the truth of that fact. After all, when I lost my ear, the rest of my head was nearly lopped off as well. Even as a newborn, I saw my whole life flash by. (It was milk and diapers, mostly.)

Ben, though, was already twelve so he had more to view in that fateful moment. And among the many faces of his family and the people of Boony Point, he saw Mayor Olympus—and his mind locked on the mayor's big brave grin.

Mayor Olympus never gave up, not once. Not when he had those horrible boils; not when he faced down that ferocious bear to save Norman; not when he took up Norman's leg bone and vowed to make his Marching Moose the state champion. No matter what, Mayor Olympus would never give up...

It all happened in a heartbeat, before the ogre could take a single step his way, but Benjamin Boyd somehow found the will to continue.

The Giant Heart bongos boomed to life again.

The ogre's eye fluttered shut; its head began to rock. Ben watched the monster sway until finally there was a pause—then its eye snapped open and away it went with a lovely leap.

But Ben could only shake his head. *Where's Dad? Why hasn't he come looking for me? He wouldn't forget about Leech Lake...*

He pushed aside these thoughts of his father, though—they would only sap his strength.

Instead, he fixed his mind on Mayor Olympus.

The Bloody Tutu

I PRAY YOU NEVER CROSS PATHS with a white widow. The black widow, that's bad enough, but you might as well just lay down with your flowers if the white widow bites. You'd think the white widow would be no different, really, from the black widow. After all, it's just an albino type, white as a grub with pink eyes and a pink hourglass on its back. But scientists say (at least the ones who survived their experiments) that the poison of the rare white widow is far deadlier…

These were the unpleasant thoughts in Walter Boyd's mind as he barreled down Mule Creek Highway, his eyes squinting on the road. His toadskin boot was flat to the floor and the old truck was roaring like a rocket. It was rattling so madly, in fact, that it's a wonder it didn't just fall apart right there on the road. The windows were down (they hadn't rolled back up in years) and the wind was screaming, threatening to strip his lucky fishing hat from his head.

Henry the Eighth might die any minute, right there in the trailer, and they were still a long way from Boony Point.

Doc Sprinkle was in the back, kneeling beside Henry the Eighth. His mouth was pressed against the two red bite marks he had discovered on the llama's furry, quivering rump. He was sucking out the bitter poison that hadn't already slipped into the animal's bloodstream—sucking and spitting, sucking and spitting. *The less venom in the bloodstream, the better his chances,* the old doctor knew. *The more time we have.*

Ben's mother continued to hold Henry's hoof and stroke his cheek. "You'll be okay, Henry," she whispered to him, over and over, in a choked voice. "Doc Sprinkle is taking good care of you."

But poor Henry the Eighth could only grunt and grimace in reply.

Then, all of a sudden, a terrible moan rose from deep in his throat and he began wailing like a windstorm. His eyes bugged and his heart thumped wildly. His whole body flew into a fit of shaking and flailing and frothing from the nostrils. Doc Sprinkle could no longer keep his mouth on the quaking animal's rump.

"Doc, what's wrong with him?" Ben's mother cried, trying to hold onto Henry's jerking head so he wouldn't snap his own neck.

"It's the poison!" Doc Sprinkle shouted, spitting once more into the straw. "The poison has reached his heart!" He flung open his doctor's bag and rummaged through it for something, anything, that might help save Henry the Eighth. He burst into tears of frustration.

"Do something, Doc! He's *dying!*" Ben's mother fought back her own tears as she wrestled with the llama's twisting, pop-eyed head.

"I need the anti-venom!" the old doctor sobbed. Through his tears, his eyes fell on the torn scrap of bloody tutu lying in the straw by the llama's kicking legs. Henry's heart was revving like a race car now, like it would explode any second.

"Doc, please!"

Then Doc Sprinkle's eyes narrowed and he reached back into the black bag. He pulled out an empty syringe and grabbed up the scrap of Stanley's bloody tutu. He yanked out the glass vial from the syringe and thrust it toward Ben's mother.

"Here, hold this steady!"

"What?"

"Hurry, take this vial! There isn't time to explain!"

Ben's mother was reaching for the vial when Henry's body shuddered violently. Unleashing a long blood-chilling howl, he thrashed madly on the floor of the trailer, every muscle gone haywire, his eyes throbbing from their sockets, his tongue waggling fast from his mouth, his nose spurting white like milking time.

And then, Henry the Eighth, the most majestic in a long line of state champion llamas, farted like a cannon and fell dead.

For a moment there was only the roar of the Rambler; the trailer was a silent tomb.

Ben's mother crumpled into tears on the llama's chest.

"Lollipop, hold the vial!" Doc Sprinkle demanded.

"Henry, Henry..." sobbed Ben's mother into his furry chest.

"Lollipop, listen to me!"

"Henry, Henry..."

"Lollipop!"

Ben's mother lifted her head. "Doc, Henry is dead!" she wailed. "He's *dead!*"

"Just hold the vial! Do it!"

In a wet-eyed daze, Ben's mother sat up and reached for the vial. Her hand was shaking.

"Hold it steady!"

Doc Sprinkle took the torn scrap of lavender tutu in his hands and carefully wrung it over the vial. Stanley's blood dripped into the clear glass tube. He flung the torn tutu back into the straw and grabbed the vial of blood from Ben's mother.

"Close your eyes, Lollipop!" he said, snapping the vial into the syringe. He tapped the needle and a drop of Stanley's blood appeared at the sharp point.

"What—What are you doing, Doc?"

"Close your eyes! It's Henry's only chance!" He held the syringe in his hand like a dagger, aiming the needle at the llama's chest.

"Doc, what are you doing?"

Doc Sprinkle's hand came down, stabbing hard.

Ben's mother let loose an ear-piercing scream.

The needle penetrated Henry the Eighth's lifeless heart.

Ben's father heard his wife's cry and knew Henry the Eighth was dead. Tears quickly clouded his eyes.

He saw only a small blur waddling across the highway. Then the right front tire blew out and the truck went careening off the road.

The Miracle Worker

The front end of Walter Boyd's pickup truck was hanging above a muddy ditch off the side of Mule Creek Highway. They were still miles from Boony Point.

Behind in the trailer, the empty syringe was sticking out of Henry the Eighth's chest and quivering in the air. Before the truck swerved, Doc Sprinkle had plunged the needle into the llama's heart and pumped in Stanley's blood.

"Lollipop?"

The old doctor pushed himself up from a pile of hay in the corner. His spectacles were cock-eyed on his thin face. His white hair was wilder than a patch of cootgrass, and dotted with bits of straw. He had done a somersault over Henry the Eighth when the Rambler lurched off the road.

"Lollipop, are you okay?"

Doc Sprinkle saw Ben's mother hunched on top of Henry. He crawled to her and gently raised her up. She rubbed her temple. She had toppled over onto the dead llama, cracking her head against Henry's skull.

"Doc, what happened?"

"We ran off the road. I think we blew a tire." He pulled a piece of straw from his nose.

"Oh no... Walter!"

Fearing the worst, Doc Sprinkle said, "Lollipop, you wait here. I'll check on Water Boy."

He grabbed his doctor's bag and his cane and pushed open the trailer gate. He waded through the tall stinkweed to reach the driver's side of the truck. Ben's father was still sitting in his seat, gripping the steering wheel, his seat belt fastened tight. His eyes were open and staring straight ahead. They were wet with tears.

"Water Boy?" Doc Sprinkle leaned into the open window. "Water Boy, are you all right?"

Ben's father blinked. He winced at the sound of his nickname. "I heard her scream," he said, speaking in a soft, flat voice. "And I knew Henry was gone. Then I saw something in the road. I hit something in the road."

"What was it, Water—"

Another cry came from the trailer.

"Lorelai!" said Ben's father, quickly alert. He unbuckled his seat belt and pushed open the door. "What's wrong with her, Doc? Is she okay?"

"She knocked her head in the crash, I think, but she seems all right."

"Lorelai!"

Ben's father and Doc Sprinkle rushed back to the trailer and climbed inside. They found Ben's mother sitting beside Henry, stroking his cheek. Tears were streaming down her face.

Ben's father removed his hat. "Poor Henry," he said, his voice breaking.

"No, Walter!" She smiled through her tears. "Henry is alive! He's *alive!* Look!"

Ben's mother pointed to the llama's chest. It was rising and falling softly, the syringe still stuck there like a dart.

"But I heard you scream! I thought he was dead!"

"He *was*, Walter! I don't know what Doc did, but he's a miracle worker! Henry is *alive!*" Ben's mother laughed happily and looked down at Henry. The llama's eyes fluttered and opened to slits. His mouth stretched slowly into a weary grin.

"Doc, what happened?" asked Ben's father. "I thought the anti-venom was back in Boony Point."

"It is, Water Boy. But I had that scrap of tutu. I was praying Stanley's blood still had traces of the anti-venom from the time he got bit." He made a grim smile. "But he's not out of the woods. We've bought Henry some time, but we still need to get him back to Boony Point for the full dose of anti-venom as fast as we can."

The smile on Ben's mother fell. "Walter, how's the truck?"

"Lollipop, you stay with Henry," Doc Sprinkle said. "Water Boy and I will check on the truck."

Ben's father leaned down and laid trembling hands on his wife and his llama. "I'm so relieved you two are okay," he said.

"Just don't pull out that syringe, Lollipop," Doc Sprinkle said. "The needle pricked a hole in his heart and it's plugging up that hole now. When we're back in Boony Point, I'll remove the syringe and perform open-heart surgery to patch him up again."

"Okay, Doc," Ben's mother said, nodding.

Henry the Eighth lifted his head slightly and peered up at Doc Sprinkle. His lips curled and he showed his big teeth.

"You're welcome, Henry," Doc Sprinkle said softly.

Ben's parents teared up at the sight.

"Yes, thank you, Doc," said Ben's mother.

"Thank you," said Ben's father, patting Doc Sprinkle on the back.

The old doctor nodded, his white hair bobbing about. "Okay now, let's have a look at that tire, Water Boy."

Walter Boyd winced and led Doc Sprinkle to the front of the truck, where the wheels were hanging out over the ditch. They stopped short at the sight of the right front tire.

The tire had gone flat, but that was no surprise.

The surprise was the plump creature stuck fast to the rubber.

"Good heavens," whispered Doc Sprinkle, his eyes misting.

Ben's father gazed down at the motionless creature. "Is it dead, Doc?"

Doc Sprinkle shuffled closer and carefully laid two fingers on the animal's neck. He pressed gently and paused—then a tear spilled from one eye.

"I'm afraid she's…wait, I think there's a pulse." He pressed on the neck more firmly. "Yes, there's a pulse! But it's weak, and she isn't breathing!"

"What should we do, Doc?"

Doc Sprinkle wiped the tear from his cheek. "We have to get her off the tire."

"I have some work gloves in the truck." Ben's father raced to the driver-side door and yanked it open. He reached across the seat to the glove compartment and pulled out a heavy work glove. Shoving aside a rattling box of old shotgun shells, he fished out the second glove. Then he hurried back to Doc Sprinkle, who was holding the creature's paw and speaking softly in its ear.

"Can you grab onto it, Water Boy?"

Wince. "I'll try." He donned the gloves and gingerly placed his hands on both sides of the animal.

"Pull gently."

"Okay, Doc."

Ben's father gulped a breath and pulled. He pulled again. And again—

But the porcupine was stuck fast to the tire.

"It looks like the quills are in there pretty deep," Doc Sprinkle said. "Wait just a minute, Water Boy."

Ben's father released his hold on the porcupine and exhaled with a blow. He watched as Doc Sprinkle carefully poked his cane through the quills piercing the rubber tire.

"Now this time when you pull," said Doc Sprinkle, gripping the end of the cane with both hands, like a crowbar, "I'll try prying it off."

"Okay, Doc." Ben's father grasped the porcupine again in his gloves.

"Let's be gentle now. On the count of three. One, two, *three!*"

Ben's father pulled; Doc Sprinkle pried. Both men straining, the quills began sliding out from the tire with a horrible squeak.

"She's coming off, Water Boy!"

"I have her, Doc!" Ben's father cried. The porcupine slid away from the tire, into his hands.

"Put her down in the grass!"

Ben's father laid the porcupine gently on the ground by the side of the ditch. Doc Sprinkle knelt by the animal's side.

"Give me the gloves and I'll tend to her," Doc Sprinkle said. "You change the tire. We have to get back to Boony Point for that anti-venom."

"Okay, Doc." Ben's father handed him the gloves and hurried to get the spare tire and tools.

Doc Sprinkle looked down at the porcupine, his eyes brimming with tears. "It's a miracle you survived," he said softly. "I won't let you die now."

He wiped the tears from his eyes and pulled on the gloves. Then he rolled the porcupine onto its back.

"Stay with me, Agnes," he said, thinking this name would please the creature.

Doc Sprinkle tilted the porcupine's small chin high and pinched its nose shut with one hand. He pried open its mouth with the other, revealing large rat-like teeth and a limp pink tongue. Then he drew a deep breath, pressed his mouth to the porcupine's snout, and began puffing air into its lungs.

One Last Song

OUT ON CRABAPPLE CLIFF, the hot afternoon wore on. Ben was still high in the Queen Tartelicious, his hands like sandbags as he played the Giant Heart bongos. Through heavy, half-crossed eyes he watched the ogre dance below, still fresh on its huge feet.

He tried to fix on the grinning face of Mayor Olympus, but his thoughts swirled: he saw the portrait of Mayor Olympus in his mind—then there was Mayor Sackbutt, plopping to the floor—now he was slipping in the driveway at home, the tuba plunging onto his head, the whole world turning black...

He fought to stay alert, keep his clumsy hands alive. But he knew it was just a matter of time before the drum went silent...just a matter of time before the monster devoured him...

Benjamin Boyd made a deep, deep sigh: he would never see his family again. Blinking back tears, he whispered a farewell, thanking them all. (Even Grandma.) Then he summoned the strength for one more song—one last song.

And he played for them, with all his heart.

Remember this: Bongos or no bongos, love can do so much more than fear.

As Ben now played the Giant Heart bongos, a sudden and startling change came over his drumming...

He wasn't so bad.

And as he felt this change, he also felt a surge of energy shoot through him. It's true, he was still tired to the bone, but this new burst of energy somehow spurred him on. He found himself playing the bongos even better, which led to more energy, more drumming…

It snowballed from there: his body, nearly empty of strength, filled with a power that rose from some deeper place inside him; his hands became so quick and able he could hardly believe they were his.

And when he glanced up again at the ogre, he saw it in a different light. Oh, it was still a monstrous creature, that much couldn't be overlooked. But now he watched in wonder as it danced, finally seeing the beauty too. And as the ogre went sailing past the crabapple tree, he saw the crooked smile on its face and realized that the monster was filled with the same sort of energy now flooding through him...

Ben played with abandon, making the Giant Heart bongos ring the air like church bells. And like a ten-ton angel, the monster took flight, its feet gliding over the rocky ground, its arms grasping for the heavens.

Ben lost all track of time. He no longer noticed the sun, now falling in the sky. The drumming and dancing had carried him away, freeing him of everything but the wild, wonderful energy—the pure, heart-thumping joy—that was pulsing through him, pulsing through them both.

* * *

BACK AT THE HOUSE, GRANDMA wasn't feeling so chipper. When noon came and went, and Ben didn't appear, she just expected the dawdling boy would be back in the next minute. And as each minute led to another, she supposed it would be the next minute, then the next. Her hunger was growing, of course, but she wasn't about to leave the cool farmhouse and trudge all that way to Crabapple Cliff in her rain suit on such a hot afternoon.

And where was Water Boy? Surely he'd be back soon. And if Ben hadn't returned by then, Water Boy could drive her out to the edge of Grizzly Woods.

In this way, as she sat in the living room and scowled at the cuckoo clock, the time slipped past. By mid-afternoon, she wasn't only hungry, she was sleepy: it was time for her nap. So she shuffled out to the porch, lifted old Alf from the floor, and dropped down on the porch swing. And there she dozed, with the pug snoring in her lap, both as peaceful as prayers…until a loud rumble from her belly jarred her awake.

Grandma replaced Alf under the porch swing and moved inside as the cuckoo bird began to caw.

It was now five o'clock.

"Where is he?" Grandma grumbled. Then her eyes narrowed on the cuckoo bird. "Oh, so that's it—tit for tat. The boy is out to stoke my hunger with a little practical joke of his own: lazing the day away on Crabapple Cliff, playing those bongos instead of filling my basket."

She made for the living room closet. "And where is his lollygagging father?" she muttered, elbowing past a pile of big stuffed animals. "I'll have to march all the way out there now."

She located a metal flashlight, clubbed a hippo on the head with it, and shoved the closet door shut. Then she kicked the slippers off her feet and banged through the screen door onto the porch. Alf looked up, eyes rolling.

"At least it's dipping now," Grandma said, squinting at the sun. It was turning orange in the blue sky. "But it would be nice if a cloud or two blew by. The less I see of that hot ball, the better."

She moved to the porch swing, strung to the ceiling with chain, and stood the flashlight on the arm. Behind the swing, hanging from three hooks on the white wall of the house, were a rain coat, rain pants, and rain hat. A pair of rain boots and two rubber gloves were below on the floor.

Everything was yellow.

Grandma's stomach made a deep growl as she reached into the pocket of her bathrobe and took the false teeth. She pushed them into her mouth and clicked the horsey teeth together.

"This is hardly a humdinger, Butterfingers," she said, shrugging off the bathrobe and revealing her own pair of Marching Moose pajamas. "In fact, stoking the hunger of another human being is no practical joke at all. It's a criminal act!"

She went on grumbling to herself while pulling on the slick rain suit. Last was the hat. She took special care covering up her blond curls under it.

When she was done, the old woman was a vision: the nearest thing to a grumpy banana you'd ever hope to see.

Grandma bent and gave a quick pat to the pug's head with her gloved hand. The ancient dog croaked and sneezed. Then she grabbed the flashlight from the porch swing and clomped down the steps in her boots.

She huffed down the driveway and up dusty Route Z, muttering the whole way: "I warned his mother. I told her an overcooked imagination turns the mind to mush. And now that boy's brain is so soft he can't tell the difference between a fine prank and foul play. No grandmother on earth wants to press charges against her only grandchild, but this mischief is no laughing matter. In the eyes of the law, this amounts to *attempted starvation!*"

143 Angry Llamas

By the time Grandma approached the bend in the road, she had grown quiet—except, that is, for the steady rumbling of her stomach. The sun continued to drop, but it was still glowing hot and Grandma was slowly roasting inside her rain suit. Her coat and pants were now sticking to her pajamas.

"I could have carried it this far," she griped under her breath. "I could have put it on right here in the road and saved me some grief."

Grandma, though, was a creature of habit. She always pulled on her rain suit on the front porch. A cool morning is far different from a hot afternoon, but Grandma, fixed on Ben like a fox to a pheasant, hadn't stopped to think twice about it.

As she rounded the bend, where Route Z curved to the left and Olympus Drive went on toward town, she paused. She gazed down the long, straight, dusty road. She saw the timber fences in the distance, on both sides. Her eyes studied the unfamiliar sight of the empty fields. The only movement was the tall goldenrod waving in the early evening breeze.

"They don't know," she whispered, her tight mouth breaking into a smile.

The llamas were usually waiting for her, straining at the fences. They had long ago gotten used to the two times Grandma passed by in the morning and returned before noon. All 144 llamas would be standing there stiffly, staring at her coldly.

"I'm never on the road at this time of day," she said, an edge of excitement in her voice. "Today I'll pass right by under their big noses."

Despite the heat and hunger pangs, Grandma beamed

from beneath her rain hat. Then with light, quick steps, she continued up Route Z.

Her heart pattered faster as she neared the fences, but the llamas were nowhere in sight. She giggled to herself, giddy with victory.

"Here I am, porridge heads!" Grandma began to bray. She stopped and posed. "See my lovely coat! See my lovely pants!" She went strutting back and forth in front of the fences, a model in a fashion show. "Oh, I wish you could see me! I'm lovely as a buttercup today! But you're in the stables, aren't you, sulking over poor Henry the Eighth!"

Grandma was right about the llamas. They hadn't expected her to stroll past in the late afternoon. And it was true, they were on pins and needles over Henry. But what she didn't realize is that it wasn't only her regular times that brought the llamas down to the road.

It was also her smell.

And with the wind picking up, that sour odor was carried straight over the fields of goldenrod to the stables, where the llamas had returned after an anxious day of grazing. But Ben's father wasn't home yet, so the stable doors were still wide open.

Grandma was parading on the road, just about to pull off her rain hat, when the ground suddenly shook with the sound of hundreds of hooves.

The old woman's heart practically stopped. Her whole body froze; her eyes boggled in surprise.

The llamas came thundering through the fields on both sides of the road. Before Grandma's brain had defrosted, every llama in the herd (minus poor Henry) was lined up along the fences. They glared at her with their large round eyes, their mouths chewing furiously.

When you consider the fact that 143 llamas were standing there by the road, it was remarkably quiet. Besides the wind whispering through the fields, the only sound was the animals jawing on their big mouthfuls of goldenrod.

Grandma gaped left and right. She gulped.

Normally, it was Henry the Eighth who grunted the signal. But with Henry gone, the llamas were flustered. In that moment of indecision, Grandma ducked her head and broke into a desperate dash up the road.

She heard the llamas yelping and then that horrible chorus of mouths spitting. She felt the gobs of chewed-up goldenrod splatting like jellyfish onto her hat and coat and pants and boots. It was the dishonor she endured every time she passed by the fences, but today was even more maddening. Today she thought she had managed to outwit them, then suddenly she was getting pelted again. And all because of Butterfingers!

If he had just come back with the crabapples, like he was told, she would be at home right now eating crabapple pie!

"Sheriff Silver will hear about this villainy, Butterfingers!" Grandma shrieked as the last of the barrage hit her back.

Llamas, of course, are first-rate spitters. This is true of the species in general, but especially true of the llamas that lived on the Boyd Llama Farm. After all, when you practice something often enough, you get pretty good at it. And the llamas were spitting at Grandma every day she went out to Crabapple Cliff, and twice a day at that. This had been going on for years, ever since Grandma hurled some offending words at Henry the First.

Grandma ran for a while, as she always did, though the llamas were out of ammunition and never followed very far after their attack. Finally, she stopped running and stood hunched over, breathing hard. Her rain suit was coated with the sweet-smelling gobs of goldenrod.

She flapped her arms and kicked her legs and the bigger lumps slithered off like snails. Then she used her gloves to scrape at her body as best she could, flicking the spit onto the road in disgust. But even after much of it was removed, her rain suit was still slimy and slippery and the cheerful yellow color was now the shade of muddy butter. And, of course, there were parts of her body that she couldn't really reach, like the middle of her back, so spots like this were still globby and glistening.

"Butterfingers," she growled, bowing her head and scraping off the clumps of llama spit from her rain hat. They dripped like stringy blobs before her eyes and dropped into the dust at her feet.

"Thank heavens I didn't take off my hat," she said with a shiver of relief. "I hate to even imagine it…my beautiful curls exposed on the open road. I'd have lost what's left of my mind."

Her stomach rumbled and she went clomping off. The sun was falling fast now, turning the horizon pretty shades of pink and purple.

Old Man Fibber and Carl

At the top of the rise in Route Z, Grandma gazed down at the junk monster. It had been there by the road since early spring, but until this moment she had only seen it in the morning. Most of it was in shadow now, but the gray metal eye glinted in the fading light. With the breeze blowing stronger, the joints of the junk monster groaned across the Abernathy Pumpkin Patch.

Grandma shook her head, muttering with a chuckle, "It's even a sadder pile of junk in the evening."

As she clomped down the hill, her eyes roaming over the farmhouse and the barn and the mountains of scrap metal, she drew up short at the sight of something else: a dark figure—no, two dark figures—there at the tumbledown fence. Sometimes Grandma heard sounds coming from the barn on her hikes out to Crabapple Cliff. Besides the usual splashing, lately there had been hammering and sawing and other sounds of mischief. But she hadn't run into Old Man Fibber, in the skin, in nearly eighteen years. When she realized it was him, her thin eyebrows bristled.

Old Man Fibber knew the hours Grandma passed by his farm and he didn't stray outside during that time. Even through the spring, when he was busy building his junk monster, he would check his father's old pocket watch carefully and head back to the barn before Grandma appeared. But today was different. Today Grandma was on the road at an odd hour and Old Man Fibber hadn't expected her to be trudging toward him now. He was admiring the sunset with Carl, like every summer evening, when the old snapping turtle suddenly hissed. Old Man Fibber turned and saw a small dark figure clomping his way. When he realized it was Grandma, the red stubble on his head prickled.

Old Man Fibber and Grandma would probably have been content to hold their tongues, but Carl wasn't known for his self-control. The closer Grandma got, the louder he hissed from his perch on the fence post. He was squirming so hard in Grandma's direction that Old Man Fibber had to grip him tight with his big greasy-black hands.

"Easy, Carl," Old Man Fibber said in his deep, rusty voice. He was a shaggy yak of a man with a bushy mustache and beard so fiery red it looked like his face was in flames.

If Grandma had just grit her horsey teeth and passed by without a glance, a whole heap of unpleasantness could have been avoided. But she was in a foul mood already, and the sight of Carl hissing at her brought the old woman to a grinding halt. She stood there steaming in her rain suit, a careful distance from the fence.

"I thought Sheriff Silver told you to keep a muzzle on that monster," she said, pointing a gloved finger at Carl.

Old Man Fibber glared down at her in his oily bib overalls. He rubbed Carl's craggy shell.

"He don't need a lice-lickin' muzzle on my land."

"Don't you go using that kind of vulgar talk around a lady."

"Lady? Is that what you are under all that llama spit?"

Carl tittered as only a snapping turtle can.

"Now get your clodhoppers down this pus-gushin' road," Old Man Fibber rumbled as Grandma gave a gasp, "and let a man and his turtle enjoy a fine sunset together in peace—"

"Don't you *dare* use the name Pus in vain!" Grandma cried.

"I'll do as I please on my own property, woman."

Grandma nearly gnashed a spark with her false teeth. "I can see that," she shot back. "The two of you whiling away your time in the barn there, splashing around in the bathtub together—"

"Last I heard, it's no crime playin' with a rubber duck,"

the old man growled.

"You don't muzzle him in the bathtub, that's your business, but the sheriff said to strap that creature's foul snout when he's outside your land. And look at his head—it's sticking out over the road."

"So?"

"So I'm a tax-paying citizen and this road is *public property*. That monster needs a muzzle."

Old Man Fibber clenched his jaw to keep from erupting. If he hadn't been holding Carl back, the big snapper would have lunged right off the fence post.

"Eighteen crud-crusted years later and you still provoke him," he said. "That's how you got yourself nipped last time."

"*Nipped?*" Grandma's eyes bulged behind her glasses. She yanked off her glove. "Look at this finger! That monster chomped my pinky and wouldn't let go! It was a mangled mess—even Doc Sprinkle couldn't save it!"

Carl snapped madly at the sight of Grandma's pinky.

"And whose hairy pit-sniffin' fault was that? We was mindin' our business, fixin' Water Boy's shears, when you went and provoked him."

"That monster attacked me!"

"He was defendin' my honor!"

"He chewed up my pinky!"

"You called me Fibber!"

"You *are* a fibber!"

"I'm no scab-pickin' fibber!"

"It was the *grizzly bears!*"

There was a pause, though Carl went on snapping. Old Man Fibber's eyes, bloodshot from a lack of sleep, suddenly glistened. He spoke in a softer rumble.

"I saw what it was and it wasn't the grizzlies." He pointed his long nose up at the junk monster. "This here is what I saw, more or less. You have to imagine the hair."

Grandma gazed up at the junk monster, listening to it groan. Her mind reeled back to the time she was twelve. Everyone believed it was the grizzly bears that had gotten them—everyone but Old Man Fibber.

Back then he was just nine, a gangly red-haired kid and a whiz with machinery. He claimed he was passing by the empty field in the late afternoon when he saw it. A monster. Huge and hairy. He hid behind a leg of the water tower as it lumbered past, groaning and holding one eye, heading in the direction of Crabapple Cliff. Then he ran to the high school gym, where the whole town had gathered for a surprise party to celebrate the mayor's twenty-eighth birthday.

He tried to tell people what he saw, he tried and he tried, but no one believed him. "Monsters?" they said. "There are no such things as monsters!"

And when Mayor Olympus never appeared after marching band practice, they went hunting down the grizzlies.

Grandma turned back to Old Man Fibber and Carl. "Fibber," she said, "the only monster that's ever been in Boony Point is that turtle."

"I know what I saw!" the old man thundered. "I been puttin' up with this Fibber business for sixty-nine years and three hundred thirty-one days! I may not be the dinosaur you are, but I can hear them gates of heaven creakin' open for me! And I'm not havin' that wrongful dirt-flingin' name carved into my headstone! I started this life as Airborne and that's the way I'll be flyin' from it!"

"Well, if you take that monster with you," Grandma sniffed, pulling on her glove, "you just be sure to muzzle him before you two fly off. Heaven is *public property,* you know." She snapped at Carl with her horsey teeth and went strutting up the road.

Carl was so beside himself he chomped right onto the fence post.

"I'll show you!" Old Man Fibber called to Grandma's back. "I'll show you, *Squeeze!*"

At the sound of her nickname, Grandma stopped dead in her tracks. Tears pricked her eyes. Then she bit her quivering lip and continued up Route Z.

"I'll show you all!" Old Man Fibber railed as Carl gnawed on the fence post. "I'm no Fibber! I'm Airborne! You hear me? *I'm Airborne!*"

A Whack on the Nose

It was nearly dark by the time Grandma stepped off Route Z and tromped over to the edge of Grizzly Woods. The sun had disappeared in a blaze of color, replaced by the moon, round and bright.

The old woman's mood had grown more sour than a jug of chunky milk. Not only was she hungry and thirsty, not only was she hot and sweaty and tired, not only did she get soused with llama spit, but she had suffered another foul run-in with Old Man Fibber.

Grandma clicked on the flashlight and aimed it up the path. She squinted through her glasses and frowned. The final hike through the thick forest would be like venturing into a cave. Grizzly Woods was dark enough during the day; she had never moved through it at night. But at least she knew the path by heart, and had a flashlight in hand…

Grumbling to herself, Grandma stepped over the large root of a bigsap maple and entered the forest. The moon struggled through the treetops, giving only a faint glow. She paused and slowly swept the beam through the trees. "I'm warning you!" she called out to the darkness. "I'm in no mood for mischief today!"

She listened hard, but heard only the rumble of her own stomach. Though Ben was still playing the bongos on Crabapple Cliff, it was out of earshot. And by the time she drew closer, and could have picked up the sound, the drum would be dead silent.

Grandma trudged ahead, her rain suit rustling in the hush. About halfway to Crabapple Cliff, she noticed a white glow over the path. She stopped, pointing her flashlight at the branch of a gumnut hickory.

The eyes of a great frosty owl gleamed back like headlamps. The big bird hooted gruffly at Grandma—no owl likes a flashlight in its eyes, and least of all this brand of bird. Then it flapped its wings and swooped down. Grandma ducked as it swept over her head.

"Hey!"

She spun around and searched for the owl. She found it perched on the branch of an oak tree. The owl was gripping another overhanging limb with its talons—and in those talons was Grandma's yellow rain hat.

"Give me back my hat!" Grandma cried. "Give it back!"

The owl closed its eyes.

Grandma strode over to the tree and scowled up at the owl.

"Drop that hat, buzzard! Drop it!"

The owl just sat there.

Of course, Grandma was something of a squirrel when it came to climbing trees, and she had the fleeting notion to scrabble up that ragbark oak—then quickly dropped the idea. If she got anywhere near the branch, the owl would probably fly right off, taking the hat with it.

Instead, she beamed her flashlight at the ground and found a scatter of acorns beneath the tree. Maybe if she hurled up a handful, she could startle the owl into lifting off and leaving her hat behind.

She pinched the flashlight under an armpit, tugged off her gloves, and stuffed them in the pockets of her rain coat. Then she reached down, her hand set to scoop at the acorns—when she heard a rough snort from behind. Grandma grabbed the flashlight and whirled around—

In the beam was the face of a large moose.

"No!" she shrieked as the moose's snout closed in. "I'm in no mood—" Then the animal's big tongue flicked out and licked a lump of the wet goldenrod from Grandma's shoulder.

Grandma groaned and tromped up the path toward Crabapple Cliff. She was too tired to run and the lanky moose easily kept pace, licking at the back of Grandma's rain coat.

The sweet smell of freshly-chewed goldenrod soon attracted two more moose. Now there were three moose tailing Grandma, licking at her rain suit and jousting over the largest lumps.

Grandma always did her best to brave the licking. It wasn't just The Moose Taboo that kept her from driving them off with her rolling pin each day when they started licking at her like a lollipop. What made her grit her teeth and continue clomping on to Crabapple Cliff was the thought of Mayor Olympus.

At least they turn back when I leave the forest, she would reason to herself. They seem skittish of the cliff. And they do help with that horrible llama spit.

But this had been a remarkably bad day. On top of everything else, an uppity owl had just stolen her rain hat. As hard as she tried to hold to the image of Mayor Olympus and bear the rough licking in the darkness, her patience finally snapped when the three jostling moose bumped her from behind and nearly knocked her flat.

"That's enough!" she screeched, spinning around and whacking the nearest moose on the nose with her flashlight. The moose bellowed in surprise and turned in fright. It loped away into the forest, followed by the others.

Grandma sighed as she watched the moose disappear beyond the beam of her flashlight. Then she turned and continued plodding up the path toward Crabapple Cliff. She felt bad, in a way, about whacking the moose on the nose. It wasn't so much the moose that made her frown, it was her memory of Mayor Olympus…

Then the scene was playing in her head, like a scratchy old movie: she was sobbing in a chair in the Olympus Music

Shop; he was sitting across from her, holding her hands; she looked up to see his kind, twinkling eyes; she heard his voice, deep and musical…

"Squeeze…" he was saying.

Grandma's eyes grew wet. "I'm sorry, Mr. Mayor," she whispered to the darkness. "I'm sorry I whacked that moose on the nose." And as she trudged up the path, her hand rose to her hair and touched one of the faded yellow ribbons tied into her curls.

The Drumbeat Dies

UNDER THE FULL MOON, SHINING ONTO Crabapple Cliff like a spotlight, the ogre danced. It continued gliding gracefully through the darkness, hardly making a sound—except for that constant clinking in its belly.

Ben was playing the bongos, of course, but just barely. The burst of joy of that afternoon had finally ebbed as the sun sank into the sea. Now he was like a wind-up toy running down—any second, he thought, his hands would finally stop for good.

And he knew what would happen when the drum fell silent.

Ben peered through the gloom. The monster was matching his rhythm, slowing its movements. He watched as it drifted near the tree, then danced below him. He could see its face clearly now: the eye was still silver, but no longer sparkling, and its mouth was open and drooping, the dark tongue flopping out to one side. Above the wind and the waves he could hear its breath, hard and rough.

It's tired too. Just a little more and maybe it will stop…maybe it will leave…

But the ogre went on wiggling its hips, its great gut rattling. And before Ben realized it, his body was slumping into the branch beside him, his arms were dangling dead in the air. He had no more strength to play the bongos. In fact, he hardly had the strength to sit there in the tree. He was so tired he just closed his eyes and hoped it would all be over soon…

Now I warn you, the next part gets pretty gruesome, and I know your mother would want me to skip past it. She would probably say that children ought to be spared from things this foul. But I, for one, don't think it helps to hide under the covers when beauty turns to boils. Hug your teddy bear tight, that's fine, but look life square in the eye. Because the truth is—and it's true even when you don't believe it. The truth is, you're bigger than any boil that might rise up beside you.

Put that in your piggy bank.

Ben knew the monster had stopped dancing when the jangling in its belly quit. He then heard a throaty groan and he braced himself for the terrible roar—

But instead he heard heavy footsteps pounding away.

Surprised by the sound, Ben opened his eyes and saw the ogre moving to the edge of the cliff. It stopped there, its back to him, a huge black shadow by the crashing sea.

Ben watched, waiting and wondering. Seconds later, the shadow began to shake. It quaked and rumbled and a sickly moan filled the dark sky. And then, with a violent roar, the ogre retched, hooting right there by the side of the cliff.

Ben choked back a gag. He couldn't make out what was tumbling from the monster's mouth, but he heard clinking and clanging in the gush. Then, with a final heave, the last of the things that had been rattling around inside the ogre's belly spilled to the dust of Crabapple Cliff.

Just hearing all this secondhand is enough to turn the stomach, I know. It wasn't much fun to describe, believe me. But I think you'd agree that actually witnessing the ogre in such a state would be far worse.

It's lucky for Ben this didn't happen in broad daylight with the ogre right there by the crabapple tree. Still, he felt queasy to his toes and nearly toppled to the ground—but managed to grab hold of a branch to steady himself. In that instant, though, he took his eyes off the huge shadow hunched over in the darkness.

When he looked back, the monster was gone.

Ben blinked. His eyes fell on what the creature had left behind: a large dark mound, glinting here and there in the moonlight.

Crabapples

WEAK AND WOOZY AS HE WAS, Ben started climbing down the Queen Tartelicious as quickly as he could. But clouds were now blowing across the sky, snuffing out the moon. By the time he reached the lower branches, Crabapple Cliff was doused in darkness.

As he groped for the last and lowest branch, the Giant Heart bongos dangling from his neck, Ben suddenly found himself tumbling through the air…

The next thing he knew, his eyes were opening and squinting in the glare of a flashlight.

And the glare of his grandmother.

"Just as I thought!" Grandma said, her eyes bulging behind her glasses. "This may be your notion of a practical joke, Butterfingers, but attempted starvation is hardly a prank!"

"Yes, Grandma..." Ben replied, his head hazy and aching.

"You spent the whole day playing those bongos, didn't you?"

"Yes, Grandma, but I—"

"And you finally fell asleep here under the tree!"

"No, Grandma, I was up in the tree—"

"Up in the tree? Well, where's my picnic basket?"

Grandma swept her flashlight across the ground and found the basket nearby. As she rustled over to it, the beam flickered and dimmed. She rapped the flashlight on her hip and the beam shone brightly again.

"Grandma, listen," Ben whispered, struggling to his feet and peering off into the blackness. "We have to get away from here. I don't know where it went, but it might come back any second—"

"It's empty!" Grandma cried. She was holding open the lid of the wicker basket and staring inside. Her stomach howled in disappointment.

"Grandma, don't yell—"

"It's completely empty! You didn't pick one crabapple! Not one! This, young man, is a *criminal act!*"

"I was going to, Grandma, but...but there was a *monster!*"

Grandma dropped the lid of the picnic basket with a clap. She aimed the flashlight back at Ben. "What did you say?"

"A monster!" The words spilled out in his loudest whisper. "It disappeared just before you got here! I meant to pick your crabapples, I really did, but this morning I heard a groaning sound coming from the cliff. At first, I thought it was you, but it turned out to be a huge hairy monster—"

"Butterfingers!"

"I had to stay in the tree and play the bongos to keep it dancing around the cliff—"

"Butterfingers, you must think your grandmother has oatmeal for brains! I know exactly where you got the idea for that tall tale, using it as a ruse to cover up your shameless crime: at the sight of Old Man Fibber's junk monster!"

"But Grandma, it's true! And it looked just like that junk monster—well, you have to imagine the hair—"

"I don't want to hear any more!" Grandma cried, her stomach growling loudly. "I've had a bellyful of monsters today! Now you get up in that tree, this instant, and start picking my crabapples!" She marched the picnic basket over to Ben and thrust it in his hands. It may have been empty, but it still felt heavy as lead to Ben's worn-out arms.

"Grandma, I can't climb the tree now," he whispered. "It's so dark and I'm so tired—"

"Lordy, what's wrong with this flashlight?" The beam had dimmed again. Grandma rapped it twice on her hip and the light flickered back brightly.

"Grandma…" Ben's ear was cocked toward the cliff.

The old woman's stomach rumbled again from beneath her rain coat. "I'm not about to climb this tree on an empty stomach. I'll hold the flashlight for you and you scamper up there with the picnic basket—"

"Grandma, what's that?" Ben's heart pounded as he peered out at the darkness.

"That's the sound of *hunger,* Butterfingers."

"No, that moaning sound."

"What moaning sound?" Grandma pointed her flashlight toward the cliff. "I told you I don't want to hear any more about—"

Then the flashlight dimmed and faded to a small yellow glow. Grandma growled and rapped it against her hip, again and again. This time the bright beam wouldn't return.

"Now we can't see an infernal thing!" huffed Grandma as she watched the last tiny glow of her flashlight go out.

"Grandma, listen! There it is!"

They listened as a moan rose on the dark cliff.

"Boy, that's the wind! It picks up at nightfall, you know!" She shoved the flashlight into a pocket of her rain coat. "Now fill up that basket so I can make a pie tonight! Gather them from the ground if you must. But be careful about the wormy ones! Check each one carefully for worms!"

Ben set the picnic basket, and his bongos, on the ground. "Grandma," he whispered, "where's my Dad? I thought he might drive you out here—"

"I thought he might too," Grandma grumbled. "But they're still not back."

"What?"

"Like father, like son, when it comes to lollygagging. Now get to work!"

Ben sighed and began groping for crabapples with his grandmother. Without the moonlight, or the flashlight, they were forced to hold each one right up to their glasses to check for worms. But the truth is, the light was too dim, and their eyesight was too poor, for them to quickly tell the difference between the fine red ones and the fine red wormy ones.

"I think that's about ninety-seven, Grandma," said Ben, giving the basket a shake.

"Keep at it, Butterfingers. Fill it up. I'll need more than ninety-seven this time, I expect. I'll be needing extra if you put in any wormy ones."

Ben and his grandmother went on picking up crabapples and eyeballing them to check for worms. The small boy had no idea, really, whether each piece of fruit contained a worm or not, but Grandma seemed to be inspecting them closely and tossing quite a few back to the ground with a small *thud*, so he thought he'd better do the same or risk her wrath.

Grandma, in fact, couldn't tell any better than Ben which crabapples were the wormy ones. She couldn't throw all of them in the basket, though, or Ben would simply copy her. And so she pretended to check each one carefully and rejected about half.

There had been no sign of the ogre since it disappeared, but Ben was still terrified it would return. He tried to hurry without appearing to be careless. And, of course, he couldn't mention the monster again. That would only rile up Grandma and any yelling might draw it back to the tree.

So they worked at a possum's pace, but finally the basket was full. Grandma slapped the lid shut and rustled to her feet.

"You carry it, Butterfingers. It's the least you could do

after all the heartache you caused today."

Ben was exhausted, but he didn't argue. He draped the bongos around his neck and grasped the handle of the basket. He strained to lift it. It was a lot heavier than the usual load of ninety-seven crabapples, especially when he was so weary, but he managed to hoist it with two hands. Then he wobbled after his grandmother toward Grizzly Woods.

He was just glad to be getting far away from Crabapple Cliff.

Grandma's Hat

Grizzly Woods was now blacker than a hot bowl of crow soup.

But even with no moonlight to peek through the tall trees, Grandma knew the path so well, every treacherous root and rock, that she stepped smartly ahead.

Ben could follow the clomping of his grandmother's rain boots, not to mention the regular rumbles from her stomach, but he didn't know where the obstacles lay and it wasn't easy lifting his feet while carrying the heavy picnic basket. He stumbled a lot, and nearly fell when his foot slid fast on a walnut.

"You be careful with those crabapples!" Grandma called back through the darkness. "Don't you drop that basket!"

"Yes, Grandma," Ben puffed in reply.

As the two went along, Ben saw the faint glow of eyes watching from the forest. When he heard snuffling, he knew they were moose. The moose, of course, had caught Grandma's scent again, but this time they held back. The shocking news that the old woman in the rain suit attacked one of the herd that evening with a flashlight had swept the forest like wildfire. The moose were wisely keeping their distance.

Except for one. He was a young, reckless animal, the kind that acted on desire without a second thought, and when he smelled Grandma approach, he shuffled right toward her with his tongue drooping out.

He didn't get in one lick.

When Grandma heard the lumbering footsteps, she reacted so quickly that Mayor Olympus had no time to enter her head. Her mood was so foul, and her hunger so fierce, she instantly pulled the flashlight from her pocket and began swinging it wildly.

A second later there was a crack, like a gun shot, and a shatter of glass.

Ben froze and saw a sudden glow of yellow light on the path ahead. Grandma was gripping the flashlight and in the beam was the terrified face of the moose, its tongue still drooping out. It seems Grandma gave a hard whack with the metal flashlight to one of the moose's antlers. This broke the glass lens covering the bulb, but somehow also jarred new life into the beam.

"I'll have no more mischief tonight!" Grandma shouted, shaking the flashlight like a billy club. "Keep your tongues to yourselves!"

The young moose, yelping in fright, turned right on his hooves and fled back down the path.

This probably wasn't a good time to bring up The Moose Taboo, but Ben was stunned at what Grandma had just done. Fortunately, as the subject was about to blunder from his mouth, Ben stopped, his eyes drawn to the tree limb stretching out above her.

"Grandma, what's that?" he said.

Grandma saw that Ben was pointing up at a ragbark oak. Aiming her flashlight at the branch, she boggled behind her glasses.

"It's my hat!" she exclaimed.

"Your hat?"

"My rain hat."

"What's your rain hat doing up there?"

"An owl snatched it off my head," Grandma grumped. She swept her flashlight along the limb, around the oak tree, and to the trees nearby, but found no sign of the great frosty owl. Aiming the beam again at her hat, she said, "Don't just stand there like a stump. Scamper up to that branch and grab my hat."

Ben stared at the ragbark oak, looming in the gloom. "Grandma, I don't think I can climb any more trees today."

"*More* trees?" Grandma said, turning on Ben with the flashlight. "What do you mean, *more* trees? You didn't even climb the crabapple tree today!"

Ben gulped. He didn't dare bring up the monster again.

"Butterfingers," Grandma grumbled on, "I need that hat. I can't have my head exposed on the road, can I? I expect the herd is bedded down by now, but I'm not taking any chances with these curls." Her stomach rumbled loudly. "Now stop twiddling your toes so I can get home with my crabapples!"

Ben sighed. "Yes, Grandma." He lugged the picnic basket over to the oak tree and set it down, along with his bongos, at the foot of the trunk.

Grandma shone the flashlight at the lowest limb. "Jump for that branch. Once you grab on, I'll give your feet a push." She stood the flashlight on the ground, its beam spotlighting the tree, and pulled on her rubber gloves.

Ben eyed the branch. Thank goodness it was lower than that limb on the crabapple tree.

He took a deep breath, bent his knees, and jumped. His hands were tender, and the bark was rough, but he held on, his legs kicking in the air. "Grandma, give me a push!"

"First stop flopping like a frog!"

Ben let his legs dangle for a moment and Grandma gripped the soles of his boots with her gloves.

"On a count of three, I'll push and you pull. One, two, *three!*"

Grandma gave a grunting shove as Ben struggled to pull himself up. But just as his right leg swung over the branch, his left leg kicked out hard, like a testy mule. His boot shot through the old woman's grasp and tagged her flush in the forehead.

"*YOW!*" Grandma shrieked, falling to her seat with a

rustling thump. One hand flew up to rub the blow. "Butterfingers, you kicked me in the head!"

"Sorry, Grandma," Ben replied in a small voice from above.

"Oh, I bet you enjoyed that, didn't you? Giving your poor grandmother a frisky kick—"

Suddenly Grandma froze, her gloved hand at her forehead. *"NO!"* she screamed, like the devil himself was prodding her with a pitchfork.

She yanked the hand away, tore off the glove, and scrambled to the flashlight. She stuck her hand in the beam and studied it. Then she slowly brought her fingers up to touch her hair. She held her breath, feeling for any sign of slime in the curls bouncing near her forehead.

"Grandma, are you okay?"

The old woman heaved a heavy sigh of relief. "Butterfingers, if I had found one tiny drop of llama spit in my hair from that glove…"

Rustling to her feet, she snatched up the flashlight and aimed it at Ben. He was on top of the branch now, hugging it like a frightened beetle. "Start scampering, young man!"

With Grandma lighting the way, Ben inched along the branch of the oak tree. When he reached the trunk, his arms hugged halfway around it and he slowly stood. He gazed up at the rain hat. The slender branch it was resting on jutted from the other side of the tree. He would have to leap for it and hope he could grab on—

"Right there, Butterfingers! Jump for the branch!" Grandma was pointing the circle of light at the spot where the branch met the trunk.

It was a warm night, but Ben shivered.

"Don't dawdle! It's just a little jump! Even a toddler could do it! Jump and grab the branch, then…"

Grandma carried on with her coaching, but it was only background noise to Ben. He was summoning the confident smile of Mayor Olympus once more. He pictured Mayor Olympus in the same predicament: Mayor Olympus easing his grip on the trunk; steadying himself on the branch; bending his knees, preparing to spring…

The next thing he knew, Ben found himself leaping through the air and grabbing hold of the new limb.

"Boy, you have some flying squirrel in your blood after all!" Grandma said with a chuckle. Then she slid the flashlight beam from Ben to the yellow rain hat. "Now just pull yourself up and creep along the branch, like you did before."

Ben began struggling to get onto the branch, but as he did, the limb bobbed up and down. When a soft creaking came from beside him, where the branch joined the trunk, his whole body froze. He clung there like an ice-cold sloth, his arms and legs wrapped around the branch from below.

"Grandma, it's going to break!"

"Nonsense, a tree like this—"

"I'm too heavy, Grandma!"

"Butterfingers, you're light as a pill bug! And that branch is sturdy so don't mind the creaking. It would take far more than a scrawny boy to snap the branch of a ragbark oak."

Maybe his grandmother was right, Ben thought, but he wouldn't risk bouncing the branch by trying to crawl on top of it. He would just slide along the branch like this, dangling from his arms and legs, then knock the hat down to her.

The branch wobbled, and the creaking continued, but Ben gamely crept forward, inch by inch.

"See, Butterfingers, you're nearly there!" Grandma said. She was underneath the hat now, shining the flashlight up at it. "That's it…a little closer…now reach out your hand and knock it off."

Ben could see the yellow hat just ahead, drooping down across the branch. He slowly unhooked his right arm and stretched out his hand…

But he could only brush it with his fingertips. He strained to reach farther, but when he did, the branch shook and there was a horrible creak—

"Grandma!"

"Knock the hat off!"

Ben swiped at the hat…

"Grandma!"

Now don't worry, Grandma was right—the branch didn't snap. It might have, I suppose, but a moment after the hat fell (a bull's-eye on Grandma's head), Ben fell too. When he swatted at the hat, he lost hold of the branch.

It's lucky that Grandma was below to break his fall.

As the boy and his grandmother hit the ground like bales of hay, the flashlight flew from Grandma's hand. It sailed into the side of the oak tree, shattering the bare bulb.

And Grizzly Woods was crow soup again.

Wet Skin and Hair

Ten minutes later, Grandma stalked over the last root that lay in the path and emerged from Grizzly Woods. She trudged through the high goatsbeard—the rain hat in her hand, the dead flashlight in her pocket—and paused on Route Z to catch her breath.

The wind was gusting now, whistling across the road and wiping the moon clean. A warm light now bathed the countryside.

Ben was watching Grandma's hair glow like a halo when his foot caught the last root and he pitched forward with a cry. He tumbled from the forest and into the shaggy goatsbeard. The bongos hit the ground with a *boom;* the picnic basket followed with a *thud* and tipped to one side. The lid sprang open and half the crabapples spilled out.

Grandma turned in alarm. "Butterfingers!" she called.

Ben pushed up, sputtering dirt and ants. "Grandma, I'm okay!" he yelled. He struggled to his feet then flinched at the ribbon of blood running down his right leg. His knee had landed on a rock.

"What about my crabapples?" Grandma cried.

Ben gaped when he saw the crabapples strewn there in the moonlight. "They're fine, Grandma," he said quickly. "Only a few fell out."

"Well, pick them up and let's get going!"

Ben peeled the band-aid from one elbow and stuck it on his knee. Wincing, he dropped to the ground again. He pulled off the bongos and started scooping up the crabapples. But there were so many and they had rolled in all different directions…

"Lordy, what's taking you so long?"

"Coming, Grandma!"

Ben scooped up one last pile and dumped them into the basket. He slapped the lid shut and slung the bongos over his head. When he lifted the basket, he was half-glad to find it a little lighter than before. As he limped past a fair number of crabapples still scattered on the ground, Grandma scoffed, "Butterfingers, you're clumsy as a cow with pig's feet." Then she turned and marched off down the road.

* * *

BEN HOBBLED ALONG WELL BEHIND GRANDMA. He kept her hair in sight, though, and whenever the yellow glow dimmed from view, he would grit his teeth and trot down the road until he could spot it again.

When another dark patch of clouds finally muffled the moonlight, Grandma's hair was snuffed out like a candle. Ben could no longer see her, but at least he could hear her rain boots clomping on the road. He followed Grandma's steps for a while, walking more quickly when the sound seemed to fade. In fact, he thought he was even closing the gap some when he heard another sound—

He stopped on the road and listened…and his ears began to tremble.

Searching the darkness for the source of the sound, he saw something up ahead, something by the road: a black shape looming large in the gloom. And groaning.

Ben dropped the basket of crabapples with a heavy *thump*. Weary as he was, he pounded hard on the Giant Heart bongos.

Grandma whirled around. "Butterfingers!" she cried. "What in tarnation are you doing?"

"The monster, Grandma! It's right over there! I have to play the bongos! I have to make it dance!"

The old woman shook her head sadly. "Butterfingers, if you believe this monster can dance, then you're a whole lot softer in the head than I thought—"

"What the squirt-stinkin' skunk rump is goin' on out here?"

A rusty roar had come from the darkness.

Then the moon edged out again, giving a glow to the Abernathy Pumpkin Patch. Ben could see the junk monster, rising by the road and groaning in the wind. His hands dropped silently to the surface of the drum.

He saw Grandma now too, curls gleaming, up ahead in the road. And a burly figure stomping toward the fence with a lantern in his hand and blood in his eye.

Besides the white towel around his waist, he was just wet skin and hair.

"You *again?*" Old Man Fibber yelled. "Isn't once every eighteen ear-bleedin' years enough! Poor Carl was so stirred up today it took me an hour to coax his jaws off the fence post! And just when I get him settled down some, you're out here again raisin' a slug-stompin' rumpus!"

"Fibber, you cover up in the presence of a lady!"

"I am covered up, woman!"

"You're one puff of wind from your birthday suit!"

"That's right, just one gust from my full glory!"

Ben, of course, had heard plenty about Old Man Fibber, but this was the first time he was seeing him in the flesh—and it really was in the flesh.

"Well, I'm not about to hold forth with a half-naked man," Grandma huffed. "Butterfingers, hurry up with that basket before his towel blows off."

Old Man Fibber's glare swung to the blond-haired boy hustling up the road to Grandma. He hadn't even noticed Ben until this moment.

"Who's this salamander?"

"He claims he's my grandson."

Ben glanced up at the big man in the white towel. His red beard hugged his face like a wet fox. His gaze burned so hot that Ben quickly dropped his eyes. When he did, he saw four puncture-like scars on Old Man Fibber's bare ankle.

"Come on, Butterfingers," Grandma muttered. "As much as I'd enjoy more friendly chitchat with this big hairball, I have a crabapple pie to make." She turned and tromped away.

Ben turned too, but then looked up at Old Man Fibber and mumbled: "I'm sorry about raising a rumpus, sir."

Old Man Fibber blinked; his eyes seemed to cool. He held the lantern out closer toward Ben. "What's that you got there?" he rumbled.

"Bongos," Ben said.

"Practicin' for this year's tryouts, is that it?"

Ben nodded.

"What do they call you, boy?"

"Ben, sir."

"No, your nickname."

"Butterfingers, sir."

"Butterfingers… Well, you can't be blamed for wantin' a change."

"I was thinking Dragon Hands, sir."

The old man's soggy beard rose in a slight grin. "I'm wantin' a change too. I'm no Fibber and I never was—I'm Airborne. And I plan on reclaimin' that name soon enough." His dark eyes sparkled.

A loud groan came from the junk monster. Ben glanced up and was suddenly jarred back to Crabapple Cliff. But before he could even consider telling Old Man Fibber about the monster, Grandma's voice rose sharply from the gloom: "Butterfingers, get your rear in top gear!"

So off he went, smiling a quick goodbye, then hurrying past the forgotten pumpkin fields and finally catching Grandma at the top of the rise in Route Z. Grandma was huffing hard and gazing back down the hill.

Ben set the picnic basket gently on the road and hunched over beside her to get his breath. He saw a glow in the darkness and realized it was the lantern: Old Man Fibber was standing there in his towel, staring up at the junk monster.

"What's he doing?" Ben whispered.

"Shhh," said Grandma.

At last Old Man Fibber turned and trudged toward the barn. At the barn door he stopped and suddenly roared out at the night: "I'll show you all, you doubting hogheaded dolts! I'm no Fibber! *I'm Airborne!*" Then he tugged the door open and slammed it shut behind him. Moments later, Ben heard a big splash and a muffled sigh.

"Grandma," Ben said, "do you know much about Old Man Fibber?"

"More than I like," Grandma replied.

"What's 'Airborne'? Was that his nickname before? I mean, before he—"

"Butterfingers," Grandma snapped, her half-pinky twitching against the rain hat, "the last thing in the world I want to do right now is sit here yakking about Old Man Fibber." Her stomach rumbled. "Let's pick up the pace so I can get home for my pie. These curls could start losing their bounce any second."

With that, Grandma marched off toward the Boyd Llama Farm.

Ben lingered there a moment, gazing down at the junk monster, its steel eye gleaming. He shuddered. Then he hoisted the picnic basket and hurried after Grandma, trailing her hair as it glowed like gold in the moonlight.

Born in the Air

NOW BEFORE I GO ON WITH THE STORY of Benjamin Boyd, and how all this led to the untimely loss of my ear, I feel duty-bound to lay bare the facts behind Old Man Fibber and "Airborne." It's information that needs airing to appreciate later events, and since Grandma refused to talk about it, your Grandpa Gristle will step in to explain.

And with Grandma and Ben just trudging along the road for a while, it's as good a time as any…

You see, Old Man Fibber's first nickname was due to the fact he was practically born in the air.

It all happened seventy-eight years before, on a hot July night. Both the farmhouse and barn were shiny new buildings back then, and the Abernathy Pumpkin Patch was thick with pumpkins, a crop that would turn out to be the biggest yet, boasting jack-o'-lanterns the size of boulders.

It sounds like a nice place to be born, surrounded by pumpkins and all, but baby Old Man Fibber just wouldn't come out. And it had nothing to do with his ears, like me, or any other part of his anatomy. It was fear. Even before he entered this world, he feared for what life here would bring.

So it was a long, hard delivery, and old Doc Bladder (Doc Sprinkle's grandfather) did everything he could to make it a natural birth. But finally, with the life of the mother at stake, Doc Bladder had to resort to a more drastic course of action: he lured out the newborn with a sugar cookie.

You'd never guess it from a glance at burly Old Man Fibber, but as an infant, he was tiny. Of course, it was a surprise to everyone, since he held out longer than your average tot, but he wasn't much bigger than a mouse soaked in buttermilk.

Torch Abernathy and his wife Dainty named the baby Arnold. He was their first child, and as it turned out, their last.

He wasn't known as Arnold Abernathy for long, though. Less than an hour later, he was Airborne.

After Doc Bladder left, Arnold Abernathy was lying beside his worn-out mother and suckling milk. He was naked, except for a white diaper. His father was sitting in a rocking chair on the front porch, near the open window to the room where the baby and his mother lay.

Torch Abernathy was puffing on a pipe and listening to his wife humming a lullaby to his son. It was a muggy night, with crickets chirping in the pumpkin fields and a full moon in the sky.

Torch Abernathy was a big man and he looked even bigger in his bulky brown coat, black boots, and red helmet. He not only owned the largest pumpkin farm in the state, he was also the fire chief of Boony Point. Back then, in fact, he was the town's only fire fighter. Of course, if a fire broke out in someone's barn, everybody pitched in to fight the blaze. But it was Torch Abernathy who wore the uniform and drove the fire truck around like the family car. And since it was mid-summer now, the driest and most dangerous time for fires, he was always dressed ready for the flames. (You might be thinking he got the nickname "Torch" because he was the fire chief, but the name came long before that. Like generations of Abernathys before him, he had raging red hair.)

So Arnold Abernathy was lying there by his mother's side, suckling milk, as his proud father sat rocking on the porch, smoking his pipe and listening to a sleepy, off-key lullaby from Dainty, a woman no bigger than a biscuit.

Torch Abernathy was just glancing at his pocket watch when it happened—at exactly 3:13 a.m.

A huge owl, white as snow, swooped in through the window and snatched little Arnold Abernathy right up. Digging its talons into his right ankle, the owl carried the infant upside down as it swooped back out. It all happened so fast that Torch Abernathy wasn't even out of his chair when he saw the owl flying off with his son dangling in its grasp.

Dainty Abernathy was caught unawares too. One moment she was lying in bed peacefully, humming to her newborn. The next moment there was a flapping of wings and a tickling of feathers and her baby was being spirited out the window.

She sat up and screamed: *"My baby! My baby! The owl's got my baby!"*

Torch Abernathy leaped off the porch and charged

toward the barn. The great frosty owl had a nest in one corner of the rafters. It was good at keeping down the rats that gnawed holes in the pumpkins so, despite a prickly disposition, it had been welcome on the farm.

The nest, in fact, was above Carl's big white bathtub. Carl was just a young snapper back then, just fourteen, but he witnessed the entire thing.

It was dark in the barn, but the moonlight was knifing through the open door. Torch Abernathy looked up at the nest, glowing there in the gloom, just in time to see the owl gobble down his son headfirst, diapers and all.

"*NOOO!*" he roared.

The owl slurped in the last of the baby's toes.

Now I don't know how familiar you are with the eating habits of owls, but those habits are unappetizing, to say the least. Owls, you see, don't have any teeth so they can't chew up their prey; they just gulp it down whole. And then, after they digest it a while, they spit out a hard pellet of the stuff they don't have a taste for, like the hair and the bones.

Well, Torch Abernathy, who was prepared for pretty much any other emergency that might spring to mind, was suddenly at a loss. Maybe he should have had more foresight, but he just never expected an owl to eat his firstborn. He had to do something, though, and he had to do it quicker than a mule kick.

So he slammed the barn door shut to keep the owl from flying off. But without the moonlight, the barn was pitch-black.

Human beings, of course, aren't alley cats; you can't normally spy the world in the dark. But the same wild fight is in your heart, and if the will is summoned, it's surprising the sort of powers you can muster in a time of real need—like when a bird has just gulped down your loved one.

Torch Abernathy said his eyes nearly popped from their sockets, that's how hard he was straining to see. And suddenly something happened, something that never happened to him before and would never happen to him again: he began to make out shapes and shadows in the barn, as if a night-light had been flicked on in the corner.

He grabbed a pitchfork from a pile of hay and ran to the nest. He shook the pitchfork and bellowed at the owl. At the same time, Carl was splashing around and hissing angrily in the bathtub below. But the great frosty owl just stared down in disdain with its big orange eyes.

Torch Abernathy knew he couldn't spear the bird with his pitchfork; after all, he didn't want to spear his son too. But maybe, he thought, he could clout it from the air when it took flight. Maybe he could stun it long enough to gut his baby free with his pocketknife.

He thrust the pitchfork at the rafters to rattle the nest. He thunked at the wood, again and again. But the owl didn't flinch a feather; it just gaped down like a stone gargoyle.

He couldn't have known, of course. It was something he only surmised later. But the fact is, as small as the baby was, it still made a heavy bellyful for that bird. It probably didn't have the stomach for much flying right then.

But with Carl urging him on, Torch Abernathy kept knocking at the rafters, harder and harder. Finally, I suppose he rattled that nest so much, and shook up the owl to such a degree, it just couldn't bear the quaking.

Its eyes blinked and its feathers ruffled. Its chest heaved and its head tilted back. Then its beak opened wide and it made a horrible, sickly hoot. A second later Arnold Abernathy went shooting back out like a bottle rocket. He went soaring over Carl and over his father's head with a dazed little grin on his face.

Torch Abernathy saw his son flying through the air, but he was caught flat-footed. He threw down the pitchfork and turned. He dove, his helmet tumbling off. His arms were out, his big hands open. His son was just a foot from the ground…

He was too late. His dive was short.

But Arnold Abernathy was saved, caught in his mother's arms.

Dainty Abernathy, completely worn out by the birth, had somehow managed to stagger to the barn and push open the barn door just when the owl hooted up her baby. With the moonlight shining in over her shoulder, her eyes caught a flash of white—*the diaper!*—and she lunged, arms outstretched.

And for the first nine years of his life, Arnold Abernathy was known to all as Airborne.

The Cricket

BENJAMIN BOYD TRUDGED ALONG after his grandmother on Route Z. Dark clouds continued to blow by the moon, spilling light, then shadow, over the countryside.

As they drew near the fields of the Boyd Llama Farm, Grandma stopped on the road and waited for Ben.

The moon peeked out again, shining a spotlight on them.

"Quiet now, Butterfingers," Grandma whispered, though Ben hadn't said a word since they left the Abernathy Pumpkin Patch.

"Yes, Grandma," Ben whispered back, not sure why they were whispering.

The old woman carefully pulled the yellow rain hat over her curls. "I expect they're sound asleep by now," she said, tugging on her rubber gloves, "but you walk right beside me, just in case." She slipped her arm around his. "Now tiptoe."

Arm in arm, Grandma and Ben went slinking up the road toward the timber fences. She clung to him tight, her eyes darting back and forth at the fields of goldenrod. The goldenrod swayed and swished in the wind, but the fields were still.

As Grandma had guessed, the herd was now fast asleep. Even without Ben's father there to whistle them home, they had returned to the stables when darkness fell, and were soon snug and snoring in their beds of hay. And though their nostrils twitched at the wind-blown odor of Grandma passing by on the road, this time they slumbered on. The scent invaded their sleep, and soured their dreams, but they did not wake.

However, one young llama—a fluffy, honey-colored creature with black ears called Cornelius—was tossing and

turning next to his mother on their pile of straw. His stomach was feeling jumpy. Just before bed, he had accidentally swallowed a cricket and it was now hopping about inside him. When Grandma's odor tickled his nose like sauerkraut, and a sneeze shook his eyes open, the next second he was sitting bolt upright in bed. Young as he was, he was quick to realize that the yellow enemy of his herd was out on the road. He yelped the news to his mother who awoke and sent up a shriek to her neighbors.

The warning spread like brush fire through the stables of the Boyd Llama Farm. Moments later, 143 llamas, chewing furiously on big mouthfuls of goldenrod, were stampeding through the moonlight toward Route Z.

Of course, all that mewling from the llamas threw Grandma into a wild-eyed panic. She yanked at Ben's arm, pulling him down the road. But Ben stumbled over a rock and the llamas rushed up to the fences before they could get very far.

"Oh my Lordy!" Grandma cried. She pushed Ben in front of her, like a human shield, and froze flat against his back. The llamas loved Ben and they wouldn't spit at him, would they? Especially now, in the dark of night, with the wind swirling, they would surely think twice about hitting Ben too, right?

The llamas were all bunched at the fences now, on both sides of the road. They glared at Grandma as she cowered behind Ben. When Grandma peeked out, she saw the hard stares and the angry chewing. But, as she hoped, they seemed reluctant to spit.

Grandma studied the llamas. Their jaws were working fiercely, but their eyes were uncertain. Llama heads started to turn, exchanging quizzical looks. Without their leader, Henry the Eighth, the herd had no one to guide them in such unexpected conditions. If llamas could scratch their heads, I believe that's what they would have done next.

Then Grandma broke into a big horsey smile. Relief swept over her, and a surge of pride. At last, she had done it! She had finally outfoxed them! They wouldn't spit with Ben right there!

"Porridge heads!" she shouted, still cowering behind Ben. "I've waited years for this day—the day I would finally triumph! And it's all thanks to *this!*" She poked a gloved finger at her head. "Do you know what's inside here? It's a brain!

A brain! But you beasts wouldn't know about little things like brains, would you, because you're just big bundles of brainless instinct! And that goes double for Henry the Eighth and every Henry that came before him!"

The llamas, of course, had no idea what Grandma was carrying on about, but their ears pricked at the sound of Henry's name and they could certainly sense, from her tone, that the sour old woman was bad-mouthing him again. They began to stamp and snort at the fences, their nostrils flaring angrily.

Grandma, though, was unconcerned. Gripping onto Ben's shoulders with her gloves, she began pushing him down the road and singing a song she made up on the spot. In a high soprano that was surprisingly sweet, she sang for all to hear:

I have a brain!
Yes, I have a brain!
Break out the champagne!
Because I have a brain—

Then a sudden gust of wind blew Grandma's rain hat right off her head. It sailed to her left and landed—*plop*—on the head of an attractive, chestnut-colored llama named Eleanor. The other llamas swung their heads to look. The hat had settled on her brow at such a becoming angle that more than a few llamas felt a twinge of envy. Eleanor blushed at all the attention.

Grandma stopped and stood petrified. She was still huddled behind Ben, but her blond curls were now bouncing free in the moonlight.

The herd turned back to Grandma and stared at her gleaming golden hair. It was the first time they had ever seen it—it had always been hidden under her rain hat before. For a long moment, they were overcome with awe. They stopped chewing and stood perfectly still, wide-eyed, unblinking.

Even the wind seemed to hold its breath at the sight of Grandma's radiant curls. After gusting off her hat, it died right to a hush.

With the llamas hypnotized by her hair, Grandma had the chance to flee. But the shock of her head exposed on the open road had turned her into a pop-eyed potato. She couldn't move; she couldn't speak; she couldn't even think.

Ben could see Grandma's hat parked there pertly on Eleanor so he realized what had happened. He could also see Cornelius, the young llama with the cricket in its belly, standing next to her. (Cornelius had a boyish crush on Eleanor.) While all the llamas were still as statues, gazing at Grandma's hair, Ben noticed that Cornelius had a funny, frowning look on his face.

And then it happened.

The young llama's mouth dropped open and he began to gag. The noise stirred the rest of the herd out of its daze, and they turned toward Cornelius. The cricket had bounced up into Cornelius's throat. And spotting the moon through the llama's open jaws, it was now scrabbling up his windpipe to escape.

While poor Cornelius coughed and gasped, the cricket bounded into his mouth, right into the sloppy pool of chewed-up goldenrod. As the panicky insect slipped and squirmed in Cornelius's mouth, the young llama, with a look of utter disgust on his face, spat out a stream of goopy goldenrod, the cricket surfing on top. Ben watched as the gob of mustard-yellow spit hit the ground near his feet, splattering his boots. The cricket jumped away across the road.

Grandma had been right about two things: one, the llamas felt reluctant to spit with Ben there; and two, the llamas acted on instinct. Unfortunately for Grandma, when the herd saw Cornelius gush, instinct won out and the remaining 142 llamas

responded instantly, like when they followed Henry the Eighth.

The spit, I'm sorry to say, began to fly.

And when the air had cleared, it was a sight to behold.

As you know, the llamas of the Boyd Llama Farm were accomplished spitters. It may have been the first time they were called upon to spit at night, but with the moon shining down brightly, it made little difference to their large, sharp eyes. And even without Henry the Eighth to lead them, they had already proven, earlier that day, that they could spew with confidence to spare.

Now it's true that Grandma's scheme of huddling behind Ben was successful to some degree: the front part of her rain suit, in the shadow of his back, wasn't hit at all. But I'm afraid the rest of her was drenched again.

And the worst of it was—oh, it's so horrible I wish I could skip this part.

The worst of it was, Grandma's beautiful blond curls, her pride and joy, were now caked with llama spit. Only one lonely curl, drooping to her forehead, had managed to survive the onslaught.

And the amazing thing is—the astonishing thing is—the only spit touching Ben was on his boots, from the lump launched by Cornelius.

For a long moment Route Z was still as a cemetery. The only sound, the only movement, was one small gob of goldenrod that slid from a flattened curl on Grandma's glasses, rolled down her nose, and landed onto the dusty road with a soft *plunk*.

Grandma and Ben stood frozen as before, but the old woman was now gripping the boy's Mayor Olympus T-shirt so tightly in the back that it was clutching at his throat. Her face was warped in a look of pure horror, like she had just plunged into the fiery pit of hell itself.

The llamas stared, spit dangling from their chins. The wind picked up again and another gust blew the yellow rain hat off Eleanor's head. Eleanor, who was quietly enjoying the attention the hat had brought her, let out a quick cry of regret. All eyes turned and caught sight of the hat as it floated over the field of goldenrod, then disappeared in the darkness.

That's when Grandma snapped.

It started with a deep hungry rumble in her belly that seemed to spark a tremor from the bottom of her rain boots. As the tremor buzzed up through her like an electric shock, her whole body began to shake. When it reached the top of her matted head, her mouth flew open and she erupted with an angry, animal-like wail. Hungry and exhausted and now crazy with rage, she yanked Ben aside by the back of his shirt and took off running down the road in her rain boots, wailing the entire time.

Ben and the llamas watched in stunned silence. A few of the llamas even felt a bit bad about it all.

"Grandma!" Ben called after her. "Grandma, wait for me!" He broke into a run too, though it was hard-going with the heavy basket of crabapples and his painful left knee.

The llamas looked on until Grandma and Ben were both swallowed up by the night. Then they turned away from the road and trotted back to their stables and beds of hay. They could hear Grandma still wailing in the night and they soon grew annoyed at her for keeping them awake.

I don't know what happened to the cricket.

Near-Death Experience

Ben hurried to catch up to Grandma. If he beat her home, he could tell his side of the story first. His lungs burned and his knee ached, but he ran on down the road lugging the picnic basket as the Giant Heart bongos bounced around his neck. Grandma, running ahead in the moonlight, was surprisingly fast on her short, wiry legs.

Ben wondered how long Grandma could keep running. He also wondered how long she could keep screaming. The old woman had been wailing with barely a breath ever since the llamas demolished her hair.

Finally, as they drew near the fork in the road, Ben was relieved to see Grandma's dark figure stop up ahead in the distance. The llamas were relieved too, when Grandma's shrieking voice went silent.

Grandma had run all the way to the junction of Route Z and Olympus Drive. The bend in the dirt road, to the right, would take her home; the blacktop, to the left, led to town.

As Ben ran toward Grandma, he saw her stoop, her hands on her knees. Even from this distance, he could hear her wheezing for air.

Moments later, he heard another sound: the rumble of an engine. Then two beams of light broke into view, darting up Olympus Drive. He paused, panting, and watched his father's truck crunch onto the dirt road.

Ben's parents had arrived back in Boony Point just an hour before. At Doc Sprinkle's office, Henry the Eighth was given the shot of anti-venom for the white widow and quickly recovered from the near-fatal bite. Doc Sprinkle then removed the syringe that was still sticking in the llama's heart, performed open-heart surgery to repair the hole, and stitched him back up. After bidding farewell to Doc Sprinkle and Agnes (who survived, but had very sore quills), and offering prayers that Stanley would soon make his way back to town, Ben's parents hurried for home.

Grandma was hunched over right there at the fork in the road when the truck roared by, but neither Ben's father nor his mother saw the small, weary figure. It had been a long day and Walter Boyd felt awful about breaking his promise to take Ben to Leech Lake for his birthday. He was squinting only at the road ahead as he sped through the darkness. Lorelai Boyd, worn out from all the drama they had endured, was dozing on the bed of hay in the trailer.

In fact, the only one who noticed Grandma wheezing by the roadside was Henry the Eighth. The anti-venom had brought him bouncing back to life and he was now feeling spry as a youngster again. He was standing tall in the trailer, chewing on a mouthful of sweet honeysuckle that Ben's mother had picked from Doc Sprinkle's garden, and peering out over the back gate at the shining full moon with his big amber eyes.

Now, naturally, I understand the sort of near-death experience that Henry the Eighth just survived. After all, I nearly had my whole head lopped off, as you'll see. And when you cheat death like that, you can't help but feel reborn. I was only three weeks old at the time, but after that brush with death, I distinctly remember feeling like a newborn again.

Well, in his own llama way, Henry the Eighth was feeling reborn too. He was gazing out at the world with new eyes: the glorious full moon, the luscious scent of the sunflowers, the delightfully dusty old road. He had always been a proud and surly creature, but he now felt something stirring in his stitched-up heart that he had never felt before for anything other than himself—

He felt love. He felt love for everything. He felt love for the whole world around him.

He even felt love for Grandma.

When Henry the Eighth caught sight of her standing there as the truck rattled past, and saw what a pitiful figure she had become, from her filthy rain boots to her flattened blond curls, he suddenly felt very sorry for all the times he had spit at her. And when her wild gaze met his, Henry's big eyes filled with tears, his heart gave a thump of regret, and he made a shy, hopeful smile as if to say: "I'm so sorry, let's be friends."

Well, I wish I could tell you that Grandma reacted in the same way and that the old woman and the handsome llama mended fences then and there and began new relations as fast friends.

But the truth is, when Grandma saw Henry the Eighth grinning down at her from the truck with his pearly white teeth, she thought he was laughing at her plight. And this final humiliation was more than poor Grandma could bear: her brain shut down like an overheated motor. Instead of that brain she had brayed about, she was moved by instinct alone—and instinct at that moment told her to repay those years of misery by spitting at Henry the Eighth.

But Grandma's mouth was so dry she only succeeded in spitting out her false teeth, which dropped straight into the dust.

Of course, it isn't a good idea to spit at a llama, no matter how poorly you do the deed. Even if a llama's heart is brimming with love—as Henry's heart was then—you can be sure that all the love in the world will be instantly overridden by instinct and the animal will spit right back at you.

And that, I'm afraid, is just what Henry the Eighth did. As the truck rumbled away, the llama spit out a big gob of goopy honeysuckle and it hit the front of Grandma's head with a *splat*, fouling the last lonely curl that had survived the herd's attack just minutes before.

Henry the Eighth gave Grandma another sheepish smile. The fact is, he felt bad about what he had done as soon as the spit left his mouth and he was now grinning awkwardly in regret.

Before Grandma or Ben had enough breath to call out, the truck was already barreling away and stirring up a cloud of dust that cloaked Henry the Eighth and his remorseful smile. As the red tail lights faded into the night too, the Rambler backfired with a *bang*.

It may be hard to believe, but Grandma not only resumed her caterwauling, it was now even louder than before. And when the screaming erupted again, the other 143 llamas, who were finally drifting into sleep with uneasy dreams of Henry's fate, were jarred awake and lay grumbling in the hay.

Scooping up her dusty false teeth, Grandma went sprinting after the truck.

Ben groaned, the picnic basket heavy as a heifer in his arms. He had just caught his breath and now Grandma was running again. He broke into a run himself, and rounded the bend toward home. But he was too tired, and his knee was too sore, to run the whole way. So finally he stopped, gulping for air, and listened to Grandma's quick footsteps moving farther ahead in the distance, the wail still rising from her throat and filling the dark sky.

Just a Dream?

Ben did his best to hurry, but Grandma still beat him home by half a mile. He could hear her wailing the whole way, even after she reached the Boyd Llama Farm. When he finally drew near the house, he also heard the hiss of the garden hose and his mother's voice.

"I need you to stop screaming now, Mother," she was saying. "Stop screaming so I can rinse off your hair and you can tell us where Ben is, okay? If you don't stop screaming, the llama spit will go straight into your mouth—"

Then his father's voice broke in: "Tell us where Ben is! Stop that screaming and tell us where he is!"

Ben was too tired to run another stride, but he quickened his pace to a stumbling stagger. As grating as it was to his ears, he heaved a sigh of relief at the fact that Grandma hadn't stopped howling—this meant she hadn't accused him of anything yet. Maybe he would get the chance to tell his side of the story first after all.

He could see the yellow glow of the porch light ahead and he opened his mouth to cry out…but his throat was so dry and dusty he could only cough.

"Lorelai, she's hysterical! She won't stop screaming until you rinse that llama spit off her head!"

"Mother, I'm sorry…" And then came the sound of the hose spraying a jet of water. Grandma's shrieking quickly died to gurgles and gasps.

"Where's Ben?" his father shouted. "Where is he?"

It was at this moment that Ben wobbled to the foot of the dirt driveway. In the shine of the porch light, he saw his grandmother sputtering water while his mother showered her with the hose. His father stood by, his face wild with worry.

"Did something happen out on Crabapple Cliff?" his father demanded.

"What? What are you saying, Walter?" His mother went pale.

"I warned him!" his father said, his voice breaking.

"What is it, Walter? What's happened to Ben?"

"I warned him a hundred times to stay away from the edge!"

His mother quaked and dropped the hose. *"No, Walter! No! Not my Ben! Not my baby!"*

And just as Ben's mother was about to start screaming where Grandma left off, there came a small cough at the end of the driveway.

Ben saw his parents stop and turn. When they caught sight of him, they blazed with joy. His mother rushed down the driveway past the pickup truck and trailer, his father on her heels.

Grandma was left sputtering there alone, the hose hissing at her feet. Her hair was finally free of the llama spit, but it was now slicked to her head like a squid.

Fighting back tears, his mother gently took the picnic basket from Ben's stiff grasp and placed it on the ground. His father slipped the drum strap from around his neck and set the bongos down beside the basket.

His mother knelt and hugged him tight, then began to sob. His father leaned down, embracing them both.

Grandma stood watching the heartwarming scene through the wet curls that flopped down her forehead like tentacles. She gave another sputter.

When Ben's parents arrived home minutes before, they were alarmed to find the house dark. As the noisy roar of the pickup truck died away, they suddenly heard Grandma wailing in the distance and were terrified that something dreadful had happened.

Thinking he would have to barrel out to Ben's rescue, his father quickly led Henry the Eighth back to his stable. The other llamas, still awake thanks to Grandma's screaming, were overjoyed to see Henry again, healthy as a racehorse, and they crowded around him and snorted with delight. At the same time, they noticed a new starry-eyed look on his face…

"Ben, where have you been?" his mother said, crying and laughing.

"What happened, Ben?" his father said.

Ben blinked at them through his dusty glasses. He opened his mouth to speak and croaked out "Monster."

Except it didn't sound like that; it sounded like "Mozdoo."

"What, honey?" his mother said.

Ben cleared his throat to try again.

And just then Grandma screamed.

"Get that beast away from me!" she shrieked. Her arms were high, defending her dripping hair.

It was Henry the Eighth. He still felt awful about spitting on Grandma and had nosed open the stable door and ambled back to apologize. He was grinning with shame and gazing at Grandma with all the regret he could muster in his big amber eyes.

"He's going to spit on me again!" Grandma yelped.

"Walter, please take Henry back to the stable," Ben's mother said. "And be sure to bolt the door this time."

Henry the Eighth was naturally reluctant to leave since his apology didn't quite go as planned. In fact, the llama refused to budge when Ben's father gave a sharp whistle through his fingers. He didn't know what more to do, though, so he just stood there awkwardly, grinning down at Grandma with his big white teeth and hoping the old woman would somehow see what was now in his heart…

"He's going to bite me!" Grandma cried, cowering like a hermit crab.

Finally, Ben's father was forced to give Henry a heavy swat on the rump with his fishing hat. No one noticed, but the llama's lower lip began to tremble and his eyes welled with tears. He quickly turned and trotted toward his stable. Ben's father pulled his hat back on and followed after to shut the stable up tight.

Ben's mother peered into her son's grimy face. "Ben, what is it? What happened?"

Ben licked his lips. "Monster," he said weakly. "On Crabapple Cliff."

"What?"

Now it may seem surprising that Grandma could catch Ben's soft words, especially with water dripping in her ears, but as I've said, those ears were like an elephant when the listening was convenient.

"Lorelai, I warned you!" Grandma cried, marching down the driveway, her wet feet squeaking in her rain boots. "Didn't I say those books would turn his mind to mush? Now this boy's head is so full of porridge he can't tell what a right-minded practical joke is!"

"Grandma, it wasn't a practical joke!"

"That's correct, it was a *criminal act!*"

"Mother, what are you talking about?"

"I'm talking about *attempted starvation!* He spent the whole day sitting under the tree playing his bongos while I was waiting here for my crabapples. If he had just brought back the crabapples like he was supposed to, none of this would have happened!"

"Ben, is this true?"

"There was a monster! A huge monster—"

"Like the monsters in your books?" Grandma snorted. "Or the monsters in Old Man Fibber's head? Before you know it this boy will be making his own junk monster out of our kitchen appliances!"

"Mother, please—"

Then Ben cut in, the words spilling from his mouth in a single breath: "Yes, yes, like the junk monster! Just like that one! I climbed the tree and I pounded on the bongos! And it started dancing! But it wouldn't stop! It was dancing around the cliff the whole day! Then it got sick and it disappeared! That's when Grandma came out of the forest—"

"And I found him there under the tree, sound asleep. Oh, it must have tired you out playing those bongos all day while I withered like a houseplant from a lack of nourishment." Her stomach rumbled to back up her story. "But you'd think after reading all those books he could come up with a more sensible defense than a dancing monster—"

"But it's true! It was dancing!"

"What was dancing?" Ben's father asked as he came jogging back.

"Ben says he saw something out on Crabapple Cliff," said his mother.

"Something dancing?" said his father.

"A dancing monster!" Grandma cried. "Mark my words, if this boy doesn't get a firmer grip on the real world, he'll wind up in a bathtub with a reptile, just like Old Man Fibber!"

"My son is no fibber!" Ben's father shouted.

Ben's mother shot two withering glares for silence. Then she put a hand to Ben's cheek. "Ben, honey, you know there are no such things as monsters, right? If people hear you talking about monsters..." Her voice choked on the words.

"Maybe it was a bear," said his father.

"A bear?" said Grandma.

"Bears can dance," said his father. "Like Stanley."

"There are no bears out there," Grandma scoffed. "There hasn't been a bear in Grizzly Woods for sixty-nine years... ever since Mayor Olympus..." She swallowed a sudden lump in her throat. "Ever since Mayor Olympus disappeared and every single bear in that forest was hunted down...well, except for Stanley. And he isn't much of a dancer, either."

"It can't be Stanley," Ben's mother said. "He was in Bloat City today to dance at the governor's mansion, but the poor thing spooked again. He ran off and I expect he's now somewhere between there and Boony Point."

"It must be another bear," Ben's father said. "Another grizzly."

"Grizzlies don't grow from acorns, Water Boy."

Ben's father stiffened at the sound of his nickname. He fought the urge to shoot back with "Squeeze," remembering the promise he had made to his wife.

"It could have wandered into the forest from somewhere else," he said, frowning at Grandma. "Like a traveling circus."

"Ben, was it a bear?" his mother asked. "Is that what—Ben, you're hurt!"

Ben's mother had finally noticed his knee. Ben glanced down and saw the band-aid and the stripe of dried blood on his lower leg. He suddenly felt faint.

"You got *clawed!*" his father said, squatting and draping an arm around Ben's back. He sounded strangely hopeful. "You were climbing the tree to get away from the grizzly and it raked your leg with its claws! I don't care how well it can dance, it sounds like a man-eater! For all we know, it might even be *rabid!* It wouldn't be the first time a bear from a traveling circus got rabies when it escaped—"

"You sound rabid yourself!" Grandma snapped. "The boy fell over a root coming out of the forest! He dropped my basket of crabapples—"

"Mother, let Ben talk." Ben's mother put both hands to his cheeks. "Honey, tell us what happened. Did a bear do this to you? Is there a dancing bear out on Crabapple Cliff?"

Ben blinked. He flashed on Crabapple Cliff and the ogre dancing around the tree. It was hairy, all right, but it wasn't a bear.

He shook his head slowly.

"Just as I thought!" Grandma said.

"It wouldn't look like Stanley!" Ben's father protested.

"He was keen to play a practical joke, but he couldn't tell the difference between a humdinger and a homicide, so he fibs about a dancing monster—"

"A dancing grizzly that's now rabid would be foaming at the mouth and hard for a small boy to identify—"

"*Enough!*" Ben's mother cried, and silenced Grandma and Ben's father with two quick scowls. "Ben would never do anything to harm you, Mother, so it couldn't have happened as you're suggesting. And Walter, if Ben says it wasn't a bear, then I think we have to trust his judgment. Since we all know there are no such things as monsters, that leaves only one explanation: Ben must have fallen asleep under the tree and dreamed up the sort of monster he saw when he passed by Old Man Fibber's farm. Right, honey?"

Ben gazed at his mother. In the black pupils of her eyes he watched the ogre dance, leaping and whirling across Crabapple Cliff. It had all seemed so real, but was it any more real than the stories that came to life in his books? A huge, hairy monster dancing so gracefully, so lightly, on feet the size of rowboats? It was ridiculous! Impossible! It must have been his imagination. It must have been a dream after all. He just didn't pinch himself hard enough—

"Ben? Honey?"

He nodded. Then his eyes fluttered shut and he slid through his mother's hands.

"*Ben!*" she cried.

His father managed to catch him before he crumpled to the ground.

"Walter, take Ben into the house!"

Ben's father cradled him like a baby and hurried up the driveway.

Ben's mother grabbed the bongos and followed quickly. They went through the screen door and the house lit up with light.

Grandma watched them disappear, then stooped for the basket of crabapples. A wet curl dropped with a *slop* onto her glasses. She gave a heavy sigh.

Then Alf woke up and croaked for a dog biscuit.

Shish Kebab

NOW DON'T YOU WORRY ABOUT BEN. He was just worn down as a bald tire, that's all. A long bubble bath put the tread back on him. As he soaked in the warm water, his mother sat perched on the edge of the toilet seat, fighting off her own exhaustion to tell Ben about their trip to Bloat City. She didn't want him dozing off and sliding down under the bubbles, after all.

Finally, his mother helped him from the bath and put a fresh band-aid on his knee. Then he slipped on his Marching Moose pajamas and followed her to the kitchen for a late birthday dinner.

As soon as the door swung open, Ben fell into a coughing fit. Heavy smoke hung above the kitchen table. His father was at the stove with a pointy party hat on his head. He was frantically patting out the flames leaping from a tray of black shish kebab.

"Oh, Walter. Not on Ben's birthday."

"I was waiting and waiting…" He snuffed out the last small flames with the oven mitts on his hands.

Walter Boyd had a fair number of talents, but cooking wasn't one of them. Normally, Ben's mother would never have allowed him to make Ben's birthday dinner. But she wasn't about to leave Ben's side when the boy was in such a delicate state. And, anyway, she thought, it's hard to ruin shish kebab. All he had to do was cut the meat and vegetables, spear the chunks onto the skewers, and grill them in the oven. Ben's father turned to them, glumly holding the tray of burnt shish kebab. "Sorry, guys."

"Dad, it's okay. I'm so hungry I could eat those oven mitts."

Ben's father chuckled. "Thanks, Ben."

Ben and his mother snapped on party hats too, and they all tucked into the birthday dinner, playing a guessing game of the black chunks on their skewers. (The game came down to the last chunk and Ben won when his mother said "meat" and it turned out to be a mushroom.)

After the shish kebab, Ben and his father started dueling with skewers from their chairs. In fact, sword fighting with the metal skewers was the main reason he always clamored for shish kebab.

While the skewers clicked and clacked, Ben's mother carried the dishes to the sink and then moved to the kitchen counter where a big chocolate cake sat covered on a clear crystal stand. She had made the cake the night before, squirting white icing into "Happy Birthday, Ben!" and the face of a smiling boy wearing a puffy hat with moose antlers. She began lighting the small candles that dotted the cake.

"Mother!" she called through the kitchen door. "Mother, we're ready to cut the cake!"

But there was no reply. Grandma was still upstairs, fussing with her hair.

The skewers finally fell silent as Ben's mother brought the flickering cake to the table and set it before Ben. While his parents sang "Happy Birthday" in tired voices, he counted the candles and felt a thrill when he reached twelve.

"Make a wish, Ben!" his parents said.

Ben was hardly in the best shape to blow out twelve candles with one breath, but he sucked in as much air as his lungs could hold. He wasn't about to endanger his wish to join the Marching Moose by leaving any candles lit.

He practically passed out from the effort, but he managed to get them all. When the wooziness went away, he started eating a big slice of chocolate cake. Ben's mother was marvelous at baked goods, and over the years she had won half-a-dozen blue ribbons for her cakes and cobblers at the state fair.

So it's easy to see how Walter Boyd gained himself a belly since his wedding day.

Well, Ben and his parents were in the middle of eating that fudgy cake when Grandma finally came plodding down the stairs after her shower to retrieve the picnic basket from the living room. They thought they heard the snarl of a wildcat too, but then realized it was Grandma's empty stomach.

"Mother, I could cut you a small piece of birthday cake," Ben's mother called from the kitchen. Grandma hadn't eaten anything but crabapple pie in years, but Ben's mother still tried.

"I'll be making my pie now, thank you," replied the living room.

Through the kitchen door came the sound of crabapples

clattering to the hardwood floor as Grandma poured them from her basket. She would then sift through the mound to select the best eighty-six crabapples for her pie.

Ben was forking another big bite of cake into his mouth when a scream split the living room. He was so startled he gulped the cake right down.

Ben's mother rushed from the kitchen with Ben and his father close behind. They found Grandma in her yellow robe, yellow slippers, and big silver curlers. She was staring down at the floor, her eyes bugging in horror behind her glasses. She was pointing with a quivering finger at the crabapples poured into a large mound in the middle of the room.

"Worms!" she cried. "They're full of *worms!*"

Small green worms were slithering over the pile of red crabapples.

"I told you not to put in any wormy ones!" Grandma shrieked, her gums chomping the air. "You did it on purpose, didn't you? You deliberately stuffed my basket with wormy ones so I would starve!"

"I didn't, Grandma," Ben protested. "It was dark out there. I did the best I could."

"The best you could! Look at that! I can't even bake a pie now! You dumped out half of them stumbling from the forest—I'll barely have enough good fruit for a mug of crabapple cider!" Grandma's stomach rumbled again. She clutched her belly with both hands and gave a whimper.

Ben's mother went to her, arms wide. "Mother, maybe we can make a small pie. Maybe a crabapple fritter."

But Grandma dropped to the floor and fell into a frenzy. Pawing through the crabapples, she snatched up a shiny red one and exclaimed, "See? No worm holes! I put in this one!" She found another. "And this one! I put in this one too!" Then another, holding it high for everyone to see. "I put in all the ones like this, all the ones that are healthy and wholesome, and he put in all the ones with *worms!*"

As everyone stared at the crabapple in Grandma's hand, a small green worm popped its head out. Some say it even winked at her, though I think that may be stretching the truth. Grandma dropped the crabapple with a gasp and collapsed to the floor. To everyone's surprise, she curled into a ball and burst into tears.

"I'm *hungry!*" she sobbed. "I'm hungry as a billy goat!"

Grandma's head was on the floor, near the mound of crabapples. Attracted by the glint of the silver curlers, several curious worms crawled into her hair.

Ben's mother knelt next to her. She gently brushed off the worms and raised Grandma's head. "Don't worry, Mother," she said, holding her and patting her curlers. "We'll get a wonderful basket of crabapples tomorrow, bright and early."

But Grandma sniffled and said, "I'm so tired. I'm so weak." Then she broke down and bawled: *"My hair is so limp!"*

"Well then, Walter and Ben will go," volunteered Ben's mother, glancing up with a gaze that made them both eye the floor. "They can take the truck to the edge of Grizzly Woods to get back even faster. And they'll be sure to bring home the best crabapples they can find."

Ben and his father exchanged a look. They weren't used to feeling much sympathy for Grandma. In fact, Ben's father had already decided to set out for Crabapple Cliff in the morning, well before Grandma's misery on the living room floor. But not to pick crabapples.

You see, when you're eager to believe something badly enough, it isn't hard to convince yourself it's true, no matter how outlandish it may seem to others. And Walter Boyd, he was eager as a bag of beavers to think that Ben had a run-in that day out on Crabapple Cliff. Not with a monster, no, but with a bear—a rabid, foaming grizzly that might easily be mistaken for a monster by a small boy in a panic. And now his mind was churning with a plot to stop this deadly danger to the people of Boony Point and become a hero in their eyes—and at last earn himself a new nickname.

Ben's father squinted down at Grandma and cleared his throat. "That's right, Grandma. We'll bring back the finest crabapples you ever saw."

Grandma sniffled. "No wormy ones."

"No wormy ones, Grandma," Ben's father said. He put his arm around Ben's shoulders.

Grandma looked up at Ben with small red eyes.

"No wormy ones, Grandma," Ben said.

"And pick them while the dew is on the fruit."

"Yes, Grandma," Ben's father said. "Bright and early."

"Yes, Grandma," Ben said.

The old woman smiled weakly. Ben's mother smiled too.

Then Grandma slumped to the floor and fell fast asleep.

Wonder Boy

Grandma was still asleep when Ben's mother went into her bedroom the next morning.

Grandma was usually the first one stirring so it was strange to find her in bed at nearly seven o'clock. Normally she was awake even before Ben's father rose at five to feed the llamas their sunflower seeds. She would shuffle down the hall to the bathroom in the early morning darkness, take out the silver curlers, and spend the next hour and a half fluffing and fingering. Then, with every hair coaxed perfectly in place, and the yellow ribbons carefully tied, she and her curls would bounce down the stairs to mash the remaining eleven crabapples from the day before to make her morning mug of hot crabapple cider. By seven o'clock she was out the door in her rain suit, clomping toward Crabapple Cliff to pick another basket of fruit for that day's pie.

But Grandma had spent a very restless night. After nodding off in the living room, she was carried to her bed by Ben's father. It wasn't long, though, before her rumbling stomach jarred her awake and then growled at her each time she was about to drift back to sleep. By three in the morning she had gotten so crazed with hunger that she stumbled down the stairs to the living room to find eleven decent crabapples for a cup of cider.

But when she stepped into the dim kitchen to mash them up, she froze at the sight across the room: sitting quietly on the counter was Ben's chocolate birthday cake, half-eaten, spotlighted on the crystal cake stand by the moon shining through the window.

Grandma gazed at the cake like a badger eyeing its first chipmunk after a long hibernation. Her tongue suddenly quivered with the long-lost taste of chocolate cake. Her mouth flooded; her stomach thundered; her hands dropped open and her crabapples hailed to the floor. Before a second thought could restrain her, she was there at the kitchen counter, yanking off the glass cover and attacking Ben's birthday cake with both hands. She pushed the fistfuls of cake into her greedy mouth, wolfing down every last crumb and sucking the frosting off her fingers.

Almost four hours later, when Ben's mother awoke and didn't find Grandma downstairs in her easy chair, sipping cider, she went into her bedroom. Grandma was sound asleep, though she wasn't exactly resting easy. Her body was jerking and her head was jiggling, like she was dreaming of being zapped by lightning. And all around her mouth were thick smears of chocolate frosting and cake crumbs.

Ben's mother got a warm washcloth and gently wiped Grandma's face clean as she slept. Later, when Ben and his father asked about the birthday cake, Ben's mother told them she woke up hungry and ate it herself. Any further questions they might have had were stopped cold by a hard look.

The sun was just starting to rise behind a sheet of steel-gray clouds when Walter Boyd, wearing his lucky fishing hat, returned from the llamas and moved to his truck. (He had already deposited the trailer by the stables, first thing that morning.) He squinted toward the house and made a small smile when the only one he saw was Alf, who was busy gnawing on his tail instead of his dog biscuit.

Reaching through the open window on the passenger's side, he removed a shotgun from the gun rack fixed behind the seats. It was a Serenity 66, made of cherry and black steel, with a single barrel and a brown sling to carry on the shoulder.

Then he opened the glove compartment and rummaged in the rear, finally fishing out that old box of rattling shotgun shells.

His eyes flicked toward the house again. He paused, watching Alf chew his tail. Then he quickly broke open the shotgun, loaded six slugs into the chamber with a series of clicks, and snapped the gun shut. He pushed the box back into the glove compartment.

It had been a long time since Walter Boyd held that shotgun in his hands. He was once the best shot around, ever since his youth when he became known far and wide as "Wonder Boy." In fact, he won the Boony Point Shootout ten years in a row, tying the record first set by Mayor Olympus.

But everything changed with one fateful shot. Now he was "Water Boy" and he couldn't even bring himself to aim a squirt gun at a toy clown when Corky's Carnival rolled into town each year for a few days. The big stuffed animals he used to win practically blindfolded—the hippos and giraffes and whale sharks—were gathering dust around the house, along with the ten gold trophies he earned from the shootout.

He made another careful glance at the porch. Alf hiccuped and spit out his tail.

Then Walter Boyd raised the shotgun. He squinted, taking aim at the red mailbox standing on a post at the end of the driveway. His heart beat quickly as the mailbox became a grizzly bear, ferocious and foaming, rising to its feet and roaring with fury.

Bang!

The screen door slammed. Ben's father whirled toward the house. He tried hiding the shotgun behind his back but the barrel was peeking over his shoulder.

On the porch was Ben's mother, her arms folded across her chest, her mouth fixed in a frown.

Alf hiccuped again.

"What are you doing, Walter?"

Ben's father forced a smile. "Nothing," he said.

"What are you doing with that shotgun?"

"Shotgun?"

"That shotgun behind your back."

Ben's father revealed the rifle. "Oh, you mean *this* shotgun."

Ben's mother narrowed her eyes and headed toward her husband. "Walter, I thought we settled this last night. Mother had a hard day yesterday and I don't want her getting riled up again about Ben. Ben dozed off and had a bad dream, right?"

Ben's father nodded eagerly.

"If you really think there might be a bear," Ben's mother said, lowering her voice, "I better call Sheriff Silver to take a good look out there before you and Ben—"

"No, no," said Ben's father, the hairs on his neck bristling at the mention of Sheriff Silver's name, "you're absolutely right. Ben just had a bad dream. There aren't any bears out there. No bears at all."

Ben's mother cocked her head. "Then what are you doing with that shotgun, Walter?"

"Oh, well, I was just... I was just *dusting it off.*" He pulled a handkerchief from his pants pocket and began rubbing the barrel of the shotgun.

Ben's mother softened at the sight of his grin. "I haven't seen you with that Serenity 66 in your hands in a long time," she said. "You haven't touched it since... Well, it's just nice to see you holding it again, Walter. Maybe you'll try shooting it again too."

"Oh, I'm just dusting it off today."

"Well, that's the first step, isn't it? Step by step, you might even make it back to this year's shootout. You just need to swallow your pride and get a pair of glasses from Winky at Olympus Eyewear before you start shooting again—"

The screen door opened and Ben's mother turned. Ben's father squinted to find his son stepping onto the porch. The curly-headed boy was in his second-favorite Mayor Olympus T-shirt and another pair of cut-off jeans. He had a band-aid on his knee and a headless gingerbread boy in his hand.

"Ben, your boot's untied," Ben's mother said. "You'll trip and hurt your other knee." She returned to the porch and crouched to tie Ben's boot. He went on munching his cookie.

Ben's father pushed his handkerchief back in his pocket. He moved around the truck, tugged open the creaky driver's side door, and replaced the shotgun in the gun rack. Sliding into the seat, he cranked the key. The engine roared to life and the truck backfired three times—*bang! bang! bang!*—before settling into its loud rumble.

"You ready?" Ben's father called out over the noise.

"I can't find my Giant Heart bongos," Ben shouted through a mouthful of cookie.

"Ben, you can play your bongos when you get home," his mother said. "Just pick the crabapples quietly today and get them home quickly to Grandma."

For a moment Ben's stomach flip-flopped with fear, remembering how the bongos had saved him from the dancing monster—

But then he reminded himself it was all just a dream.

Ben's mother stood and kissed his head. Ben popped the last of the gingerbread boy into his mouth and hopped down the steps. As he climbed into the truck and pulled on his seat belt, Ben's mother approached the open driver's side window.

"Bring back those crabapples right away, Walter. Maybe you can even get back before Grandma wakes up."

Ben's father tipped his hat and flashed a grin. "Yes, ma'am." He thrust the gear shift into reverse with a grinding sound, then began backing away down the driveway.

Ben's mother waved. Ben waved back.

Alf had one eye on his tail, the other on his biscuit.

As the truck reached the foot of the driveway, a scowling face appeared at the screen door. It was Grandma, in her bathrobe and silver curlers. And in her hand with the twitching half-pinky was the brown wicker picnic basket.

The Picnic Basket

Now it's important to remember that Grandma ate half a chocolate cake just hours before she spotted the picnic basket in the living room. If you think back to the times you ate half a chocolate cake, maybe that will give you some idea of Grandma's state that morning. I mean, even when a person eats sweets every day and has the cavities to prove it, all that sugar from eating half a chocolate cake gets the body buzzing like a hive of honeybees. But when a little old woman who hasn't eaten sweets in years, not even a peppermint drop, puts a tidal wave of sugar into her system, you've now got yourself a whole nest of hornets.

Grandma was so wound up, it's a wonder she didn't sprout a big stinger on her backside.

"*STOP!*" she screeched from the screen wire, her piercing cry practically blowing out another tire on the rumbling truck. Ben's father instinctively slammed on the brakes. His eyes squinted, then widened, at the sight of Grandma charging through the screen door—*bang!*—and stomping off the porch in her yellow slippers. She brushed past Ben's mother, who chased her down the driveway.

Alf looked up, his mouth full of biscuit and tail both.

Ben turned to his father. "Dad, you forgot the picnic basket."

"I can see that," his father murmured from the corner of his mouth. Then he poked his head out the window and gave an eager grin. "Grandma, thanks! We were in such a hurry to pick those crabapples for you…"

Grandma said nothing as she approached, but her toothless gums were grinding away and the rest of her was twitching. When she reached the trembling pick-up truck, her curlers barely cleared the bottom of the open window. She glared high at Ben's father, her eyes huge behind her glasses. Ben's father shifted in his seat.

"Here, we'll take the basket," he said. He reached out and got a hand on it, but Grandma wouldn't let go. She just glared and went on grinding her gums.

"Grandma, we need the basket to pick your crabapples." Ben's father gave a small tug, but Grandma had a death-grip on the handle. "Grandma?"

Then the old woman's mouth spread into a gummy smile. She spoke in a soft, dangerous voice: "What are you up to, Walter?"

Ben's father tugged again at the basket, harder, but Grandma's arm was an iron bar. "Grandma, just give me the—"

"How come you're so eager to pick crabapples without a basket? Where were you planning to put them all? In your cheeks?"

Ben's mother shot her husband a scolding look from behind Grandma. "Mother, he must have forgotten it."

"Forgotten it? How could a person forget—"

"Yes, Grandma. I'm sorry. I forgot it."

And that much was true: Walter Boyd did forget the picnic basket.

"Well," Grandma said, studying Ben's father for the telltale signs of fibbing, "if you forgot the basket, the basket you need for crabapple-picking, that must mean you have something else on your mind besides picking crabapples, now doesn't it?" Her gaze drifted to Ben, then came to rest on the Serenity 66 in the gun rack. Her eyes narrowed at the barrel, wiped clean…

"I was dusting it off today, Grandma," Ben's father said quickly. "I guess I got distracted."

"Dusting it off?" Grandma said. "Dusting it off for what? For a foaming grizzly bear—"

Ben's mother jumped in. "Maybe he'll start shooting again, Mother. Maybe we can even get him to enter the shootout this year. Wouldn't that be nice?"

"The shootout? After what happened last time?"

"I was just dusting it off," Ben's father said.

The old woman peered up at Walter Boyd. Then her gaze fell to the picnic basket, still gripped in a tug-of-war. Ben's father was about to plead for the basket again when Grandma's eyes suddenly flashed with fire.

"You think I've forgotten how you used to practice for your shootouts?" she snapped. "Blasting away at my crabapples with your shotgun! So that's why you're feeling so forgetful today! Your mind is fixed on a comeback at the next shootout! You're more antsy to blast my crabapples than pick them for my basket!"

"No, Grandma—"

"Mother, calm down—"

But Grandma had already ignited.

"Well, let me tell you something!" she cried. "You're welcome to shoot at that tree all you want, because you won't hit a single crabapple, anyway! Not even a *wormy* one! And when you've spent every shell blasting holes in the air, you climb up and start picking my crabapples!" She thrust the picnic basket through the window. *"The dewiest ninety-seven crabapples on that tree, Water Boy!"*

Walter Boyd's face flushed red. His lips pursed tight, a reply building behind them like wild water set to burst a dam.

Lorelai Boyd saw the reckless look in her husband's eyes. "Walter, don't," she warned. "Just go get the crabapples—"

But then the words were rushing from his mouth: *"I've had it up to here with that nickname! I miss one time—one time—and I'm Water Boy for the next ten years! Well, you won't be calling me that much longer! I've had it! You hear me? I've had it, Squ—"*

"Walter!"

"Squ...Squ..."

"Walter, no!"

Grandma steeled her ears.

Ben dropped his eyes.

Ben's father fought to say it, and blurted: *"Squish kebab!"*

Now I know that sounds funny, but the mind is a funny thing. The fact is, Ben's father had every intention of shouting

"Squeeze!" but his promise to his wife had gotten him flustered, and he couldn't force the word from his tongue. That's why *"Squish kebab!"* finally barged out instead. I suppose if he had eaten something else for dinner the night before, he would have sputtered *"Squirloin steak!"* or *"Squeet potato!"*

No matter how you slice it, *"Squish kebab!"* was a surprising thing to say and it caught everyone completely off guard. They all froze in confusion, even Ben's father. (Well, except for Alf, who finally spit out his tail and started gnawing on his biscuit.)

Then, without another word, Walter Boyd flung the basket into Ben's lap and slammed his boot on the gas. The truck lurched backward and spun out onto the road. As you might imagine, he already felt humiliated by what just happened—he wasn't about to linger there and try explaining why he shouted *"Squish kebab!"* at Grandma.

As the Rambler went barreling away in a cloud of dust, Grandma regained her voice.

"And no wormy ones!" she shouted, jittering in the driveway. "You hear me, Water Boy! No wormy ones!"

The Last Shootout

BEN'S FATHER HAD A HABIT OF DRIVING FAST on the country roads around Boony Point, but today he was pushing the old Rambler so hard it was practically a rusty rocket. Dust whirled around the truck; rocks thunked its belly; wind screamed through the windows. It's a wonder his head wasn't whipped off, let alone the lucky fishing hat.

Ben gripped the door handle with one hand and the handle of the picnic basket with the other. He stared at his father as they flew by the rows of sunflowers. This wild ride was frightening enough, but he was even more terrified by his father's face: he had the look of a man gone loco. Squinting into the gray horizon, his eyes gleaming fiercely, he was growling to himself: "Water Boy, Water Boy…"

Ben grit his teeth as his father went hurtling around the bend in Route Z. The truck tilted off the ground and wobbled on two wheels before falling back to the road with a jolt. His father didn't even seem to notice—he just went on speeding straight ahead and grumbling "Water Boy" under his breath.

Ben had been afraid to disturb his father, but now he was more afraid that the truck might fly right off the road.

"Dad," he began, but his voice was drowned out by all the din. His father continued glaring out the gritty windshield and muttering to himself.

"Dad!" he shouted as loudly as he could.

His father turned. "What is it? You don't have to yell—"

"I don't think we have to go so fast, Dad. I know Grandma is waiting for her crabapples, but—"

"Crabapples?" his father replied. "I don't give a squat about crabapples!"

"What? But Dad, why—"

"Because I've been Water Boy long enough, that's why!"

The llamas came dashing through the goldenrod as the truck raced up the road. Like Ben, their eyes were wide with alarm.

Ben had heard people call his father "Water Boy" for as long as he could remember. At first, he thought they were just saying his father's name, "Walter Boyd." But as he got older and noticed how his father's face would flush red every time, he finally listened more closely. Then he heard the difference. He had never found the courage to ask him about it, though. He was worried it would just upset him more.

And the one time Ben approached his mother, tears quickly came to her eyes and she said his father would tell the story himself when the time was right.

Well, Ben figured, if he wouldn't live to see another birthday, the time was as right as it would ever be.

"*Dad!*" he shouted again.

"I'm right here. You don't have to yell—"

"Why do people call you that?"

There was a long pause as his father continued squinting up the road. Then he turned...

When Ben saw the pain in his father's eyes, he wished he hadn't said anything at all; he wished he could crawl right inside the picnic basket. And yet, before he knew it, he found himself blurting out: "Why do they call you Water Boy?"

Ben held his breath. His father turned back to the road, his face flushing red. Then he stomped his foot on the gas pedal, clear to the floor, and the truck bellowed like a bull and charged even harder up Route Z. The old Rambler was now roaring and rattling so madly that Ben thought it would either blast off into the sky or just fall right to pieces all around them.

It's a good thing he was wearing his seat belt.

Finally, Walter Boyd turned to his son and cried: *"One miss! One miss and I'm Water Boy!"* His right hand came off the steering wheel and the truck began skidding back and forth on the road. Making a fist, he pounded his chest and appealed to his son: "My name is Walter Boyd! MY NAME IS WALTER BOYD!"

Ben gaped at his father, as frightened by his outburst as he was by the truck lurching out of control. The Rambler had nearly slid into the ditch by the side of Route Z when his father turned back to the road and grabbed the steering wheel with both hands. He jerked the truck straight, but didn't slow down.

"They used to call me *Wonder Boy*," he said, squinting at the road, his eyes tearing up. Ben strained to hear him. "I was your age when I started winning those stuffed animals."

Ben flashed on all the big stuffed animals around the house. "You have a lot of stuffed animals, Dad," Ben shouted.

"I practically put Corky's Carnival out of business," said Ben's father with a sad chuckle. "From the first time I picked up a squirt gun, I could hit that toy clown dead in the nose. My eyes were like lasers. I never missed."

"You won a lot of big trophies too."

"That was later, when I turned eighteen."

The truck barreled on down the road, alongside the Abernathy Pumpkin Patch. Ben's father began to glow with pride as he recalled the days he was known as Wonder Boy. His eyes sparkled, his voice came to life. "I won the first year I entered and I was champion ten years in a row! Ten years! I tied the record set by Mayor Olympus! No one could touch me back then, me and my Serenity 66, not even Sheriff Silver!"

But as he spoke Sheriff Silver's name, he faltered. "One miss..." he moaned. "Just one miss..."

Ben's father fell silent as the truck roared up the high hill on Route Z. Before he could urge his father to finish the story, they were suddenly at the top and the truck was shooting into the gray sky. It then bounced back to the road and went on roaring down the hill toward Old Man Fibber's junk monster.

Ben stared at the junk monster as they raced toward it. He pictured it dancing around the cliff as he played the Giant Heart bongos from atop the Queen Tartelicious. He shuddered, but quickly shrugged off the vision. It was just a dream, right?

As the pickup screamed past, Ben swung around to keep his eye on the junk monster. When he did, he caught sight of two faces—one human, one reptile—peeking out from the old red barn. They were staring daggers at the truck as it sped away.

Ben turned back to his father. "Dad, what happened? How come you're not Wonder Boy anymore?"

Walter Boyd bit his lip. His eyes again clouded with tears. "You were there when it happened," he said.

Ben's eyebrows rose. "What? I was there?"

"I don't expect you remember. You were just two years old, sitting there in the grass on the Olympus Gun Range and chewing on a leaf. But the rest of the town has a long memory…" He swallowed hard. "It was the last shootout I entered. For ten years running I was the champion and Sheriff Silver was the runner-up. But Sheriff Silver won that year and then every year since. He tied the record last year, Ben. He's won ten years in a row too. If Sheriff Silver wins again this fall, that'll make it eleven, a new record."

"But what happened, Dad? Why did your nickname change that year?" He waited, fighting to hear above the Rambler and the raging wind.

A tear rolled down his father's dusty cheek. "When that first clay dove went up, I missed. I missed by a mile…"

"But everybody misses sometimes, right?"

Ben's father shook his head at the memory. "That slug hit the water tower. It blew a hole right in the side and all the water spilled out before it could be plugged up. Nobody in town could take a bath for a month. Grandma never forgave me for that. She says her hair hasn't had the same bounce since."

He wiped his eyes with his handkerchief and squinted up the road. The speeding truck was drawing near Grizzly Woods.

"That's why my name changed. That's why they started calling me Water Boy." Ben's father sighed…then a fire returned to his eye and he vowed: "But I plan to earn myself a new nickname today."

Ben was set to ask about his father's plan when a flashing red light appeared in his mirror. Then a siren split the air. He turned to see a black and white police car racing up behind them.

The Sheriff and His Deputy

A LOUDSPEAKER BOOMED ABOVE THE SHRIEK OF THE SIREN: "PULL OVER, SIR!"

Ben turned to his father. He was scowling in the rearview mirror. Then he took his foot off the gas and rolled the truck to a stop on the side of the road. Grizzly Woods now loomed to the right, across the patch of goatsbeard. When he turned off the engine, the truck sputtered, backfired twice, gave a shuddering gasp, and fell silent.

"Dad…"

"Shhh, be quiet. I can handle him."

Ben's father eyed the rearview mirror again. He took his handkerchief and wiped away all evidence of tears as the police car came crunching up behind. The siren whined down, but the red light continued spinning on top of the roof. Two men stepped out of the police car, as different as barbed wire and bunny whiskers.

The first to emerge was the driver. He was lean as a lizard, and cold-blooded to boot. His uniform was tan, with a matching cowboy hat. And everywhere he saw the opportunity, he sported gold: he had gold-tinted sunglasses; a gold badge on his chest; gold buttons on his shirt; a gold belt buckle and a gold-plated pistol in his holster; he even had a gold zipper on his pants.

His name was Sheriff Silver.

The other man took longer to get out of the car. In fact, Sheriff Silver stood stewing for half a minute while Deputy Thunk squeezed out the other side, like a big clown rising from a little clown car.

Deputy Thunk was twenty-six and still growing. Not only was he the biggest man in Boony Point, he was the biggest man in the whole state. His uniform was tan, like the sheriff, but it was much too small for him—it was a wonder, really, that he managed to wrestle into it. And the cowboy hat on his huge head was so small he had to hold himself very straight or it would topple right off. This was actually the uniform worn by the last deputy, a man called Minnow. Deputy Thunk's new uniform was too big a job for the tailor in town, Dandy, so it was now being custom-made by three tailors (triplets, actually) in Bloat City.

I suppose your average giant wouldn't be feeling so jolly in pants which cut off the circulation in his legs. But that was the thing about Thunk: he was always grinning and chuckling and chomping on a big wad of gum. The fumes from his Powermint gum, you see, helped keep him awake and alert. Deputy Thunk may have been a giant, but he suffered from nervous fits that sometimes made him faint dead away.

The two men walking up to Walter Boyd's pickup truck amounted to the entire police force in the town of Boony Point. Sheriff Silver had been the sheriff for many years, but he was dreadfully rude to his deputies and none of them lasted very long before Thunk. Besides Minnow, eight others had quit within days or weeks. (Goose Guy, Elbows, Itchy, Weatherman, Polyglot, Pork Chop, Caboose, and The Crown Prince of Crumbs, though people usually just called him Crumbs.) Normally, of course, a giant would make an ideal deputy, but a giant with a habit of keeling over unexpectedly from stress might not. Still, when the sheriff finally ran out of other options, he turned to Thunk. At least a happy-go-lucky giant like Thunk probably wouldn't quit as easily as the others, he thought. And it seems he was right: Deputy Thunk was already starting his second month on the police force.

"Good morning, sir," Sheriff Silver said as he sauntered up to Walter Boyd's window. He may have been rude to his deputies, but he prided himself on being polite to the public.

"Morning, sir," echoed Deputy Thunk, looming behind the sheriff like a mountain crowned with a cowboy hat. He smacked his gum in a friendly fashion and gave a chinny grin.

Ben's father forced a tight smile. "Morning, Sheriff." He then tilted his gaze so high Ben heard his father's neck crack. "Morning, Deputy."

Sheriff Silver slowly removed his gold-tinted sunglasses and hooked them to his shirt pocket. He peered down at Walter Boyd with a hard, unblinking gaze. Then he showed his teeth—the closest he could come to a smile—and revealed a big gold tooth in front.

"Sir, you seem to be in a serious hurry again. Yesterday it was a sick llama. What is it today? A sick child?" Sheriff Silver narrowed his eyes at Ben. Ben looked down at the picnic basket in his lap.

Deputy Thunk blew a bubble.

"No, we're just off to pick crabapples for my mother-in-law." Ben's father waved toward the basket and Ben promptly held it up for inspection. "We're headed out to Crabapple Cliff."

"Crabapples, huh?"

"That's right."

"You seem awfully keen to pick crabapples, sir." The sheriff turned and looked skyward at his deputy. "Deputy Thunk, have you ever been this keen to pick crabapples?"

"I'm not much for crabapples myself," said Deputy Thunk with a grin. "But I do like figs."

Ben's father forced another smile. "Well, write me up a ticket and we'll be on our way."

"Write you a ticket?" said Sheriff Silver, flashing his gold tooth. "Why, sir, just yesterday you didn't want one.

Yesterday you made a fuss about getting a ticket."

"I was speeding, fair and square." Ben's father pulled his driver's license from his wallet and held it out for the sheriff. "Here's my license."

Sheriff Silver studied Walter Boyd's face. He reached for the license, thanking him politely. Then he turned and barked, "Deputy, hand me the ticket book."

But the large pad for writing traffic tickets was trapped in Deputy Thunk's back pocket. He struggled to free it from his pants, even tugging with both hands.

Sheriff Silver frowned. "Deputy, stop playing with your posterior and give me that ticket book."

"Sheriff, it's stuck..."

"Thunk!"

Deputy Thunk's eyes began to jiggle, the first sign of a nervous fit. He jawed on his Powermint gum, trying to stay alert. Then he pulled so hard on the ticket book that the whole pocket tore off—*RIIIP!*—and dropped into the dust.

"Here you go, Sheriff," Thunk said with a nervous chuckle.

Sheriff Silver snatched the ticket pad from Deputy Thunk. He turned back to Ben's father and slipped a gold pen from his shirt pocket.

"So you like picking crabapples?" he said as he began scribbling up the speeding ticket.

"Yes, I absolutely adore it," Ben's father said.

The sheriff paused and looked up, taking in his old rival. The two men locked eyes in a long staredown. Finally, Sheriff Silver's gaze drifted to the Serenity 66 in the gunrack.

"Sir, that gun looks different today."

Ben's father swallowed. "Different?"

"As an officer of the law, I notice such things. That gun has been dusted since I pulled you over for speeding yesterday."

Sheriff Silver leaned into the window, so close to Walter

Boyd's face their noses nearly touched. He went on in a low, but mannerly voice: "I know how you used to practice for the shootout—back when you were known by another name. You used to take potshots at that Queen Tartelicious out on Crabapple Cliff. Maybe now that I'm set to break the record, you're groping for the nerve to enter again."

Walter Boyd's lips curled into a smile. "Sheriff, I have more important things on my mind today."

Sheriff Silver studied his rival in silence. The only sound came from Deputy Thunk's great wad of gum. Then, still in tight, he said: "Sir, you can blast every crabapple off that tree, if you like—assuming you can manage that much. Because there's no way in this wicked world you'll beat me at the shootout." The sheriff showed his teeth again, the gold one winking at Walter Boyd. "You'll probably just drain the town of its water supply for another month."

Sheriff Silver went back to calmly writing up the speeding ticket. Ben saw his father's face flush red, his nostrils flare, his jaw clench like a fist.

The sheriff then slowly, loudly tore the ticket from the pad. "And another thing, sir," he said, handing Ben's father the speeding ticket and his driver's license. "I'm sorry I didn't mention this yesterday, but please fix this little mistake on your license."

"What mistake?" Ben's father said.

"It says Walter Boyd."

"That's my name," Ben's father replied sharply. He glanced at the speeding ticket and saw that Sheriff Silver had scrawled across it in block letters: WATER BOY.

"My name is Walter Boyd!" Ben's father snapped.

"Good day to you, sir," the sheriff said, clicking his gold pen closed and returning it to his shirt pocket. He slipped on his gold-tinted sunglasses then took a step toward Deputy Thunk. "Here, Thunk," he grunted. The giant reached down for the ticket book.

Ben watched his father staring at the ticket in his hand. His face was practically purple. His nose was fit to spurt steam. His teeth were grinding like the gears of his truck.

Then Walter Boyd did something he normally would never do. Something downright dangerous.

He looked up from the ticket and hissed back at the sheriff: "Good day to you, Sheriff *Silver*."

Back when Ben's father was Wonder Boy, the sheriff had always come in second, even when they were children. Long before the Boony Point Shootouts, the sheriff could only win the medium-sized stuffed animals at Corky's Carnival. Never the big stuffed animals, like Ben's father—the hippos and giraffes and whale sharks. In fact, the sheriff's attic was still crammed with woodchucks, warthogs, and baboons, along with the silver second-place cups he won when Walter Boyd was collecting his gold first-place trophies. But even after Ben's father hit the water tower and the sheriff began his own winning streak at the shootout, the people of Boony Point continued to call him Sheriff Silver. And the more he sought for people to call him Sheriff Gold instead, in ways that became barely courteous, the more stubborn they all grew about sticking fast to his first nickname. It was one thing, though, when other people called him Silver; to hear his old rival say it now, the nickname he despised, well, a rush of rage finally overwhelmed his good manners.

Sheriff Silver whirled back toward Ben's father. "That's Sheriff *Gold* to you, Water Boy!" he barked, pointing his finger rudely at Walter Boyd. "I could run you in for disrespecting an officer of the law! That's a second-degree offense, mister!"

Walter Boyd was set to answer back, and probably get himself arrested for something of the first degree, but he was saved by a sudden *crack* from Grizzly Woods. Ben jumped and turned toward the trees. His heart raced as he flashed on the day before…

Something was crashing toward them through the brush.

Happy Hibernation

"Who's there?" shouted Sheriff Silver.

Deputy Thunk stood big and frozen as an iceberg, the ticket book gripped in his hands. Even his jaws had stopped in mid-chomp. The only movement, if you looked closely, came from his eyes: they were jiggling with alarm.

The crashing continued from Grizzly Woods.

"It's coming!" Ben yelped to his father, who was reaching for the rifle.

"Identify yourself!" shouted Sheriff Silver, unsnapping his holster.

"Ben, lean back," his father whispered. "And cover your ears." He stretched across Ben with the shotgun, sticking the barrel out the window. He raised the gun to his shoulder and squinted toward the crashing sounds.

Ben pressed his hands to his ears. He gaped at the trees, suddenly wishing he had brought his bongos. *No, it was just a dream,* he told himself. *There are no such things as mon—"*

Then a huge head poked out of the forest.

Attracted by the odor of Deputy Thunk's Powermint gum, a large moose had come to investigate. It snorted at the air, its eyes zeroing in on Deputy Thunk.

The giant instantly toppled to the ground.

Thunk.

The small hat spilled off his head. The wad of gum popped from his mouth and dropped into the dust. Then, with the ticket book still clutched in his hands, he began to snore happily, like a grizzly bear in hibernation.

"Thunk! Thunk!" Sheriff Silver barked. It was the second time this week Thunk had fainted in the line of duty. (The first time involved a wad of gum on the bottom of Sheriff Silver's gold-toed cowboy boot.)

"Thunk, it's just a moose!" The sheriff drew his gold-plated pistol and fired a shot in the air. The moose bellowed in fright and fled back into the forest. But Deputy Thunk went right on snoring.

As Sheriff Silver stalked over to the sleeping giant, Ben's father reached across Ben and opened the passenger-side door. He nudged Ben out and then climbed out himself with the shotgun in his hand. He was about to close the door when he stopped. He stuck his head back inside the truck and plunged his other hand behind the seat. Fishing about for a moment, he pulled up a dark leather strap…and the glittering Giant Heart bongos.

He passed the bongos to his surprised son, put a finger to his lips, then softly closed the door of the truck.

Sheriff Silver, his back to Grizzly Woods, was crouched by Deputy Thunk. He sighed and squirmed his hand into the giant's tight shirt pocket to produce a fresh pack of Powermint gum. Tearing it open, he waved the gum under Thunk's nose. Thunk went on snoring, but the sharp smell made Sheriff Silver grimace and turn away. He then caught sight of Walter Boyd and his son tiptoeing through the tall goatsbeard: one clutching a shotgun, the other carrying a pair of bongos.

Sheriff Silver narrowed his eyes. "Water Boy, I think you're forgetting something!" he shouted. "I think you're forgetting your picnic basket!"

"Dad—"

"Shhh. Don't turn around." Ben's father put his arm around Ben and pulled him close as they continued moving toward Grizzly Woods.

"Blast away, Water Boy!" the sheriff yelled, still waving the pack of gum under his deputy's nose. "Even if you manage to turn that tree bare as a newborn, you still won't beat me in September! And after that I'll have the record all to myself!"

"Sheriff? Is that you, Sheriff?" Deputy Thunk's eyes fluttered halfway open.

"Yes, Thunk, it's me."

"Sheriff," Thunk mumbled, "let's fill up our basket with figs. I like figs." He gave a chinny grin.

"Thunk, we don't have a basket."

Sheriff Silver turned back to Walter Boyd and his son. He frowned as they disappeared into the dim forest.

"And for your information, I hate figs."

Heavy Breathing

Grizzly Woods was even gloomier than usual that day. With the sky slate-gray, the bit of sunlight from the day before was gone and the forest was now deep in shadow.

Walter Boyd gripped the shotgun tighter than a vise. His eyes darted from side to side as he tiptoed up the path through Grizzly Woods. His ears were pricked for the slightest sound.

Ben stepped along gingerly behind his father. The bongos felt heavy on his neck. His heart thumped against the wood. When they first entered the forest, Ben had asked his father about the plan for earning a new nickname—but his father quickly hushed him. It was dangerous to talk in the forest, he said. They had to keep quiet, keep alert.

So father and son, two pale ghosts in the gloom, slunk ahead in silence.

As each step brought them closer to Crabapple Cliff, Ben's heart seemed to beat a little faster. He told himself there were no monsters out there, that it was all his imagination. At the same time, he was glad his father had a gun.

And then, from the murk, they heard a low sound. Ben's father froze and quickly raised his shotgun. He squinted, searching the trees.

Hoooo.

"Dad—"

"Shhh."

Hoooo.

"Dad, I—"

"Ben, quiet—"

"But Dad, I see it," Ben whispered. "Over there."

Ben's father followed his son's finger, pointing at the branch of a hickory tree by the path. As they crept closer, Ben's father found a large white owl, its eyes glowing orange.

Hoooo.

"It's a great frosty," he whispered.

Ben nodded. "It looks like the one I saw yesterday."

The owl glared down at Ben's father—no owl likes a shotgun, and least of all the great frosty.

"It pulled my hair. And then it stole Grandma's hat—"

Hoooo. The big bird spread its wings, set to swoop…

But before Ben's father could be scalped, he grabbed the brim of his fishing hat. The owl paused on the branch and ruffled its feathers with fury. As Ben's father passed by the tree—one hand on his hat, both eyes on the owl—he shook the shotgun to warn off the bird. The owl glowered down, unblinking, but didn't budge from the branch. Ben followed his father up the path, glancing back several times until the orange eyes faded from sight.

* * *

MINUTES LATER A POINT OF LIGHT APPEARED, like a bright star, at the far end of the path. They had nearly reached Crabapple Cliff.

Ben stopped in his tracks. "Dad..."

Ben's father turned. "What is it?" he whispered. "You hear something?"

The small boy shook his blond curls. "I can't go out there, Dad."

Though his brain was trying to remind him it was just a bad dream, his body was now scared stiff at the thought of returning to Crabapple Cliff.

Ben's father squatted to gaze into his eyes. He put a warm hand on Ben's shoulder.

"Don't you worry, Ben," he whispered with a smile. "Here's my plan."

He glanced around, as if someone might be eavesdropping from behind a tree, then spoke in a low, feverish voice. "When we get to the cliff, we'll head for the Queen Tartelicious and climb to a high, safe branch. You start playing the bongos—that lured it out yesterday, right? It goes dancing near the tree, waltzing by on its back legs, and then"—there was a gleam in his eyes that sent a shiver through Ben—"I'll blast it with my shotgun! And when everyone finds out how I saved the town from a man-eater, I'm bound to get a new name! They'll start calling me Bear-Killer! Bear-Killer Boyd!"

The truth is, Walter Boyd had never shot at a living creature in his whole life—he had only fired at crabapples and clay doves. In fact, just the thought of harming a living creature would usually upset him, like the day before when he hit little Agnes driving back from Bloat City. But ten years of shame had made him blind to everything but gaining a new nickname—even a name that didn't really fit—to at last remove the curse of Water Boy.

"But Dad, I didn't say—"

"Shhh, what's that?"

Father and son froze in the dim forest. From away in the gloom came the sound of soft, heavy breathing.

Walter Boyd's face, rosy with excitement just a moment ago, was now chalk-white. He raised the shotgun and gripped on for dear life. With a jerk of his head, he motioned for Ben to follow him off the path.

Hearts thumping, they stepped like burglars through the trees. Dark limbs scratched at their skin as they edged toward the sound. The closer they got, the louder the breathing became.

Ben's father normally had heavy footsteps, but he was hardly making a rustle as he moved over the leaves and twigs on the forest floor. Ben, too, was trying hard to step gently in his boots. In fact, he was gazing so intently at his feet that he didn't realize he was advancing more quickly than his father...until it was too late.

Ben walked right into him. The Giant Heart bongos swung into the butt of his father's shotgun. The drum made a sudden *boom*.

Ben's father spun around and threw out a hand to muffle the sound. Father and son stared at one another, their eyes wide, their breath caught in their throats. They were listening so hard, they could have sprained their ears.

They heard a snort, then a grunt. Ben's father swung the shotgun toward the sound, his finger trembling on the trigger. The steady, heavy breathing returned.

They stood rigid for another minute, then Ben's father stepped toward the sound again. Ben followed, very slowly.

Finally, as they approached the trunk of a massive old sawtooth sycamore that had fallen to its side, Ben's father stopped cold. Ben stopped too, about ten feet behind his father. Up ahead in shadow, behind the great trunk, was the source of the sound. And with each rumbling breath, something was appearing above it, then disappearing on the exhale: a dark, hairy mound, rising and falling, rising and falling...

Ben and his father stood watching, listening, the same thought chilling them to the bone: *It's sleeping right there, over there behind the tree.*

Bear-Killer Boyd

WALTER BOYD HAD A CHANCE TO GET CLOSER, get a better shot. But the fact is, he was terrified to approach any further. He was rooted to the spot, and pale as a grub, peering at what seemed to be the bear's belly jiggling behind the sycamore. Still, he could blast it in the stomach, he thought. And if that didn't do the job, when the grizzly rose up with a roar, he would shoot it right through the heart.

He raised the Serenity 66 and aimed. Squinting through the gloom, he watched the big belly rise and fall. He drew a deep breath and blew it out slowly, trying to calm the quivering barrel of his gun. The next time that belly bulged above the trunk, he vowed, he would fire. He would kill the grizzly.

"Bear-Killer," Ben heard his father whisper just before the shotgun blast.

But before that blast, Ben heard something else too. He was about to press his hands over his ears when he recognized it: a soft, familiar sucking sound. In fact, his father heard the same sound, but it didn't register. The only thought in Walter Boyd's head right then was becoming Bear-Killer Boyd.

The sound they heard came from Stanley. He was sucking two big claws on his right front paw—a habit from the days he was an orphaned cub. Doc Sprinkle said it gave him comfort in times of distress.

After the terrible turn of events at Governor Glutty's mansion in Bloat City, Stanley had fled back to Boony Point, hustling the whole way. By the middle of the night he had collapsed in Grizzly Woods and fallen asleep, utterly exhausted.

The moment Ben realized it was Stanley, his mouth flew open to warn his father: *"Dad, no! Don't shoot!"*

But at that same moment Stanley's belly rose above the trunk like a hairy mountain.

Ben's shout had come a split second too late.

Walter Boyd fired—

BLAM!

And missed.

The shotgun blast woke Stanley with a start. He scrambled to his feet, his lavender tutu torn and soiled with dirt and blood. In a panic, he stood tall, raised his arms in the air, and roared.

Of course, Stanley's roar was actually a cry of fright, but to Walter Boyd it sounded only like the mad bellow of a man-eater. And when he spotted the foamy white drool around the bear's mouth (a common side effect of claw-sucking), his eyes popped at the sure sign of rabies. In a panic himself, he was unable to comprehend, even with that ragged tutu around its waist, that the great grizzly looming before him in the shadows was really Stanley.

He fired again—

BLAM!

And missed.

Stanley stood there stiff as a stuffed bear in a hunting lodge: arms high, claws curled, jaws open, fangs bared. On the outside he may have looked ferocious, but on the inside he was petrified.

Even Walter Boyd's eyebrows were quaking as he aimed his shotgun at the bear again, this time at its chest.

"Dad, stop! It's Stanley!"

Ben rushed to his father and pushed the rifle barrel down as the third shot rang out.

BLAM!

The slug whizzed between Stanley's legs. The big grizzly then burst into tears, turned on his heels, and fled into the forest.

Ben's father listened to the bear's sobs fading away, suddenly recalling the sound of Stanley crying as he ran from the governor's mansion the day before. He stared into the dark forest with wide, horrified eyes.

"That was Stanley…"

"Yes," Ben said.

"I almost shot Stanley…"

"Dad—"

"I almost killed him…"

"Dad, listen—"

"Stanley-Killer…"

"Dad, listen to me—"

"Stanley-Killer Boyd…"

"Dad, it wasn't a bear."

Walter Boyd blinked. "What?"

"I tried to tell you—"

"But—But you said…" he sputtered, turning to his son. "You said it was a monster."

"Yes."

"A grizzly."

"No...a monster."

Ben's father blinked again. The rifle slipped from his hand and fell to the ground. He tugged off his hat and ran his fingers through his hairless head. Then he squatted and peered into Ben's eyes. "What are you saying, Ben?"

"Dad, I don't want to take a bath with a snapping turtle!"

"What?"

"Like Old Man Fibber! I don't want to end up like that!"

"Of course not, Ben."

"So it must have been my imagination, right? It must have been a bad dream, like Mom said."

Ben's father pulled his hat on and put both hands on Ben's shoulders. "Ben, tell me exactly what happened yesterday."

Ben swallowed. Then he told his father all about the monster: how it looked a lot like Old Man Fibber's junk monster, how it chased him up the crabapple tree, how it attacked him with the branch, how he played the Giant Heart bongos and it danced around the cliff, how it finally got sick and then disappeared. By the time Ben finished pouring out the whole story, with all the emotion that had shaken him the day before, his father's eyes were bulging in wonder.

"But it was just my imagination, right, Dad?" Ben whimpered. "Monsters aren't real, right?"

Walter Boyd stared at his son. Two days ago, he would have agreed: monsters aren't real. But the boy's story was so vivid and he knew Ben was no fibber. On top of that, he now wanted to believe there might be a monster. After all, the news that there were no rabid grizzly bears terrorizing the community had come as a huge disappointment. The possibility that another horrible creature was stalking the countryside instead had suddenly filled him with fresh hope. If he killed something the size of Old Man Fibber's junk monster, he could have any nickname he wanted! He could even reclaim his old one!

Ben saw the feverish light return to his father's eyes. "Dad?"

"Wonder Boy," his father breathed as he grabbed up his shotgun and cracked it open. His eyes narrowed, then hardened, at the sight of the three remaining shells. "I'll be Wonder Boy again." He snapped the gun closed and stood.

Ben felt his stomach drop to his toes. "Dad, maybe we should go back and get Sheriff Silver and Deputy—"

But at the sound of Sheriff Silver's name, Ben's father blurted: "I can't have the sheriff horning in on this monster!"

Ben made a small yelp in surprise.

His father's eyes gleamed as he laid his hand again on Ben's shoulder. "Don't you worry, Ben," he said, more gently. "We'll just follow the same plan. We'll get a safe spot high in the tree and lure it out with the bongos—and then I'll blast it."

He smiled, with too much teeth, and squeezed Ben's shoulder. Then he brushed by and trudged back toward the path. Ben followed, his fingers trembling on the Giant Heart bongos. He could hear his father mumbling up ahead: "Wonder Boy, Wonder Boy…"

The Big Mound

As father and son approached the end of the path through Grizzly Woods, they slowed to a tiptoe. The sky over Crabapple Cliff was deep gray, but their eyes had grown used to the gloom of the forest and the daylight made them squint. Hiding behind a thick bitterwood tree, they heard the waves crashing against the cliff and smelled a sharp odor in the air…

They peered out. Ben's father, clutching the shotgun in one hand, shielded his eyes with the other. He gazed across the cliff at the mighty Queen Tartelicious. Wind whistled through the branches, jiggling the crabapples.

Then he saw, with a shiver, that a high limb had been torn from the trunk. His eyes searched the ground and found the branch not far from the tree, just as Ben had described.

He gripped his rifle tighter.

Ben stood behind his father, his small hands on his father's waist, peeking out through his wire-rimmed glasses. His heart thumped at the sight of the crabapple tree, the branch on the ground, the crabapples strewn all about…

"What's that over there?" his father whispered. He had noticed something perched at the edge of the cliff: a big purplish-black mound.

Ben's whole body shuddered. He saw the huge shadow standing there in the dusk the day before; he heard the grunting and gasping and spitting…

"Let's take a closer look, son."

Ben's father led the way through the horsetail, past the crabapple tree, across the windy, rocky-red bluff. The sharp odor grew stronger, prickling their nostrils.

Ben plodded behind his father. He felt dazed, like he was dreaming, or like he had stumbled right into a book.

His hands crept from his queasy stomach and came to rest on the Giant Heart bongos.

The dark mound was wider than the trunk of the crabapple tree and taller than Ben's father. It was shaped like a haystack, with things jutting helter-skelter from the sides and the top. And it was all coated with something like blueberry jam, though bits of shiny silver and gold were peeking through in spots.

The stench now stung their noses.

Ben's father laid his gun on the ground and pulled out his handkerchief. He bit into it, then ripped it in two. "Cover your nose and mouth with this," he said, giving half to Ben.

Masking himself with one hand, Ben's father reached out with the other. He scraped a finger through the dark goo from a part protruding on top. It felt sticky between his finger and thumb. Then his skin began to tingle. He quickly wiped his fingers clean on the handkerchief and stuffed it in his back pocket.

A glitter of gold appeared in the spot where he had removed the goo.

"What is it, Dad?" Ben asked, talking through the handkerchief.

Ben's father studied the streak of gold. "It looks like metal." He stepped back and gazed again at the whole purplish-black mass. Then he turned, his eyes wide with awe. "The monster got sick and hooted up *this?*"

Ben's stomach squirmed again. "I didn't actually see it, because its back was toward me. But I heard it."

His father reached for the shotgun. "And then it disappeared? How could a monster that size just disappear?"

"I don't know. I looked away for a moment. When I looked back, it was gone."

As Ben's father scanned the empty cliff, Ben added, hopefully, "Maybe it fell over the edge. It seemed kind of dizzy."

Ben's father frowned at this suggestion, then stepped carefully to the edge. He peered down at the boulders far below, afraid he might find the battered body of the monster sprawled out over the rocks. No one would be moved to call him "Wonder Boy" again if the creature had simply tumbled to its death.

But he was relieved to see only the ocean, angry and hissing.

"I don't see anything down there," he said.

"Maybe it hit a rock and slid off into the sea. Or it missed the boulders and dropped right into the water and drowned."

His father huffed and turned to Ben, who was creeping up by his side. He was about to scold his son for his poor attitude when something terrible happened: Ben tripped.

It's hard to say exactly what occurred. It may be that his foot caught on a small root—as you know, roots from the Queen Tartelicious went snaking through the cliff toward the sea. Or it may be that he just stumbled over his own feet—it wouldn't have been the first time, of course.

No matter how it happened, the upshot was the same: he pitched headlong into the air, as if diving into Leech Lake, the torn handkerchief fluttering away. In fact, Ben would have plunged right off the cliff if his father hadn't managed to shoot out a hand and grab the back of his T-shirt. His father yanked him backward and the two fell hard to the ground, the lucky fishing hat jarred from his father's head.

But when his body pitched forward, then was jerked back, the bongos were whipped off Ben's neck. As he fell, he saw them in the air, arcing in slow-motion, glittering ruby-red. They hit the ground with a great *boom*, bounced once, twice…and then the Giant Heart bongos disappeared over the edge.

Delirious

"MY BONGOS!" BEN SCREAMED. He scrambled to his feet and pushed his glasses into place. *"My new bongos!"*

Ben's father reached up and clamped Ben's wrist. Then he rose, leaving the shotgun on the ground. His hands moved to Ben's arms and held them firmly from behind. He wasn't about to let his son suffer the same fate as the Giant Heart bongos.

Ben burst into tears. "Now I'll never be Dragon Hands," he sobbed. "I'll be Butterfingers for the rest of my life."

His father teared up too. He needed those bongos for his own nickname. Without the bongos, his plan was botched. How could he lure the monster out now to shoot it from the tree? Even if he ran home for the old birch bongos, they were hardly a good substitute; they might not even work. Anyway, he couldn't return home now, without the crabapples. And that would mean first going to the truck for the picnic basket…

Ben's father was in the middle of this brooding when they suddenly heard a soft *boom*.

Father and son gave a quick gasp. They looked at each other with wide, puzzled eyes.

Ben's father nudged him forward, his hands holding fast to the boy's thin arms. Inch by inch, they eased back to the edge of the cliff and peered down.

"Ben, look!"

Ben blinked through his tears. He could scarcely believe what he saw: the Giant Heart bongos were dangling right there, not far from the top of the cliff. The leather strap had caught on a root and saved the drum from plunging into the sea.

"Dad, my bongos!" He moved to kneel, but his father held him tight.

"You can't reach it, Ben. Let me do it."

They took two steps back. Ben's father got to his belly. Ben went to the ground beside him.

"Son, stay right where you are."

"Okay, Dad."

Ben's father squirmed forward until his head poked over the edge. He eyed the ruby-red bongos, rocking in the wind, knocking against the face of the cliff. He dug into the ground with the toes of his boots and the fingers of his left hand. Then he stretched his right arm down toward the drum…

He reached as far as he could, straining at the shoulder, but the bongos were still farther below. Even worse, he could see that the strap might easily be jostled off the root by the next strong gust of wind.

"Dad, do you have it?"

"I…I can't reach it," his father grunted.

Ben crawled to his father's side.

"Ben, get back."

"But my bongos!" Peering down, Ben saw his father's hand above the swaying drum. A sudden gust sent it swinging into the rock wall with a louder *boom*. "Dad, do something!"

Ben's father tried again, stretching and grunting with all his might…but even with the arm of an orangutan, it would have been impossible. He brought his arm up and lay on his side facing Ben.

"I'm sorry, Ben," he said, breathing hard. "I'm sorry for us both…"

There was another loud *boom* from below.

"Dad, lower me down!" Ben cried, his desperation overriding his fear. "Hold my ankles and lower me down!"

On any other day, Walter Boyd would have at least thought twice about dangling his only son upside down over the side of Crabapple Cliff. But at that particular moment, with the bongos set to plunge into the sea, he was just as delirious as Ben.

"Good thinking!" he exclaimed. Then he scrambled up and crawled behind Ben to grasp his ankles.

"Ready, Ben?"

Ben pushed his glasses firmly behind his ears. "Ready, Dad!"

Ben's father again went to his stomach. With his hands locked on Ben's legs, he pushed against the rocky ground with his feet, nudging them both forward. Ben's head, then shoulders, then chest, poked into the air above the cliff. When his stomach slid free of the ground too, his body dropped and he began descending toward the drum.

He saw it swing into the cliff with another ringing *boom*.

"You okay, Ben?" he heard his father call.

"Fine, Dad!" he yelled back over the sea, slamming into the boulders far, far below. "I'm almost there!"

Finally, Ben's body slid completely over the edge. Ben's father dug in with his boots and stretched out his arms, lowering Ben as far as he could. With his face turned to the side, flat against the ground at the very edge of the cliff, he was unable to see Ben drawing close to the bongos, his small hands reaching for the drum strap...

Then something caught the boy's eye.

Below the bongos, from a spot halfway down the side of the cliff, something sprang into the air. A small rock, no bigger than a meatball.

Ben froze, his fingers open over the strap. He watched the rock fall, then disappear into the sea.

"Do you have it?" came his father's voice.

But Ben was holding his breath. His eyes were fixed on the face of the cliff.

"Ben?"

From the same spot, a burst of dust and rocks now shot into the air. Ben's heart nearly stopped.

"Ben, answer me!"

But before Ben could say a word, a huge head erupted from the side of Crabapple Cliff.

And an eye, gray as doomsday, gazed up at him.

One Split Second

SOMETIMES A SINGLE MOMENT LASTS FOREVER.

In that moment, as Benjamin Boyd gaped at the ogre, the rest of the world disappeared: his father shouting his name; the bongos swaying within reach; even the fact that he was hanging headfirst, hundreds of feet above a boiling sea. In that moment it was just the boy and the monster, three eyes staring at one another...

And then, *boom*.

Ben blinked. The ogre blinked. And as the bongos rebounded off the rock, the drum strap finally slipped from the root. Ben gave a sharp cry, watching the Giant Heart bongos begin to plummet…then suddenly his right hand was darting out, his index finger was hooking the leather strap.

"Ben, what is it? What's wrong?"

"Dad, pull me up!" Ben screamed, closing his fingers around the drum strap.

Ben's father, his blood suddenly ice, jerked back on his son's ankles.

At the same time, the ogre seemed to emerge from the side of the cliff, like a huge root pushing through the rock. First came its hands and arms; then it reached up with its ragged fingernails and dug into the rock with a horrible scrape.

Ben eyed the monster as his father lifted him through the air. The creature was pulling with its powerful arms, bringing its body into view. Once the chest appeared, it yanked its fingernails free and reached higher to claw back into the stone. It made another grunting pull, then seemed to get stuck. It strained and groaned for a moment before the huge belly came jelloing out. Again the monster reached for a higher hold. With a final pull, its stocky legs slid into the air and the toenails on each foot scratched into the rock.

Clinging to the face of the cliff, the ogre glared up at Ben and snorted. That was Ben's last glimpse of the monster before he was hauled over the edge and into his father's arms.

"Dad, it's coming!" Ben cried, flinging the drum strap over his head.

Ben's father leaned out to look, kneeling there at the edge of Crabapple Cliff. The ogre was now heaving its hulking body up the side, its fingernails digging into the rock like grappling hooks.

Ben jumped up and tugged at his father's sleeve. "Dad, run!"

But Walter Boyd just sat there, staring wide-eyed at the ogre as it continued its slow, relentless climb. Picturing Old

Man Fibber's junk monster was one thing; seeing the monster in the hairy flesh, clawing and drooling its way toward him, was something else—something so petrifying it had turned his body to rock.

"Dad, the tree! Run to the tree!"

Then the ogre caught the fishy scent of Walter Boyd's hat lying quietly by the purplish-black mound. It paused, sniffing the wind, and gave a hungry roar. Fortunately, this bellow at last jolted Walter Boyd into a suitable state of panic. He flashed to his feet and father and son broke into a run, racing for the crabapple tree. Behind them they could hear the ogre grunting and scraping up the side of the cliff. They were halfway to the tree when Ben's father suddenly stopped, his eyes bulging in horror.

"My shotgun! I need my shotgun!"

At the sound of his father's shout, Ben whirled around. He saw his father pointing at his gun, still on the ground near the edge of the cliff.

"Ben, get to the tree! I'll be right behind you!"

Ben's father spun away.

"*Dad!*" Ben screamed, watching his father bolt back for the shotgun. But at the same moment Ben's father reached the Serenity 66, the ogre's enormous right hand rose over the edge, its fingernails raking into the rock.

"*Dad, look out!*"

Ben's father gasped and snatched up the shotgun. He turned and ran.

"*Ben, go! Go!*" he cried.

At the foot of the crabapple tree, Ben's father stood the shotgun against the trunk. He grabbed Ben by the waist and boosted him within reach of the lowest branch. From there the small boy scrambled up the tree, the Giant Heart bongos clunking around his neck.

Now Ben's father seized his gun. He watched as the ogre

dragged the last of its bulk over the edge. For a moment the monster sat hunched, breathing hard. Then it slowly rose to its terrible, towering height.

"Dad, hurry! Climb the tree!"

But instead, Walter Boyd raised the shotgun to his shoulder. His heart was pounding in his throat. He squinted, taking aim at the ogre's heart.

"Wonder Boy," he said under his breath, mustering the days he had laser eyes.

The ogre sniffed the wind. It glanced down at the dark mound nearby and wrinkled its nose.

The barrel of Walter Boyd's rifle quivered in the air, as it had minutes before when he fired the first three rounds at Stanley. "Wonder Boy, Wonder Boy," he chanted softly to himself, steadying his breath, steadying his gun…

Remember this: One split second can change the whole course of your life—one second too soon, one second too late. The fact is, if Walter Boyd had fired right then, rather than blowing out a final breath, your Grandpa Gristle would probably still have a full set of ears today. Chances are, with his nerves settled some, Walter Boyd would have hit the huge brute. And even if he missed its heart, wounding it in the chest or belly would have made it easy to finish off with his last two rounds.

But as that final breath came, his finger curling on the trigger…Walter Boyd lost his careful aim. The ogre bent over and reached down with a long arm. It picked something up from the ground.

"My hat!" he cried. "My lucky hat!"

"Dad, just climb the tree!"

The pale green fishing hat resembled a breath mint between the giant thumb and finger. The ogre held the hat up to its eye, studied it, sniffed it, and devoured it.

"My hat!"

The ogre turned back to Ben's father and replied with a roar. It was clear that one shabby hat, as fishy as it was, wouldn't be enough to satisfy the monster's appetite.

Then the ogre took a long, lumbering step toward Ben's father.

"Dad!"

If the loss of his lucky hat hadn't been enough to ruffle Walter Boyd, the sight of a gigantic ogre storming toward him was all the reason he needed to feel a fresh burst of fright. The monster would have made a wide target, but he was in no shape to take aim. And with the ogre stomping heavily across the cliff, the shotgun wasn't just quivering in his hands now, it was quaking.

Walter Boyd knew he had only three shots left. And he couldn't risk squeezing off those shots wildly, like he did in the forest. If he climbed the tree and collected himself, his plan could still work…

He slung the rifle over his shoulder and leaped for the lowest branch. He couldn't climb a tree much better than Ben, and the weight he had gained over the past ten years didn't make it any easier. But as Ben had already discovered, the fear of being gobbled up alive can quickly put an extra spring in your step. Branch by branch, Walter Boyd climbed madly toward the high perch that Ben was approaching.

Still, slow and blundering as it was, the ogre could cross the cliff faster than Ben's father could climb the Queen Tartelicious.

"Hurry, Dad!" Ben screamed as the ogre closed in on the tree.

Ben's father glanced back to find a giant hand reaching up toward him. The fingers, big around as timber, were drawing together, drawing near…

Ben heard his father cry out—and saw the monster move to pluck him like a ripe crabapple.

BLAM!

BOOM-BOOM-BOOM-BA-BOOM!

High in the tree, Ben pounded on the Giant Heart bongos. He was back in his perch from the day before, the deep booms throbbing in the air around him.

He watched as the ogre paused, its fingernails brushing the leg of his father's pants. His father's eyes and face were scrunched tight, waiting for the monster to snatch him from the tree.

But the ogre's gray eye blinked, then fluttered and closed. Its arm sank to its side. Its head rocked back and forth.

Ben's father cracked open one eye, then the other. He gazed in amazement, watching the ogre sway. Soon its shoulders were bobbing, its arms were swinging. When its hips began to wiggle, and its big belly jiggle, Ben's father quietly scuttled up the tree.

He wedged into the crook of two branches, beside his son. He was a lot heavier than Ben, though, and could only hope that the slender, upper limbs of the Queen Tartelicious would hold his weight. He wrapped his arms around the two branches to free both hands and reached for the shotgun riding on his shoulder. Then he took a deep breath and raised the gun.

The ogre was still standing in place by the tree, its whole body now moving gently to the rhythm of Ben's bongos.

Walter Boyd smiled grimly as he took aim at the great head, rolling from side to side. He would shoot it in the eye, the closest target. If that didn't drop the monster outright, the shot would blind it. Then the next shot would stop its heart.

Ben couldn't look. As he thumped away on the bongos, he screwed his face shut, waiting for the blast.

"It isn't much of a dancer," Walter Boyd sniffed. Even the monster's small movements were now tapering off. Then, as it fell perfectly still, he zeroed in.

"Wonder Boy," he whispered, his gun fixed on the closed eye...

And that's when the eye popped open.

Ben's father was so surprised he jerked backward, without firing. He would have toppled right out of the tree if his left hand hadn't managed to grab hold of the nearest branch.

Ben felt the tree shake and was all eyes in an instant. He saw his father scrambling back into position with the shotgun. Then he looked over at the ogre, just as it gave a great leap. He let out a breath, somehow relieved to see the monster dancing across the cliff, its eye silver and staring once again.

But Ben's father was fuming behind his rifle. Not only had he lost another golden opportunity to kill the monster, but now it was impossible to get a good shot. The problem wasn't the ogre's steps shaking up the cliff—after all, it was back to being light on its feet. The problem was its movement, dancing about in all directions, which made it a far more difficult target.

Ben's father lowered the Serenity 66. "I better wait until it gets tired out," he grumbled.

Of course, Ben knew this might take all day, especially since the monster was no longer burdened by that rattling mass in its belly. But he also knew it would follow his rhythm faithfully, and that meant he could slow it down and give his father a good shot.

But he just couldn't let his father shoot it…not yet.

The truth is, as beautifully as the ogre had danced the day before, it was even a finer dancer that afternoon. Its feet hardly roused a whisper as it made running leaps and soaring jumps, swift spins and gliding turns. Back and forth the ogre danced, around and around Crabapple Cliff, and all the while its eye gazed into space and its mouth curved in a crooked smile.

It's a wonder Ben could even play the bongos, the way he sat there spellbound. And his father, well, Walter Boyd wasn't exactly a fan of dancing, but he was so dumbstruck by the sight that his jaw had dropped practically to his lap. In fact, father and son were so mesmerized by the monster that the world around them disappeared. They took no notice of the darkening clouds and the stronger gusts of wind that seemed to lift the ogre even higher toward the heavens.

Finally, though, there was a soft rumble in the sky and Ben stirred. He watched the monster twirl past the tree, then he turned to his father.

"Dad," he whispered, "we can't kill it."

Walter Boyd blinked and remembered the shotgun in his hands. Here he was, with the chance to regain his old nickname, and it turned out this devil could dance like an angel.

"Ben, I understand your feelings," his father began gently, as they watched the ogre make another breathtaking jump. "It's a terrific dancer, I can see that. But it's also a cold-blooded monster and it'll eat us alive—it'll eat the *whole town* alive—if we don't stop it."

He left out the part about "Wonder Boy."

Ben made no reply. For several minutes he sat quietly, pounding on the bongos and peering at the ogre. He tried to imagine another outcome, like capturing the monster instead, but he could dream up no practical way to subdue it. He swallowed hard. His father was right.

The boy turned. "I can slow it down for you, to give you a good shot," he said. "But first, let me watch it dance just a little longer."

His father nodded.

So Ben went on playing. If this was his last chance to play for the monster, he would put his whole heart into it.

He began thumping a new rhythm, faster and louder, and the booms of the Giant Heart bongos filled the air like fireworks. The ogre instantly followed, its dancing even more spirited, even more spectacular: it leaped, it jumped, it spun, it swished, it twisted, it twirled, it whirled, it dove, it rolled, it romped, it skipped, it kicked, it pranced, it bounced, it bounded—it did everything but defy gravity. It was such a glorious dance, so full of life, that it brought tears to the eyes of Ben and his father. In fact, Walter Boyd suddenly felt a pang of guilt about shooting it dead.

But finally, he turned to his son. "Ben, it's time," he said quietly.

Ben blinked back his tears. He started playing more slowly. The monster followed. Its brisk movement fell off and it went floating toward the tree to hear the softer sound of the drum. It began dancing in front of them, its eye shining silver, as another low rumble came from the sky.

Walter Boyd wiped his eyes and raised the shotgun. But the ogre was moving about below the tree and his aim wavered.

"I can't lock onto it. Can you make it stop?"

"Dad, it won't stop until I do—and if I do…"

"Don't worry, son. Once it stops, I'll shoot." He squared his jaw. "When I'm ready, I'll say the word."

Ben's heart thumped so hard it ached. As soon as he stopped playing the bongos, the monster would be dead. His hands continued tapping the slow, soft rhythm. He looked over at his father and saw him squinting hard down the barrel of his gun, the gleam back in his eye.

Then his father shouted: *"Now, Ben!"*

Ben's hands tapped two last times and then drooped, tingling there on the surface of the drum. He shut his eyes and steeled his ears.

The ogre froze. It blinked up at Ben.

At that instant, Walter Boyd pulled the trigger of his Serenity 66 and fired at the monster's eye.

BLAM!

And this time, he didn't miss.

A Ringing Burp

Yes, he hit the monster, but not in the head.

Ben opened his eyes to find that the shot had streaked wide to the right, shredding the monster's left earlobe.

It wasn't a shotgun blast that claimed my own ear, but I can sympathize, of course. Even the loss of an earlobe is no picnic, as you might imagine.

The ogre grimaced, its fingers flying to its ear. When it found the ragged end, now oozing thick, sticky blood, it sent up a terrible roar.

Ben and his father practically leaped out of their skin. Still, Walter Boyd held the shaking gun as steady as he could. He had two shots left. Two more chances. He squinted hard, aiming again at the gray eye.

"Wonder Boy… Wonder—"

Then father and son were suddenly gasping and coughing and rubbing at their eyes. The monster's foul breath had blown over them like a cloud of mustard gas.

And in that moment, before Walter Boyd could fire, or his son could strike the bongos, the monster charged. It took a thundering stride toward the tree and seized the trunk in its right fist. Then it shook the tree violently as the fingers of its left hand continued to poke at the pitiful earlobe.

Ben flung his hands out, grabbing for the tree. His eyes were burning; the whole world was a blur. He heard the ogre snarling, the branches swishing, the crabapples showering to the ground.

"*Dad!*" he screamed.

"*Ben, hold on!*" yelled his father, gripping the tree with his left hand, clutching the shotgun with his right.

The bongos bounced wildly around Ben's neck. If he

could just outlast the shaking, like he did the day before, he would start playing the bongos again. He would stop the monster's furious attack. His father would have another chance—

But Ben's father was the first to fall. With only one hand to hold on, he was finally thrown from the tree as it jerked toward Grizzly Woods. Ben heard him cry out and knew the ogre had jarred him loose.

"*Dad!*" he wailed. "*Dad, are you okay?*"

Of course, it was a dangerous fall—a deadly fall—yet Ben's father managed to land on his soft belly, and survive. But when he hit the ground, he broke his right arm, the one with the shotgun, and the weapon lurched from his hand. It clattered to the cliff and discharged with a *bang*.

"*Dad! Dad!*" Ben screamed, fighting to stay in the Queen Tartelicious. But seconds later, as the tree rocked toward the sea, he fell too. He tumbled down, down, down and landed on the leafy branches of the limb that the ogre had torn from the trunk. The limb broke his fall, but he still crashed through the branches and hit the ground hard. The bongos were jolted loose, bouncing with a *boom* and rolling away…

On the other side of the tree, Ben's father lay moaning on his belly. His arm was broken, his head was spinning, yet he pushed up with his left hand and fought to open his burning eyes.

"Ben!" he cried, squinting about madly. He couldn't see Ben, but he caught sight of the shotgun on the ground. He grit his teeth and dragged himself toward it. "Ben!" he called again.

Ben was hidden among the branches of the tree limb. At the sound of his father's voice, he struggled up, blinking.

"Dad, where are you?" he yelled, rubbing the sting from his eyes. He found his glasses clinging to one ear, hanging at his chin, and hooked them back in place.

"Ben, play the bongos! I have the gun!" Ben's father was sitting up now, the Serenity 66 in his left hand—but his right arm was twisting in about six different directions.

"Dad, the bongos! *Where are the bongos?*"

It was then that the ogre stopped fingering its ear and went stomping toward Ben's father.

Walter Boyd had one last round in his shotgun. One last chance. As the monster came looming over him, leaning down to him, reaching for him with its bloody fingers, he raised the gun with his left arm. His body screamed from the blinding pain, but he willed his shattered right arm to rise and take the trigger...

"Dad, I see the bongos! They're not far!"

Squinting hard, Walter Boyd aimed at the ogre's heart...and fired...

BLAM!

At the sound of the blast, Ben turned. But instead of the monster toppling dead to the ground, he saw his father dangling in the air, held upside down by one leg, above the ogre's gaping mouth. Just as Ben's father had squeezed the trigger, the ogre plucked him up by the leg. His rifle jerked toward the sky. And his last shot was lost in the clouds.

"Dad, hold on!" Ben cried. But when he tried to stand, he felt a sharp stab of pain in his right ankle. So he took to his hands and knees. He went scrambling through the tree limb and over the rocky ground, scraping the band-aid from his leg, shredding his skin again.

His father, hovering above the black hole, was now howling and thrashing like a bobcat. He jabbed at the ogre with the barrel of his shotgun and managed to prick its upper lip. But the monster snarled and slapped the gun down to the ground.

The sky rumbled. The bongos were almost within Ben's reach—glowing there in the open, ruby-red. He was set to lunge for the strap—

But at that instant he heard the ogre roar and his father cry out, "Ben, I love you! Tell your mother I love her too! As for Grandma—"

Then a great gulping sound and an awful, awful silence.
Ben turned and screamed, *"NOOO!"*
The ogre made a ringing burp.

Then the creature frowned and stuck a long finger into its mouth. It had no teeth, of course, but it dug around in a dark cranny with its fingernail. Finally, it tugged out a brown boot, there on the end of the ragged nail, and flicked it off.

The boot fell with a *thud* in front of Benjamin Boyd.

Red Leather Case

At the very moment Ben was staring in horror at his father's toadskin boot, his grandmother was on her knees, digging through her closet like a badger. Still buzzing from the birthday cake, she was grabbing things up, gaping at them, and flinging them over her shoulder.

A frying pan. A toilet plunger. A large polka-dot purse.

It was now past noon and her curls were starting to sag. She was hunting for something to replace the rain hat that had blown off her head the night before.

A dog's water bowl. A baby's bib, stained with dribble. A white Santa Claus beard.

Grandma never threw anything away. Her closet even contained things from her childhood, buried deep under decades of possessions. To Ben, it was like the layers of the earth, with new layers piled up over old ones. When he was smaller, he imagined he might find something valuable in there if he dug down far enough, maybe even dinosaur bones.

Finally, Grandma paused, a hat-like object in her hand. It was a bonnet, an Easter bonnet, made of pink silk, full of ruffles and flowers and bows. She had worn it to the annual Boony Point Easter Egg Hunt long, long ago. She gazed at the pretty bonnet, remembering that happy spring morning. A wistful expression crossed her face…

Then she hacked and spat on it. She rubbed a finger over the inside and found a damp spot where the spit seeped through. She frowned.

"This won't do," she muttered, then tossed the bonnet aside and continued to dig.

And then, peeking out from under a sparkly silver fairy dress she had worn to the Abernathy Pumpkin Patch one

Halloween, she saw it. She stopped short, her eyes bugging behind her glasses. She had never really forgotten about it, but this sudden discovery now gave her heart a jolt.

For a long moment, lost in memory, Grandma forgot all about the crabapples that Ben and his father were expected to bring home hours ago. She peeled away the sparkly fairy dress to reveal a red leather case, like a suitcase, trimmed in rusting brass. She gazed at it, gumming her lip. Then she ran her fingers, lightly, tenderly, over the crackled surface of the case.

The metal clasps had rusted tight, but Grandma forced them open with her fingernails. She lifted the lid…and a musty smell escaped.

But it looked the same, exactly the same as the last time she saw it. She recalled the moment she put it back in the case, how happy she was then—and how that very night she shoved it deep into her closet, and never took it out again.

Her eyes clouded, her hands drifting to the faded yellow ribbons in her hair...

Her hair.

She slapped shut the lid to the red case and rose. With a shove from her slipper, the case disappeared back into the mountain of clutter. She wiped her eyes and turned, wading past the bonnet, the beard, and the rest of the rubble from her search.

"Butterfingers must have a baseball cap," Grandma muttered. "Every boy on this earth has a baseball cap."

She made a beeline for Ben's room and flicked on the light. She scanned the room like a chicken hawk, but saw only the mounds of books.

"Books," she grumbled. "Who in his right mind reads books?"

Grandma was headed to Ben's closet when she heard the murmur of her daughter's voice from downstairs.

Ben's mother had just finished a flurry of anxious baking: sugar popovers, chokecherry fritters, wild gooseberry tarts. There was a quiver in her voice as she strode to the kitchen door. "Mother, I think I should go out there to check on Walter and Ben." She pushed into the living room. "Mother?"

The television was blaring the noon livestock report, but Grandma was no longer fidgeting in her easy chair.

"Mother, where are you?" She switched off the television. "Mother?"

That's when Grandma came pounding down the stairs.

The old woman was wearing a football helmet with the Marching Moose mascot emblazoned on the side. It was the helmet Ben's father had given him for his tenth birthday, hoping that Ben might become interested in something besides books. But Ben had worn the helmet only once. He tried it on that day, and after the struggle to get it off his head, he banished it to the closet.

"What's that you're saying?" Grandma yelled. "I can hardly hear a thing with this contraption on my head!"

Ben's mother raised her voice to a shout. "Mother, why are you wearing Ben's football helmet?"

"I couldn't find a baseball cap! Every boy on this earth has a baseball cap except your son!"

Ben's mother made a baffled look. "Baseball cap? Mother, what—"

"My rain hat disappeared last night and I need something to protect my curls! I'm not about to have my head exposed again today!" She reached the bottom of the stairs and peered toward the screen door.

Ben's mother pulled off her apron. "Mother, I'll go. You stay home today and rest."

"Rest? I can hardly rest when those two hooligans are conspiring against me!"

"Mother, please, you had a hard day yesterday and you didn't get much sleep last night—"

"Lorelai, I have more energy today than I've had in years!" Grandma said, her eyes flashing from the football helmet like a restless panther. "Now it isn't easy to see out of this contraption, either, so you hunt up the umbrellas. It looks like rain."

Ben's mother frowned. "Why don't you at least take off that silly helmet and we'll find something else—"

"Because it's stuck, that's why! It's stuck tighter than a tick!"

"Mother, let me try." Ben's mother reached down and gripped the sides of the football helmet. "This happened to Ben. It took a little tugging, but we finally got it off."

Ben's mother gave a sharp pull and Grandma made a shriek. "Stop that! You'll take my ears off along with it!"

"Mother, I'm sorry." She reached out to caress Grandma's head, but could only stroke the moose on the side of the helmet.

"As long as it protects my curls, I'll put up with it until I get back here with my crabapples. By then it'll probably slide right off." She blinked away a bead of sweat and broke for the porch. "You get those umbrellas. I'll wrestle into my rain suit." She went through the screen door with a *bang*.

Alf looked up and croaked for another biscuit.

Ben's mother sighed. She moved to the living room closet and fought past the hippo to reach two long umbrellas. Then she shoved the stuffed animals back, shut the closet door, and headed off, heavy with worry, to find her husband and her son.

River of Tears

OF COURSE, SEEING A FAVORITE FAMILY MEMBER get gobbled up alive is a pretty big shock. So it isn't all that surprising that Ben just sat there goggle-eyed as the ogre lumbered toward him. The sight of the monster devouring his father had turned his curly head completely numb.

At the same time, the Giant Heart bongos weren't far from Ben's grasp. He just needed to make a good lunge for the strap. But the boy was in a fog, like he had forgotten all about them. In fact, the only thing in his head right then was a picture of himself getting gobbled up too.

If this were a movie, here's where you'd start shouting: "THE BONGOS! THEY'RE RIGHT BEHIND YOU! GET THE BONGOS!"

But it wasn't a movie—it was real as rats in your pants—and there was no one around, not for miles, to save the small boy from his fate.

And so the ogre came looming over him, its eye gray and glaring, its lower lip drooling like a broken tap. Ben gaped as the monster's hand plunged—he wanted to scream, but no cry would come. He could only sit there, glued to the ground, his eyes fixed on the fingers, closing in…

Then thunder rumbled again above Crabapple Cliff.

It was another soft rumble, but the ogre noticed it now. With its hand hovering over Ben's head, it glanced up and snuffled at the wind. It searched the clouds with a wary eye. Then it turned back, smacking at the sight of Ben, when a second rumble rolled through the sky. This time the ogre let loose a roar and shook its fists in the air.

Ben blinked, the outburst jarring him to his senses. He felt the throbbing in his ankle again. With a wince, he lunged for the bongos. Pulling the drum into his hands, he flung the strap over his head and quickly pounded out a rhythm.

* * *

THE AFTERNOON STRETCHED ON. The sky grew darker; the wind blew harder; the waves crashed against the cliff.

But the ogre was dancing now and took no notice, even when thunder growled overhead.

Ben sat there in the open, which might seem like a dangerous spot with a ten-ton monster dancing about. But besides the fact his ankle made it tough to crawl away while playing the bongos, he quickly discovered the ogre somehow knew exactly where he was: it would whirl by close, even leap over his head, but Ben was never really worried about getting flattened by a false step. The ogre was still incredibly light on its feet, despite the extra weight it was now carrying. And all the while Ben's eyes were on the jiggling belly. From time to time he thought he saw the belly bulge slightly: a lump here, a bump there. Then finally, as the ogre went twirling around him like a top, he saw the shape of his father's body poke out from the monster's skin.

The boy gasped—and at last the tears came. The shock of seeing the ogre gulp down his father had held them back for a time, but now they streamed down his cheeks and dripped onto his hands. He cried and cried, thumping blindly on the drum, until the river of tears at last ran dry.

That was when he felt the first drop of rain on his head. With the second drop, he heard the faint sound of shrieking from Grizzly Woods.

Something about shish kebab.

Grandma and Ben's mother had reached the pickup truck minutes before. Of course, the moment Grandma stepped on that big smelly wad of gum made for some colorful fireworks.

But it was nothing compared to when she peeked inside the truck and saw the picnic basket sitting there quietly on the seat. In fact, Grandma felt such a burst of sugar-fueled rage that her head was in danger of blasting right off her shoulders.

"*Shish kebab!*" she roared, stabbing her umbrella in the air. "*You two hooligans are shish kebab!*" Then she snatched up the basket and stalked off to the forest, shrieking in alarming detail about skewering father and son.

Now it's true, Grandma had gone giddy at that point and was capable of just about anything, but I don't think she was really out to make a meal of those two. She might have been gnashing her gums pretty hard, but her teeth were in the pocket of her rain coat. Still, Ben's mother didn't want to see anyone get skewered with an umbrella, if she could help it, so she hurried to catch up.

Grandma was tromping along so quickly, though, that Ben's mother, who wasn't used to the long hike out to Crabapple Cliff and hadn't eaten half a chocolate cake the night before, soon began to flag and fall behind. She pleaded with Grandma to slow down, but the old woman either didn't hear her daughter's cries, what with the helmet on her head and her continuous ranting, or if she did, she didn't find it a convenient time to listen.

"The son couldn't finish me off with his bongos, so the father goes gunning for my fruit! Well, your criminal minds have underestimated this old woman. My hair and I won't go down without a fight!"

As the sound of Grandma's voice grew louder, Ben's ears flinched. He quickly studied the ogre and was relieved to see that it didn't seem disturbed. It was still in its own world, he thought, deaf to everything around it but the bongos. As long as it could hear the drum, it would keep dancing.

Thankfully, that turned out to be true, for when Grandma drew near the cliff, her ears finally detected the low booms. And the fact that she hadn't even known Ben brought the bongos again made her all the more furious.

"*Butterfingers!*" she screeched, her voice reaching the pitch of a chainsaw. "Stop playing that drum this instant!"

As the rain came sprinkling down, Grandma emerged from the forest. The second the raving old woman caught sight of Ben sitting there on the cliff, drumming away, she stopped short. The glare blazing from inside that football helmet practically fried the boy's eyeballs.

"*Shish kebab!*" she screamed, shaking her umbrella at Ben. "I'm having shish kebab for supper!"

Now you may be wondering why Grandma didn't quickly notice an ogre that was fifty feet tall and flitting about like a fairy. But the fact is, when Grandma came clomping out of the forest, the ogre was dancing on the far side of the cliff. And the old woman was so blinkered by the football helmet, and so blinded by her fury, that she instantly zeroed in right on Ben and his bongos.

"Grandma, the monster!" Ben yelled, trying to point across the cliff with his nose, since his hands were busy beating on the drum.

"*Monster?*" shrieked Grandma. "You want a monster? I'll show you a monster!" She let loose a ghoulish howl and broke straight for Ben, charging through the horsetail in her rain boots.

"Grandma, it's behind you! Over there! It's dancing! Look, it's dancing!"

"Stop that fibbing, Butterfingers! And where's your father? I suppose you'll tell me the monster ate him, right?" She was closing in on Ben.

"It did, Grandma!"

"That's enough!" She was nearly upon him now. *And stop playing that drum!*

With one quick motion the old woman let the picnic basket fall from her hand and snatched at the drum strap. She yanked it from Ben's neck, jerking the bongos away from him.

"Grandma, no!" His hand shot out. "I have to keep playing!"

Then Ben and Grandma each had one hand on the drum strap, the bongos dangling in the air between them. The rain fell harder as a tug-of-war began, Grandma pulling from above, Ben pulling from below. Grandma narrowed her eyes and grit her gums. Ben blinked through the rain and strained to get his other hand on the strap—

And then his eyes popped wide.

"Grandma, it's coming!" he screamed.

"Stop it, Butterfingers! Just stop all this—"

Then Grandma froze, feeling the ground throb beneath her feet.

"Grandma, give me the bongos!"

Ben lunged to get both hands on the leather strap. He tugged with all his might.

At the same moment, the ogre reached down and scooped up Grandma in its huge hand. As Grandma screamed and lost her grip, Ben lurched backward. The bongos whipped through the air and whacked Ben in the forehead as he fell to the ground. He lay on his back, still as stone, the drum strap clutched in his right hand, the rain spattering on his glasses.

Thunder and Lightning

"Mother! Mother, what is it?"

Lorelai Boyd had broken into a run when she heard the first scream from Crabapple Cliff. Seconds later, as she dashed from the dry forest into the rain, she stopped short and gasped. She saw the gigantic ogre from behind, and there was Grandma in her football helmet, gripped high in its right hand.

Grandma's eyes were burning from the ogre's breath, but she was putting up a wild fight. She was jabbing madly with her umbrella and wailing so loud it must have made the monster's head ring. Still, its jaws opened wide and the ogre swept Grandma toward its waiting mouth…

Sometimes the things that trouble us most turn out to be life's biggest blessings. It's funny to think that the llamas, which had caused Grandma so much grief over the years, wound up saving her life right then.

You might be thinking the herd, led by Henry the Eighth and his change of heart, came charging out of Grizzly Woods and saved Grandma by driving the ogre off the cliff and into the sea. That would have made a rousing rescue, no doubt, not to mention preventing a lot more heartache later on. But the fact is, all 144 llamas were huddled dry in their stables, gnawing on sunflower seeds.

You'd have the good sense to do the same on a rainy day, wouldn't you?

However, before the rain fell, the llamas had raced to the road when they caught Grandma's scent as she went stalking by, Ben's mother trailing behind. Oh, Henry the Eighth wanted them to hold their fire this time—he wanted to end that long feud with Grandma once and for all—but as soon as he opened his mouth, the herd started spitting.

In this case, it's lucky he didn't succeed at stopping them. You see, it was now raining pretty hard, but it wasn't hard enough to wash all that llama spit off Grandma's rain suit. (The poor moose, of course, didn't even think of approaching for a lick when she came raging through the forest.)

As you probably learned in school, llama spit is slimy, slippery stuff. And with Grandma wriggling there in the ogre's hand, she finally squirted right through its fingers like a goldfish, up into the air...and then down into a nosedive.

Ben's mother watched in horror as Grandma landed on her head at the ogre's feet. The football helmet hit the cliff with a loud *clunk*, the long umbrella tumbling from her hand.

"Mother!"

The ogre swung its head toward Lorelai Boyd. It glared and grunted as she stood dripping at the treeline, her own umbrella unopened in her hand. Then it turned back to Grandma and scooped her up again. This time it gripped her tight, pinning the old woman's arms inside its fingers.

The fall had cracked the top of Grandma's helmet, and left her woozy, but she started shrieking when she smelled the ogre's foul breath upon her again. As lightning flashed overhead, the ogre held Grandma above the black pit of its gaping mouth, the lower lip dripping.

A clap of thunder followed and the ogre roared at the sky—then suddenly snarled in pain.

Ben's mother had rushed up from behind with her umbrella and speared the monster in the back of the leg. The umbrella stuck quivering above its ankle, like a dart. And as the ogre flinched, Grandma squirted through its grasp again, this time from the bottom of its fist. She dropped straight down and landed, cat-like, on all fours then scrabbled away toward the crabapple tree.

The ogre turned and scowled down at Ben's mother. It reached back and plucked the umbrella from its flesh.

As the monster sniffed and snarled at the umbrella, Ben's mother searched for Grandma. She couldn't see her hiding behind the tree, but she spotted the shotgun laying there on the ground. She rushed to the gun and hurried to take aim at the monster…then suddenly caught sight of the small figure just beyond it.

"*NOOO!*" she screamed, as lightning slashed again at the sky.

The ogre gulped the umbrella and turned to Ben's mother. But another thunderclap jolted Crabapple Cliff and the monster glared at the dark clouds and roared a warning. With the rifle in her hand, Ben's mother flew past the ogre's legs as the rain came bucketing down.

"Ben! Ben!" she cried, falling to his side. She shook him, but the boy lay still, a purple lump on his forehead. Then her eyes lit on the empty toadskin boot nearby and she released a furious wail. She raised the shotgun high, training it on the ogre's huge head. Squinting through the rain, she saw its cold, gray eye staring back at her.

She squeezed the trigger—

Click.

She fired again—

Click. Click. Click.

The ogre reached down and snatched the shotgun from her hands. It sniffed the gun and swallowed it. Then its hand stretched for Ben's mother, now shielding her son. She gave a cry as the ogre's fingers closed around her and swept her away from Ben. Squirming in its grasp, she managed to slip one arm free and stab her fingernails into its thumb.

The monster grimaced. At the same moment, a shower of crabapples stung its hairy hind end.

Grandma had tugged off the broken helmet and rubber gloves and was now scooping up a second handful of fruit from the ground. When the ogre turned, she reared back and fired another barrage, this time at its belly—but it wasn't enough to save Ben's mother. She scarcely got out a scream before the ogre stuffed her in its mouth and gulped her right down with a mouthful of rain.

And now it was Grandma's turn.

The old woman and the ogre, their hair dripping wet, eyed each other through the downpour. But there was rain on

Grandma's glasses, and tears in her eyes, and she could barely make out the scowling monster as it towered above her.

The ogre gave a great snort—then was drawn by another burst of lightning and thunder. It roared again at the dark sky, giving Grandma a moment to grab a fistful of crabapples. When the monster looked back, Grandma hurled the hard fruit as high as she could. Most of the crabapples missed their mark, but one hit the ogre flush in the eye. The creature snarled in surprise and its hand shot up to rub the sting.

Grandma bent to gather more crabapples…but huge fingers wrapped around her and lifted her into the air. She shrieked and squirmed, but the slippery llama spit had washed away in the hard rain and the ogre now had a firm grip. It gave a grunt, its head tipping back, its mouth caving open…

Then the ogre gobbled up Grandma too.

The Dark Belly

It was pouring ponies out on Crabapple Cliff.

Benjamin Boyd lay there on his back, eyes closed, rain battering his glasses. The Giant Heart bongos were by his side, the fingers of his right hand curled around the drum strap.

After gobbling up Grandma, the ogre now turned to Ben. Its eye narrowed and it peered down at the boy for a long moment, grunting softly. Then it reached with its right hand and scooped him up.

The ogre held Ben flat in its hand, studying him, sniffing him. It studied the bongos too, and its eye grew wide when it poked them with a finger and a *boom* rang out. It was set to poke the bongos again when the sky was lit by lightning and a loud clap of thunder shook the bluff.

The ogre snarled, quickly taking Ben in its left hand to protect its prey. Ben's upper body was peeking from the top of the ogre's fist and flopping about like a puppet. The bongos swung in his hand.

Now the monster's head dropped back. It lifted Ben above its mouth and its jaws opened wide, steaming the dazed boy with a blast of hot breath.

If the ogre had just uncurled its fingers, he would have plunged down its throat headfirst. But suddenly a sound cut through the storm and the monster paused—a shrill voice was rising from the darkness of its own belly...

"Butterfingers!"

Through burning eyes, Grandma had caught sight of Ben at the top of the creature's throat. Her cry roused Ben's mother and father, who fought for a glimpse of their son as Grandma carried on, clamoring for help.

The shrieking from inside its stomach must have puzzled the ogre. Its mouth hung open, the rain drumming on its tongue. Ben hovered there face down over the black hole, his body still limp as wet laundry.

Then his parents were crying out: *"Ben! Ben, help! Help us, Ben!"*

The boy finally stirred at the sound of his name. His head throbbed as he returned to the world. His eyes opened to slits. He quickly felt the sting of the monster's breath.

"Ben, help!"

He fought to see, squinting down into the darkness of the ogre's throat.

"Ben! Ben!"

"Butterfingers!"

Puzzled or not, the ogre would probably have gone ahead and gobbled him up, but lightning again flashed overhead. And in that instant, as the lightning lit the monster's dark belly, he saw them: three purplish-black shapes and six pleading white eyes.

"Ben!"

Then the ogre roared at the thundering sky, and Ben's eyes were burning in a fresh blast of foul breath.

But his family was alive!

Ben's heart soared—then quickly crashed.

And he was about to join them in the ogre's belly.

As the monster moved to devour him, time slowed to a crawl. His eyes burned behind his glasses, but he could hear his family's cries, deep and draggy in his ears. He could smell the awful fumes rising from the ogre's throat. He could feel the ogre's fingers beginning to uncurl...

It was then, at the border of the ogre's open lips, a split second from plunging toward his family and perishing together in the monster's gut, that Benjamin Boyd came surging back to life. He jerked the drum strap over his head and thumped furiously on the Giant Heart bongos.

The ogre blinked. Its mouth drooped back to an underbite, the lips nearly brushing Ben's head. The cries from the dark belly grew muffled, then fell silent.

The ogre's eye fluttered shut. Its body began to sway in the driving rain...

As you might imagine, it was a relief not to be eaten alive. But now Ben had a new worry: the monster's arm would soon fall to its side, the fingers would open, and Ben would be dropped right on his head. And, unlike Grandma, he wasn't wearing a football helmet.

At least this is what Ben feared, recalling how the branch had dropped from the ogre's hand the day before once he started playing the bongos.

But to Ben's surprise, when the ogre's arm fell, its hand didn't open. It went on swaying with Ben still in its grasp. In fact, a moment later, he suddenly felt himself drifting up again into the air. The rain had eased his eyes and he squinted to find he was being lifted toward the ogre's left ear. The shredded earlobe, crusted with dark blood, came into view.

Why the ogre didn't drop Ben on his head, I can't say for sure. But the best guess is that the sound of the bongos became harder to hear above the storm when its long arm fell to its side. And so the monster brought him back toward its ear to keep the bongos close.

Soon the ogre's eye snapped open in the silver stare. It leaped into the rain with Ben held high in its hand.

As the storm raged over Crabapple Cliff, Ben hammered on the drum. The rain lashed at him; the wind whipped at him; the thunder and lightning exploded above his head; and every part of his body either ached or throbbed. But through it all Ben willed himself to play the bongos. He drove his hands to beat the fastest, most furious rhythm he could muster.

The ogre held Ben near its ear while it danced through the storm. But now, forced to follow Ben's wild rhythm on the slick rocky ground, it couldn't move with the same grace—in fact, it was careening around the cliff.

For Ben, it was like another crazy, dizzy carnival ride. And though the rain had washed the sting from his eyes, he could hardly see a thing through the downpour. At times he felt the ogre skidding and sliding and he worried it might crash to the ground, even right on top of him. But he knew he couldn't slow his rhythm; he had to drive the monster on…

It's hard to know how long this madness lasted. To Ben it felt like forever. The whole time, though, he was blinking through

his wet glasses, watching the monster's face. And finally he spied the signs he had been praying to see: the silver eye was losing its sparkle; the mouth was going slack; the tongue was creeping out to one side.

Ben continued pounding on the bongos, but the ogre could no longer dance. It could only lurch through the rain, gasping and grunting. And then it staggered to a stop halfway between the crabapple tree and the edge of the cliff. It doubled over, its hands dropping to its knees. Ben was still curled in its fist, but he was suddenly tilted toward the ground and the drum strap slipped from his neck. His hand darted out and grabbed the strap before the bongos went tumbling to the bluff.

He turned his head and blinked up at the ogre. It was hunched over him, blocking the rain with its head and back. Its eye was now closed; it was grimacing and groaning. Then its belly was jumping—its chest was heaving—its jaws were opening—its mouth was making a horrible, retching roar...

And the ogre hooted.

Ben gagged as he watched the steaming river of dark, rank goo come gushing from the ogre's mouth. It poured down, the foulest of waterfalls, not ten feet from his head. And spilling out on the end of the violent wave was Ben's father. He landed on his back below the ogre and lay still in a purplish-black pool. He was smeared with the stuff from head to toe; even his eyes were blotted out.

"*Dad!*" Ben cried.

There was no reply.

The ogre spat the terrible aftertaste onto Ben's father.

"*Dad! Dad!*"

No reply.

The ogre spat again.

"*Dad, answer me, please!*"

Ben held his breath, straining to hear something, anything, through the raging storm and the ogre's heavy snorts.

But his father made no sound.

"Dad..."

Ben's head sank. His eyes closed.

I'm too late, he thought. *He's dead... They're all dead...*

The Giant Heart bongos still dangled from his hand, but he would play them no more. He would just wait in the monster's grip now. He would wait for it to gulp him down.

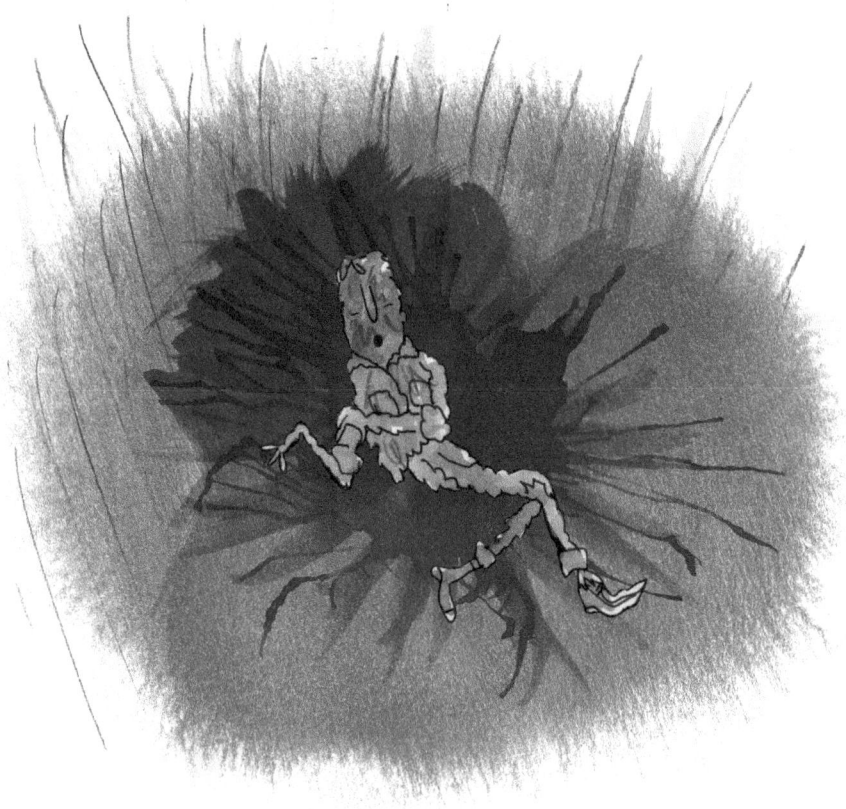

Sad as the Sky

THE STORM HOWLED AROUND HIM as Ben quietly mourned the loss of his family, the loss of his own short life. Above his head, he could hear the sounds of rough breathing and tired spitting.

And then, from below, he heard another sound.

His eyes flew open. He peered down at his father—

His father! His father was coughing!

"*Dad!*" he cried, watching him cough up a coil of the dark goo that was coating his body. It came slithering from his mouth like a coal snake…then his father was gasping for life.

"*Dad!*"

Ben's father cracked open an eye through the sticky mask. He found his son in the ogre's hand.

"Ben..." he croaked, fighting for breath. "Don't stop... Your mother..."

There was another burst of lightning and thunder. The ogre opened a gray eye and straightened up with a grunt. Nothing blocked the rain now and Ben and his father were pummeled by the downpour. As the ogre gave a worn-out snarl at the sky, Ben looped the strap back over his head and began pounding the bongos again.

The ogre was hardly in the mood for more dancing, but it obeyed the drum. Holding Ben near its ear, it went leaping across the cliff.

But this time, Ben wasn't only frightened for himself, he was frightened for his father. When the monster could move gracefully, it would dance around anything in its path. But now it was skidding over the slick rock, sliding dangerously close to where his father lay.

Ben screamed for him to hurry to the crabapple tree, but his father barely twitched; he would only stare in terror. Ben didn't know it at the time, but his father could hardly move a muscle: the dark goo from the ogre's stomach had left his limbs numb.

When the monster's huge foot came within inches of his father's head, Ben's heart nearly stopped. After that, he couldn't look at all. Banging on the bongos, he shut his eyes tight and just prayed that the monster would quit moving before it crushed his father.

Thankfully, I don't have to describe that fate for Walter Boyd.

The ogre staggered past him one last time, then fell to its knees with a great *boom*. As its hands went to the ground too, they opened and Ben dropped from its grasp. He didn't fall far, but a bolt of pain shot from his bad ankle as he went skidding away on his side.

Ben turned his head to look back. He pushed his glasses

into place and blinked through the rain. The ogre was hovering behind him on its hands and knees, its head hanging down, its mouth drooping open. And then, before Ben knew it, the monster was making a horrid roar and hooting another raging river of dark goo. Ben's mother came pouring out into a pool beneath the ogre's head, less than twenty feet from Ben.

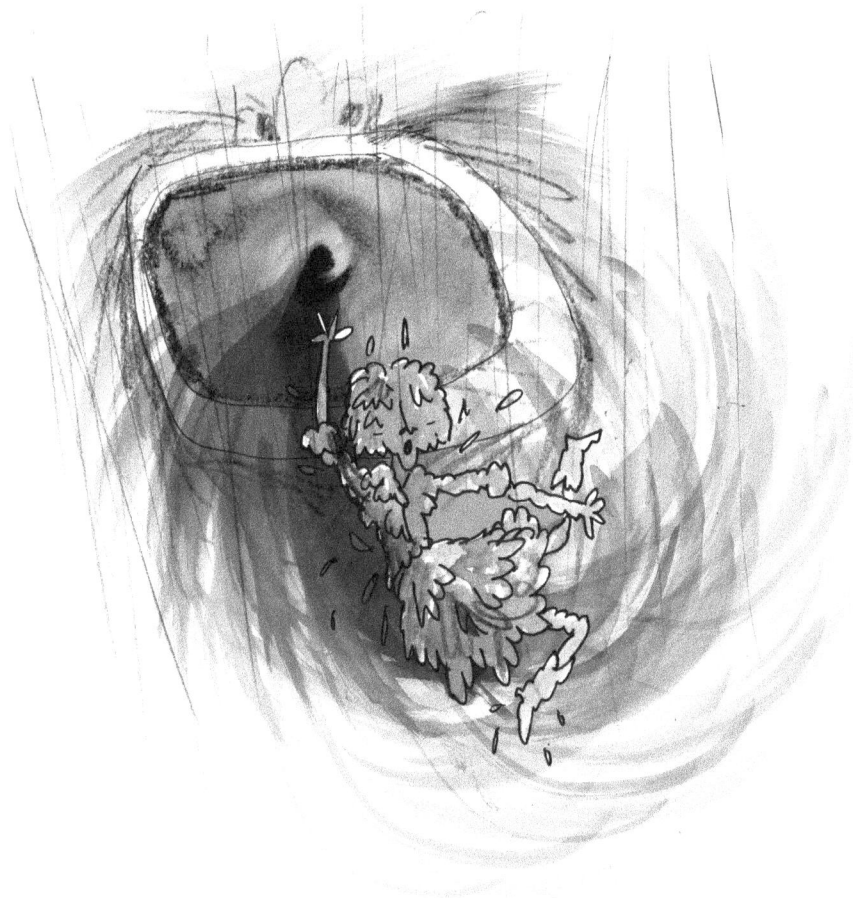

"*Mom!*" he cried. She was on her back, her head turned toward the ogre. "*Mom, are you okay?*"

Ben's mother lay still, coated in the sticky muck. Her wavy blond hair was now a matted mess.

"Mom! Mom!"

Then Ben heard her cough.

Relief rushed over him as she coughed up her own long coil of goo.

The ogre's eye was closed. It was breathing heavily as the rain pelted its hairy head and back.

"Ben..." he heard his father croak from behind the ogre.

But before his father could continue, lightning flashed closer, thunder clapped louder. The ogre, though, barely lifted its head to look. It just went on spitting the vile taste from its mouth.

"Ben...the bongos..." his father called.

By now, Ben was dizzy with exhaustion and pain, but he knew he couldn't quit. Gritting his teeth, he pushed himself up and reached out for—

The bongos! Where are the bongos?

He peered about, squinting through sheets of rain. They must have rolled away when he fell...

There they are!

He spotted the ruby-red glow near the side of the cliff. Then he shuddered: if the monster's mound hadn't been there, they would have rolled right off the edge.

As Ben dragged himself toward the bongos, he heard the ogre groan. He stopped and swung his head. It was struggling to its feet. Then it was lumbering toward him—no, he realized, it was heading for the sea.

Ben flashed on the day before. *If I don't stop it, it will disappear again—and this time with Grandma.*

As the monster came stumbling his way, Ben crawled for the drum. The Giant Heart bongos were upside down in a puddle of water. At the same moment he reached for the glistening strap, he caught sight of the ogre, nearing the edge of the cliff.

His father saw the ogre too. *"Ben!"* he cried.

Goo on her face, his mother fought to open her eyes.

Ben pulled the strap over his head. He slumped back by the dark mound and struck the drum again.

Keeping the bongos in earshot, the ogre now danced near Ben. It matched the quick rhythm, of course, but this time Ben didn't fear a misstep from the monster. Since it was sticking close, it couldn't make the same wild, skidding moves it made before.

Ben's father watched the monster dance through his open eye. Ben's mother watched too, her eyes barely slits.

It wasn't long, though, before Ben's arms were aching so badly he didn't know if he could continue. But moments later, he saw the ogre start to grunt and stagger in the rain.

A little more, Ben thought, willing his hands down on the drum. *A little more and the monster will give up Grandma too. Then it will go away...*

As hope rose in Ben's heart, and the ogre began to groan, it happened.

A great bolt of lightning, like a streaking dragon, shot from the sky. It exploded into the piece of gold-glinting metal jutting out on top of the mound. There was a huge *BOOM* and burst of fire.

Ben jerked back from the mound, his ears ringing.

The ogre went reeling back too. And as it lurched away, it lost its footing on the wet rock. It started skidding backward, its arms flying up and flailing in the air.

"Mother!" Lorelai Boyd cried out.

Ben stared in horror, his hands frozen on the drum heads. He saw the monster's hairy feet slipping over the rock. And then, in a moment that seemed to stretch forever, the ogre moaned to the heavens and its heels slid off the edge.

Maybe it was Ben's imagination, tricked by the rain. But as the monster hung in the air, far above the sea, he caught its gray eye looking back at him, sad as the sky.

Then the ogre plunged out of sight.

Like Father, Like Son

Ben and his parents gaped out in silence at the spot where the ogre had vanished. The only sounds now came from the rain, the wind, and the waves, crashing on the boulders far, far below.

Then lightning crackled out over the sea.

Ben's mother called out in a broken voice: *"Mother... Mother!"*

Her cry was met by something so foul I wish I had it in me to fib.

Plunging down, and nearing the bottom of the cliff, the ogre erupted with a tremendous roar. Jaws wide, it hooted like a volcano blowing its top.

Grandma was blasted right out of its belly. She rocketed into the air on a geyser of the dark goo.

She was still alive, but her head looked like it had a good dunking in hot tar. The rest of her body was coated in the gummy stuff too. Her hands had gone numb, but the waterproof rain suit had blocked the numbing effect on her limbs. She tried to open her eyes, but they felt glued shut by the goo. On the bright side, her glasses were still sticking to her face.

As she went soaring up the side of the cliff, her arms and legs thrashing in the rain, the sheer terror of that moment pried her lips apart. She coughed up a gob of goo and let out a long raspy shriek.

Of course, Grandma would have plunged right back down again, but she flew headlong, shrieking all the way, into one of the scraggly roots from the Queen Tartelicious that dangled from the face of the cliff. Her arms shot out blindly and her sticky hands, more like flippers now, clamped together on the root.

The shock of it all turned her mute as a mushroom. Then somehow she forced open an eye. As lightning flashed again, Grandma realized she was hanging from a thin root, high above the raging sea.

"Mother?" Ben's mother called. "Mother, is that you?"

"HELP!" Grandma shrieked.

"Mother!"

"HELP!"

Ben squinted back and forth at his parents. They were wriggling on the ground like night crawlers, but he knew neither one of them could move across the cliff.

"*HELP!*"

Ben pulled off the bongos and set them on the ground. Wincing from the pain in his ankle, he went crawling through the punishing rain, his parents urging him on. The edge of the cliff wasn't far from his spot by the mound, but it was a slow, agonizing crawl, digging his fingers into the rock, dragging his ankle behind him.

Grandma's shrieks continued, cutting through the storm and growing louder in his ears as he approached. At first she was screaming for help; finally, she was just howling in fright.

When he reached the edge of the cliff, his hand slipped on the wet rock. He collapsed and lay panting at the very edge, cringing at Grandma's piercing cries. Then he gulped his fear of the great height, pushed his glasses into place, and craned forward. Lightning lit the sky as he peeked over the side.

There was Grandma, just below the edge of the cliff. She was smeared with the dark goo from head to toe. One green eye could be seen through her streaked glasses, goggling up at the scraggly root in her grasp.

She was screaming frantically.

The root was shredding in Grandma's hands!

Ben knew that Grandma might pull him down with her, like a drowning swimmer, but he had no time to think twice. He dug in with his left hand; with his right, he reached as far as he could. His fingers waggled just above the root.

"Grandma!" he shouted over the storm and the old woman's screams. "Grandma, take my hand!"

But his grandmother's eye was fixed on the shredding root. Did she see him? Did she even hear him?

"Grandma, my hand! Take my hand!"

But Grandma went on wailing and gaping at the root. Any second, the root might tear away from the cliff and Grandma would go plunging back down into the boulders and sea.

But she was hysterical. How could he get her attention?

"Mother!" Lorelai Boyd now cried out. *"Mother, listen to Ben!"*

At the sound of her daughter's voice, Grandma's frenzy fell off. Her eye flicked up and spied a face peering down at her.

"Lorelai?" she said faintly.

"Grandma, it's Ben! Take my hand!"

"Ben?"

"Yes, Grandma, it's me! Now give me your hand!"

Grandma's hands were numb and powerless. But her arms, protected by the rain coat, still had strength.

The old woman gave her right arm a yank, pulling the sticky hand free.

But the tug on the root caused it to snap—and Grandma began to fall...

In that split second she flung her right hand up and Ben's fingers grabbed—

He had Grandma!

Grandma, of course, wasn't much bigger than a grumpy banana, but she was still plenty heavy for a small boy wracked with exhaustion and pain and forced to pull her up through a raging storm from a slippery perch hundreds of feet above the sea.

If all that wasn't bad enough, Grandma quickly lost her head again after the root snapped and she was left dangling there in Ben's hand.

"Ben, what's happening?" he heard his mother call.

With Grandma wailing and flailing in the air, Ben was now inching forward on the cliff. He grit his teeth and pushed his other hand against the rock to keep from slipping over the side, but it was only a matter of moments before his strength gave out. Then he and his grandmother would both go tumbling down, down, down...

Lightning flashed again. And before Ben even realized what he was doing, he found himself crying as loud as he could: "Squ— Squ—"

"SQUEEZE!"

Only it didn't come out like that.

"*SQUISH KEBAB!*" he hollered.

Like father, like son.

And like the last time she heard that odd cry, Grandma paused, a puzzled look in her eye. Her body stopped flailing; the wailing froze in her throat. And in that instant, Ben summoned his last scrap of strength and pulled her up and over the edge.

Their sticky hands tore apart. Grandma rolled over and lay on her side, quivering and gasping for breath.

Ben collapsed on his belly. He hardly had enough energy to breathe at all. For a long moment he just lay there, listening to his parents croaking for joy, feeling the rain drubbing the back of his Mayor Olympus T-shirt.

Finally, with a grunt of pain, he groped for the edge of the cliff. He inched his eyes over the side and peered down. Lightning flared above the sea, revealing the boulders and the waves far below.

But there was nothing more at the bottom of Crabapple Cliff.

Part Three

A Scrumptious Day

THE DAY OF THE MARCHING MOOSE TRYOUTS dawned bright and blue. Not a lamb's tail of a cloud was seen in the sky that afternoon.

Mayor Sackbutt stepped from the Olympus Music Shop and closed the door with a loud belch. It was nearly three o'clock and he had just swallowed the last big bite of a jelly doughnut. Sucking powdered sugar off his fingers, he paused to admire his reflection in the shop window. The brown band uniform he wore was now stretched to the breaking point, but all the mayor saw was a dapper sight.

He straightened the moose hat, just so, then licked his fingers again. He was carefully smoothing his sideburns when he heard a weary voice: "Nice day for the tryouts. Not a lamb's tail in the sky."

Mayor Sackbutt turned and found Doc Sprinkle, his wispy white hair sticking out like cotton candy. He was shutting his office door with his shoulder, the Stanley-head cane in his left hand. Despite the warm day, he was dressed in a thick wool sweater. On his right hand was an oven mitt, and Agnes was cradled against his chest. The porcupine was nibbling at a sweet potato clutched in her front paws. Doc Sprinkle smiled—but there was no twinkle behind his spectacles today.

"Afternoon, Doc," boomed Mayor Sackbutt with a big grin. "Afternoon, Agnes." He turned back to the shop window and continued fussing with his hair. "Yes, it's a scrumptious day. I was worried the field would still be soggy for the tryouts, but we haven't had a drizzle since the storm. Three weeks of sunshine and it's now dry as a doggy's bone."

"I'm glad you didn't have to postpone it," Doc Sprinkle said as he clicked his cane over to the mayor. "It's good to have something to help take my mind off matters."

Mayor Sackbutt pushed the comb into his pocket and turned. "Well, I'm happy to see recent events aren't keeping you away, Doc."

"I haven't missed one yet, you know." Doc Sprinkle tried a lighthearted tone, but there was a catch in his voice.

Mayor Sackbutt laid a plump hand on the old doctor's shoulder. Agnes looked up from her sweet potato and narrowed her eyes.

"I'm sorry about Stanley," the mayor said. "But he'll be back soon enough, you'll see. It's odd he got spooked when he saw Water Boy, but he won't stay hidden in Grizzly Woods much longer. He'll be knocking on your door any day now."

Mayor Sackbutt saw the tears welling in Doc Sprinkle's eyes. He added with a grin, "Doc, that's one beautiful porcupine."

Doc Sprinkle forced another smile. Agnes blushed and returned to her sweet potato. They waited as the mayor squeezed his silver baton under his arm and pulled on a pair of white gloves.

Then the two men and the prickly rodent crossed the street and stepped onto Olympus Field. The rest of the town was there too, chattering away as they piled into the big, wooden bleachers by the field to watch the annual Marching Moose tryouts. It was an event everyone in Boony Point turned out to see each year—everyone, that is, except Old Man Fibber.

Across the field from the bleachers, in the far corner, loomed the water tower. It looked like a huge silver egg, on its side, with four long legs poking down through the shell. The moose mascot, puffing proudly on a gold trombone, was splashed across the front. Next to the mascot were the words: "Boony Point, Home of the Marching Moose." (Mayor Olympus had done the climbing and painting himself.)

Below the water tower was the big bronze statue of Mayor Olympus. He stood there strong and grand, a great grin on his face, baby Norman on his shoulders. The shiny toes sparkled in the sun.

It was this water tower that Walter Boyd had accidentally hit ten years before in the Boony Point Shootout. You could still see where the slug had struck: right in the big moose's belly. Loudmouth, the town's annoying welder who most folks wished would keep his welding mask on all the time, had proudly patched the hole with a round sheet of steel.

It looked a lot like a belly button.

And since that time, when people caught sight of Ben's father at the marching band tryouts, they would point to the tower and chant: "Water Boy! Water Boy!"

That's why Walter Boyd was sitting at the very top of the bleachers. He always sat up high so he wouldn't be easily spotted.

Your Grandpa Gristle was in the bleachers too, there in the middle. I was just three weeks and a day now, wrapped in a colorful quilt Mama had made for me. I was cuddled in her arms, my two big pie-pan ears sticking out merrily. Papa sat next to us in his black suit. He was the town undertaker and always dressed for duty (just in case).

Down below us was Ben. He was in the front row, with the thirteen other hopefuls. Most of them were twelve, like him, but a few were older and trying out again. The ones with smaller instruments were resting their flutes and trumpets on their laps; the ones with bigger instruments propped their tubas and tenor drums beside them on the bench.

The Giant Heart bongos, polished again to a ruby-red glow, were draped around Ben's neck and perched on his lap. His hands trembled on the drum heads. The ugly bruise on his forehead had faded, but his ankle still bothered him. He hadn't broken it, but it was badly twisted and heavily taped. It hurt when he marched.

He glanced up and down the row. There was Stepstool. She seemed a shoo-in. Her legs were short, but she had been playing the French horn from the time she was two. Mayor Sackbutt had even heaped praise on Stepstool, saying her tone was as close to the bellow of a moose as he had ever heard.

And Noggin. He squawked a lot on his clarinet, it's true, but rumor had it he was marching in his backyard every waking minute, memorizing the steps to all the formations the band had ever performed.

And what about Stork? He was fifteen, and had been passed over three years in a row, but there was no denying he could strut like, well, like a stork, and he could play his trumpet louder than anyone around. Mayor Sackbutt liked loud instruments…

"Water Boy! Water Boy!"

Ben turned at the sound of a sing-songy shout. It was Loudmouth, the beefy welder with the tattoo of a howling hyena on one of his bare shoulders. He had spotted Ben's father. Others joined in the heckling.

Ben saw his father sitting in the stands, his right arm in a stiff white cast. His mother and his grandmother were beside him, along with Doc Sprinkle and Agnes.

Walter Boyd was now wearing a pair of large, goofy-looking glasses with thick black frames. He was staring out with a stony face, but when he caught sight of Ben gazing up at him, he broke into a smile and drummed playfully on his bald head with his left hand. His mother smiled at him too, and waved. Ben returned a small wave and gave them a nervous grin.

His mother's blond hair had already begun to sprout again. But underneath that flowery silk scarf her head still looked like chick fuzz. The ogre's sticky stomach goo—gastric acid, actually—had gotten her hair so hopelessly matted there was no choice but to cut it all off and let it grow back.

Ben's father used the llama shears to shave the snarled hair. Ben's mother kept a stiff upper lip during the ordeal, but poor Grandma… She wailed like a baby in a beehive when her blond curls were buzzed off. Afterwards, she gingerly touched her scalp and the feel of bare skin sent her fainting straight to the kitchen floor.

Grandma sat glumly next to Ben's mother. She didn't look all that different, thought Ben, since she still had a head of bouncing blond curls. But everyone knew it was actually a custom-made wig from Bloat City.

Unlike his mother, Grandma's hair had so far showed no signs of new life.

Ben turned back toward the field. He watched Mayor Sackbutt puff up the steps to a small stage that had been placed in front of the bleachers. The sides of the stage were decorated with colorful pictures of moose playing musical instruments, drawn by the children of the Olympus Nursery School.

Mayor Sackbutt moved to a microphone, mounted on a silver stand. He raised a white glove and tapped on it with his finger. A hush came over the crowd.

The mayor now leaned in close, his lips on the microphone. "Citizens of Boony Point!" he boomed, then paused to milk the moment. "Welcome to this year's tryouts for your Marching Moose!"

The whole town sprang to its feet in the traditional Marching Moose cheer: hands shot to the tops of heads, fingers stretched wide, mouths began to bellow.

As Ben hollered along with the others, he felt his heart pound against the gleaming wood of the Giant Heart bongos—along with a painful twinge in his ankle.

Mayor Sackbutt gave a big grin, basking in the roar of the town. Then he raised his baton and the crowd sank quietly to their seats.

"I know our fourteen young contestants are eager to strut their stuff for the three openings in the band this year," Mayor Sackbutt went on with a wink. "But as always, we first have two traditions to observe." His smile fell and his voice dropped low. "It was sixty-nine years ago that Mayor Olympus and Norman, along with eighteen of our dear children, vanished from this field. My friends, let us take a moment of silence to honor them today."

Mayor Sackbutt turned to face the shining statue by the water tower. The whole town rose and gazed silently at the bronze hero and his moose. Even your Grandpa Gristle had the good sense to hold back from babbling right then.

Finally, Mayor Sackbutt wiped away a tear and motioned for the crowd to sit. "And now," he said, his grin returning, "your Marching Moose will perform the town anthem, composed, arranged, and choreographed by Mayor Olympus himself. As you know, Gusto, Shimmer, and Glimmer are now graduates of Olympus High and this will be the last time they wear the Marching Moose uniform. So let's cheer them on, my friends!"

Mayor Sackbutt blew a loud blast on his whistle and the sound of a bass drum boomed in the air. Then the Marching Moose, fifty strong, marched out from behind the bleachers and onto Olympus Field.

The Marching Moose

THE MARCHING MOOSE ALL WORE THE SAME glittering brown uniform and tall moose hat. To the beat of Brawny's booming bass drum, they marched quietly in single file, their instruments in hand. When they reached the middle of Olympus Field, they split crisply into five rows of ten and spun to face the bleachers. Now they marked time, lifting their knees high.

With the bass drum thumping and the Marching Moose strutting in place, Mayor Sackbutt left the stage and high-stepped across the field. The silver baton was clutched in his right hand and his arms were pumping hard. The whistle was clenched between his teeth and beads of sweat were soon trickling down his forehead.

When he arrived at his spot in front of the band, the mayor turned smartly toward the crowd and marked time with the others. Seconds later, he blew two long blasts on his whistle, followed by three short tweets. The Marching Moose stopped instantly, their right legs snapping to the ground at the same moment. They stood motionless, staring out at the crowd. They didn't even blink.

At the sound of the whistle, the bleachers fell silent too. The crowd waited, holding its breath.

Your Grandpa Gristle stifled a gurgle.

Mayor Sackbutt bit the whistle and let the silence linger. The sweat rolled into his eyes, but the mayor never flinched. In fact, until they heard that whistle, the Marching Moose would have stood there forever, frozen in time. They were so well trained, it's a wonder they weren't trickling sweat exactly like Mayor Sackbutt.

Finally, the mayor blew his whistle again. Ben felt a chill as the Marching Moose shot into motion, high-stepping toward the bleachers, instruments blaring the first bars of the town anthem, "Boony Point, We Praise Thee!" The crowd leaped to its feet, moosing loudly with delight.

With Mayor Sackbutt flashing his baton in the sunshine, the Marching Moose strutted straight toward the crowd. Ben stood wide-eyed, favoring his ankle. He picked out the three who had graduated from Olympus High School in June and would be leaving the band: spirited Gusto, puffing his heart out on the tuba, and the identical twins, Shimmer and Glimmer. Those two looked so much alike, right down to their dimples, that the only time you could tell them apart was when they were marching: Shimmer on her piccolo, Glimmer on her glockenspiel. The next time the band assembled, there would be three new members to take their places. Ben pictured himself in the Marching Moose uniform, high-stepping with the others, drumming on the Giant Heart bongos...

He was jarred from his daydream by a cymbal crash. Astro Gal's long blond hair went flying behind her cymbals. Then Mayor Sackbutt and the Marching Moose made a smart turn to their right. As they strode down the field, the five lines of marchers broke in different directions. There was a joyful blat from Gusto on his tuba, and the people of Boony Point burst into song:

Boony Point, we praise thee!
Our paradise by the shining sea,
With woods of moose and lofty trees,
And fields of llamas running free,
Boony Point, we praise thee!

Boony Point, we praise thee!
Where people live in harmony,
Children play together gleefully,
And babies enter eagerly,
Boony Point, we praise thee!

Boony Point, we praise thee!
Home as well to the great grizzly,
No beast could be more bloodthirsty,
Just poke its poptic artery,
Boony Point, we praise thee!

As the crowd sang out the anthem, they thrilled to the formations made by the Marching Moose. Of course, the formations for the song were the same every year, just as Mayor Olympus had devised them back when grizzly bears still roamed the forest. But to the people of Boony Point, it was all a sacred tradition, like church on Christmas Eve (though a lot louder), and their excitement for this performance never dimmed.

The band first formed the waves of the sea crashing against Crabapple Cliff, followed by a frisky llama running through a field of goldenrod. After huddling into a moment of two children bouncing merrily on a seesaw, the band expanded across the field to form a big happy baby shaking a rattle. Then, in a change I found terrifying that first time I saw it, the baby became a ferocious grizzly bear, claws raised high, ready to slash at the crowd. But the bear quickly dissolved as the band launched into the last verse and the town belted out these words:

Boony Point, we praise thee!
Yes, some prefer the big city,
But we will always want to be,
In this small town of vast beauty—

And then, just as Mayor Sackbutt and his marching band were strutting toward their final stirring formation of a big bellowing moose with three legs, a police car came speeding up to Olympus Field, siren wailing, lights whirling.

New Evidence

The people of Boony Point turned from the Marching Moose to the police car, now squealing to a stop. The final verse of "Boony Point, We Praise Thee!" died in their throats.

As the siren whined away, Sheriff Silver stepped from the police car. His face was grim and he waved a white paper in his hand.

Wrestling out the other door, and jawing on another wad of Powermint gum, was Deputy Thunk. One hand was clamped to the small cowboy hat on his head, the other clutched a bulging paper bag.

At first glance, we all thought it was just the giant's sack lunch.

The light on top of the police car still spinning behind them, the two men bolted for Mayor Sackbutt.

Of course, the mayor was aware of the interruption, but he kept right on marching. He wasn't about to stop in the middle of the thrilling finish to the town anthem, with the band forming its picture of Norman. He tried to wave off the sheriff with his baton while taking up his position at the moose's snout, but they wouldn't turn back. Finally, he had no choice but to blow his whistle and bring the whole song to a grinding halt.

The half-finished picture of the proud moose now looked more like a crippled cow.

"What is it?" Mayor Sackbutt shouted from the snout.

The whole town of Boony Point gaped in silence as Sheriff Silver and Deputy Thunk rushed up to the mayor. Sheriff Silver whispered something in the mayor's ear, then handed him the piece of paper. Deputy Thunk towered behind them, gripping the brown sack and grinding at his gum.

Ben watched the mayor's red, dripping face as his eyes scanned the paper. Olympus Field was so quiet he could hear the mayor's sweat falling onto the paper with a soft *plunk…plunk…plunk.*

Suddenly Mayor Sackbutt made a strangled cry and swooned. He would have toppled to the grass too, if Deputy Thunk hadn't let go of his cowboy hat long enough to catch him.

"Mr. Mayor, are you okay?" Deputy Thunk asked with a smack of his gum.

The crowd looked on, every mouth open.

But Mayor Sackbutt just stood there, staring at the paper in horror, like he had just learned the whole world was coming to an end before suppertime.

A moment later, he blinked and clenched his jaw. He pulled away from Thunk and broke into a run, back toward the stage. The rest of the Marching Moose remained rooted to the field like tree trunks, awaiting the next blast from the mayor's whistle.

His eyes gleaming with tears, Mayor Sackbutt hurried up the steps to the stage. But the toe of his black boot hooked the top step and he went cartwheeling across the platform. Although he somehow held onto the piece of paper, he dropped his baton with a clatter, ripped the seat of his pants wide open, and sprayed sweat onto half a dozen children seated in the front row of the bleachers. He landed on his belly behind the microphone stand with a loud grunt that would have attracted a yak if one had been nearby.

Ben was hit by a few flying beads of sweat. He quietly wiped his glasses on his favorite Mayor Olympus T-shirt.

Normally, of course, a wonderful pratfall like this, complete with ripped trousers and red-striped boxer shorts, would have triggered some giggles, especially from the children. But the crowd could sense that this was no time for tittering. Instead,

they gasped at the sight of the mayor sprawling to the stage floor.

"I'm fine! I'm fine!" Mayor Sackbutt said, pushing himself up. Sheriff Silver and Deputy Thunk helped the mayor to his feet.

Mayor Sackbutt scooped up his baton and moved to the microphone. His tall moose hat was now tilted at a funny angle and the paper in his hand was badly wrinkled. Behind him the sheriff and deputy stood stiffly, trying not to eye the mayor's boxer shorts. Sheriff Silver wore a disappointed frown, his gold gun glittering in the sun. Deputy Thunk looked uneasy with the eyes of the whole town turned his way. He was hugging the paper bag to his chest like a teddy bear.

Mayor Sackbutt cleared his throat. "Citizens of Boony Point," he said into the microphone. His voice was tight. His face was ghostly pale. "I think it's best if you all sit down."

The people in the bleachers sank dumbly to their seats. The marching band still stood in their formation of the crippled cow. If they were distracted by the mayor's red-striped boxer shorts, they didn't show it.

"You've all heard the rumor that a creature of some kind was seen in our fair town," Mayor Sackbutt continued. "This rumor started swirling three weeks ago when Water Boy and his family claimed to have encountered it out on Crabapple Cliff during the storm. Since then, many of you have been wondering if Water Boy concocted the whole story and fabricated the evidence, even coercing his family to play a part in his scheme by dunking them in tar, shaving the heads of his wife and mother-in-law, giving his son's ankle a painful twist, and even breaking his own elbow—all in a misguided attempt to gain a new nickname for himself."

Ben's father glared at Sheriff Silver, who he suspected had first whispered this accusation. Sheriff Silver caught his gaze and glanced at the floor.

"I must confess, I was wondering the same thing. But as mayor of Boony Point, my duty is sniffing out truth, not snuffling up rumor. That is why I sent the evidence gathered from Crabapple Cliff to Bloat City University for testing. Bloat City University is our state's finest institution of truth, with a laboratory boasting over one thousand test tubes. Sheriff Silver has just handed me the results of the testing undertaken by the Bloat City University laboratory."

The white paper trembled in the mayor's hand as he began to read.

"Analysis of the dark, sticky substance found in the samples of blond hair was conducted using dozens of test tubes. Rather than tar, as was presumed, this analysis has confirmed that the substance is actually—"

Mayor Sackbutt paused, blinking back tears. A murmur ran through the crowd.

"—the substance is actually the gastric acid of an unidentified creature."

The crowd gasped. They turned toward the highest row in the bleachers and looked at Ben's family with new sympathy.

Mayor Sackbutt swallowed hard. "Wait, there's more," he said, raising his baton. "Other evidence was studied too. There was also a large dark mound by the edge of the cliff that the creature was said to have upchucked the day before the storm. When the gastric acid was scraped away, they discovered what was underneath…"

The mayor took a deep, shuddering breath. "This is what they found," he said, returning to the paper.

"After the coating of gastric acid was removed, the large mass was revealed to be a jumbled heap of old musical instruments. At the top of the pile was a trombone, its slide apparently blackened by a lightning strike. The other instruments, in somewhat better condition, include: one tuba, one French horn, three trumpets, two saxophones, two clarinets, two flutes, one piccolo, one bass drum, two snare drums, one pair of cymbals, and a tambourine."

The mayor blinked hard. "Sixty-nine years ago," he said, his voice breaking, "the Marching Moose, eighteen strong, led by my great-great uncle…Mayor Olympus…" He faltered, his head fell, his moose antlers drooped. He began weeping quietly behind the white paper.

The crowd gasped again.

Sheriff Silver strode forward and patted Mayor Sackbutt

on the back—then made a face when he found the mayor's marching band uniform damp with sweat. He wiped his hand on his hip.

"People of Boony Point, this is Sheriff Gold," he barked politely into the microphone. "There is no need for panic. The creature is said to have fallen off the cliff and into the sea. In the unlikely event that it didn't drown in the waves and instead returned to the scene, I headed straight for Crabapple Cliff after receiving this report." He pointed to the paper that Mayor Sackbutt was weeping behind. "But I found no sign of the creature…and I would have slain it with one shot too."

Sheriff Silver made another disappointed frown. When he learned there really had been a monster out on Crabapple Cliff, he was hoping it had somehow survived so he could shoot it dead. That would have finally gotten the town to call him Sheriff Gold, he figured.

"I did uncover some valuable new evidence, though," the sheriff continued, his gold tooth winking in the sunshine. "And I located this evidence in the creature's lair."

The bleachers buzzed.

"When I questioned Water Boy and his family after the incident, Butterfingers here"—the sheriff nodded to Ben—"told me that the creature had emerged from the side of the cliff. So I pursued that lead and proceeded to conduct a thorough investigation. I had Deputy Thunk lower me down the side of the cliff with a rope—dangerous, yes, but all in the line of duty—and I discovered the entrance to a cave right there in the middle of the cliff."

Mayor Sackbutt looked up with wet, red eyes. The town of Boony Point hung on Sheriff Silver's words.

"The cave hardly seemed large enough for a creature of that size, but I explored it carefully with my gold flashlight and I came to the conclusion that it must have squirmed its

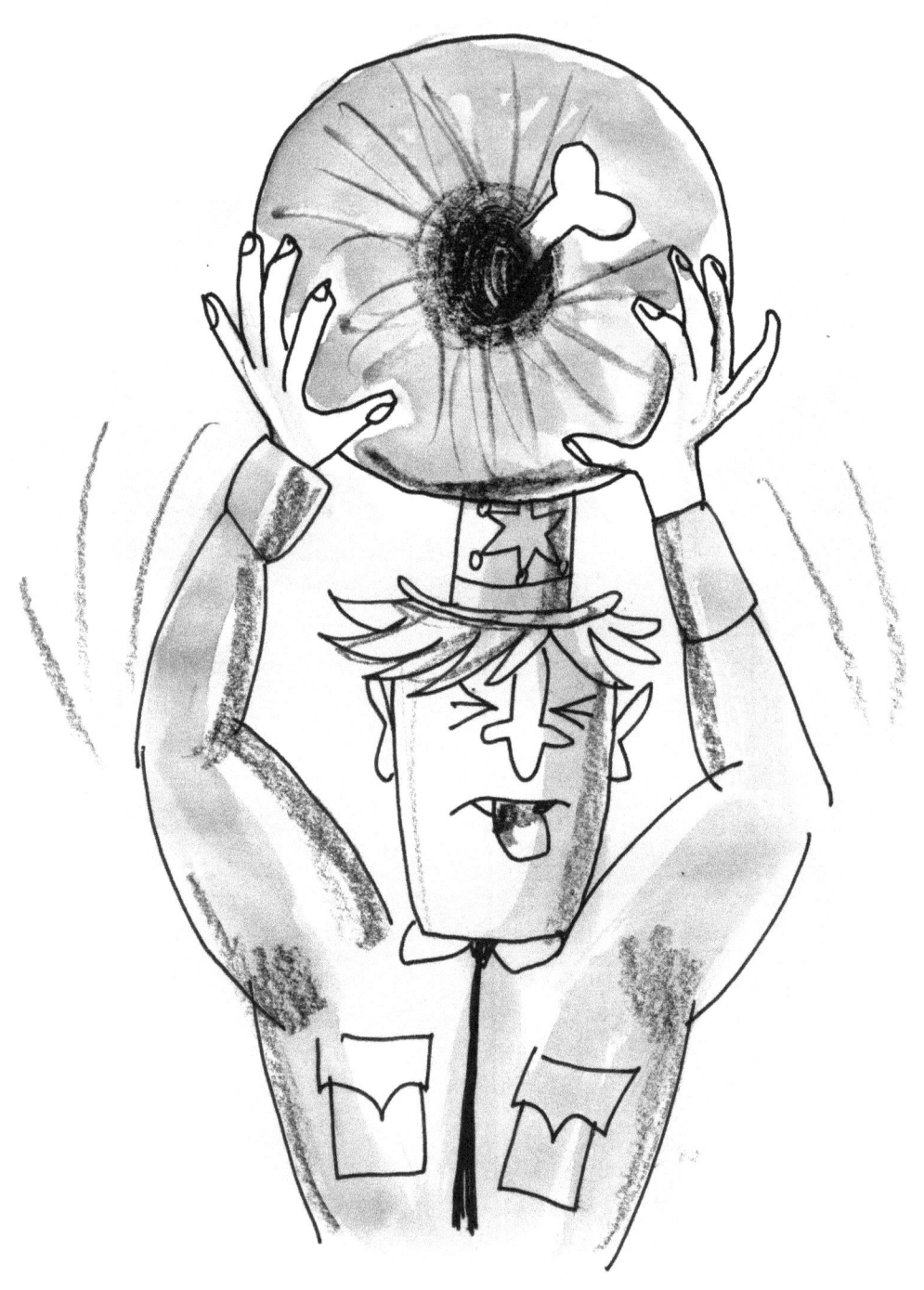

way inside to lie down. And when I reached the end of the cave, more than fifty feet from the entrance, I spied that piece of new evidence."

Sheriff Silver turned to Deputy Thunk and nodded. The giant deputy hesitated, chewing full tilt on his gum. The sheriff glared. Then Deputy Thunk set the paper bag on the stage floor, careful to keep his hat balanced on his head. He rustled open the bag, stuck his hands inside…and pulled out a big round object that resembled a large Abernathy pumpkin gone brown and leathery in the field. He made a sour face and held it up for all to see.

Shrieks and shouts went up from the crowd.

It was the ogre's left eye, staring back at them.

Defiant Cry

"Good heavens!" Mayor Sackbutt cried. "Its eyeball... Its eyeball is the size of a pumpkin!"

"I believe this accounts for the creature's missing eye," Sheriff Silver said.

"And what's that?" the mayor asked, approaching the eyeball. Something white was gleaming from the center of the great eye. He leaned in for a closer look, then drew back in shock. "No... It can't be..."

"Mayor, what is it?" said the sheriff.

"Deputy Thunk," said Mayor Sackbutt, "hold this eyeball tightly." The mayor offered his baton and report, now smudged with tears, to Sheriff Silver. Then he wiped his eyes and gripped the object in his gloves. "Hold tight, Deputy."

Mayor Sackbutt tugged hard with both hands. Deputy Thunk hugged the eyeball. A long stick-like thing came sliding out.

The crowd watched, wide-eyed, as the mayor studied the object. The end protruding from the eye was white, but the rest of its length was stained reddish-brown. When he examined the end that had been buried deepest in the ogre's eye, he suddenly let out a loud wail.

"*Norman!*" he moaned, reading the name scratched into the end. "*It's Norman's leg!*"

No one knows, of course, exactly what happened on that fateful afternoon when the ogre gobbled up Mayor Olympus and the Marching Moose. But the best guess is that Mayor Olympus was the last one left and, as you'd expect, he fought back bravely as a lion. Before the monster finally gulped him down, he managed to plunge his bone-baton straight into its eye. It was stuck there so deep, in fact, that the ogre's big fingers couldn't grab onto the end to pull it out. Back in its cave, the creature was in such agony—and I know this sounds horrible but the ogre wasn't a brainy type, remember—it finally used its fingernails to root up its own eye. Then it must have blacked out and slumbered on for years, slowly digesting that filling meal.

Until the moment he discovered Norman's leg bone, Mayor Sackbutt had fought to hold himself together. But now, cradling Mayor Olympus's baton in his hands, it was all too much to bear. He fell to his knees and broke down in big sobs. He rubbed the old discolored bone against his cheek and roared like a baby.

Sheriff Silver gave a sigh and set the mayor's baton and report on the floor next to him. Then he glanced up at Deputy Thunk, who was still holding the ogre's eyeball and jawing away at his gum. The giant deputy's eyes were brimming with tears too.

In fact, everyone at Olympus Field that day, with the lone exception of Sheriff Silver (who never even cried when he was a newborn), had begun to weep along with Mayor Sackbutt. All of us there in the bleachers had tears rolling down our cheeks as we gazed across the field at the statue of Mayor Olympus and Norman. The marching band, still frozen in position and facing the stands, fought to maintain a crisp pose as their bodies shuddered with grief.

It might surprise you to hear that Ben's grandmother was sobbing nearly as hard as Mayor Sackbutt. She had pulled off the faded yellow ribbons from her wig and was now clutching them in her small fists. Her head was bowed and her fists were pressed to her eyes.

She was remembering Mayor Olympus...

Sixty-nine years before, when Grandma was Ben's age, she was set to try out for the Marching Moose. It's true, you don't normally see an accordion in a marching band, but Grandma had been taking lessons from Mayor Olympus and she was getting so good he urged her to audition. In fact, the policy of all instruments having "an equal opportunity to wear the antlers," which Mayor Sackbutt had mentioned to Ben, was actually started by Mayor Olympus for Grandma.

But Grandma was afraid. She was afraid of making a fool of herself in front of the entire town and winding up with some awful new nickname. She tried to overcome her fear by practicing harder, marching and playing for hours on end. But the day before the tryouts, she broke down at her accordion lesson and told him she couldn't go through with it.

She remembered weeping then, as she was weeping now. Mayor Olympus pulled his chair up close to hers, his eyes sparkling like dark jewels. Then he patted her blond curls and pulled two shiny yellow ribbons from her ears. (Mayor Olympus was also quite good at magic tricks.)

He put the ribbons in her hands and smiled. He told her, in a voice like warm gravy, to wear the ribbons in her pretty hair when she auditioned.

Grandma nodded through her tears. Mayor Olympus gave her another grin.

Then later that day, he disappeared. They all disappeared. The tryouts were canceled and Grandma never did audition for the Marching Moose. In fact, she couldn't even bear to take out her accordion from its red case. Instead, she buried it in the back of her closet, deep as dinosaur bones, and never played it again.

A piercing cry now cut through the weeping at Olympus Field.

"Long live the Moose!"

The cry startled the crowd. We all paused in our sobbing and turned to the very top of the bleachers—

It was Grandma. She was on her feet, the sun shining on her golden wig, her lined face wet with tears. Her eyes were fixed on the statue of Mayor Olympus.

"Long live the Moose!" she cried again, her hands rising to her head, her fingers spreading like antlers. The yellow ribbons hung from her thumbs. *"Long live the Moose!"*

Ben looked on as his mother stood next, beside his grandmother. She opened her hands over her head scarf.

"Long live the Moose!" his mother and grandmother cried.

Then his father stood. His good arm went to his bald head.

"Long live the Moose!" all three cried.

Then Doc Sprinkle and Agnes.

"Long live the Moose!"

The cry quickly rippled through the crowd. One by one, more by more, the citizens of Boony Point rose, their eyes on the statue of Mayor Olympus, their hands on their heads.

"Long live the Moose!"

Before long, the whole town was standing tall and calling strong: the people in the bleachers, the marching band on the field, Mayor Sackbutt, Deputy Thunk, even Sheriff Silver.

"Long live the Moose!" everyone cried. *"Long live the Moose!"*

The chanting swelled, filling the wide blue sky above Olympus Field. For this one remarkable moment in the history of Boony Point, there was none of that constant friction over nicknames. There was no vanity, no envy, not a single ruffled feather among the whole flock. For this one moment the town was united, brought together in tragedy. Voices were shouting the same defiant cry. Eyes were shining with the same fierce pride.

"Long live the Moose! Long live the Moose!"

Then something moved behind the water tower.

Upside Down

BEN WAS ON HIS FEET, gazing at the statue of Mayor Olympus and cheering along with the crowd—"*Long live the moose! Long live the moose!*"—when he saw the flash of dirty brown.

His heart stopped cold.

From behind a back leg of the water tower, a large creature stepped from the shadows and staggered onto sunny Olympus Field.

It was Stanley.

The big bear had been hiding in Grizzly Woods since his terrifying run-in with Ben's father and he was now a pitiful sight. He was gaunt and filthy and his lavender tutu was in tatters. He was tottering on his back legs, the gash on his thigh now a crusty scab. His eyes were half-crossed and one ear was drooping sadly. He was sneezing and coughing, like he had caught a bad cold.

Heaven knows how poor Stanley even survived those three weeks out in the forest by himself. A bear that's been hand-fed jello from the time he's a cub hardly knows a thing about foraging in the wild. I expect it was blind hunger that finally forced him to overcome his fears of another shotgun blast from Ben's father and creep out of hiding to find Doc Sprinkle.

All eyes now flicked from the statue of Mayor Olympus to the grizzly bear. The chanting died away. Hands dropped from heads.

And then, in the silence, broken only by the bear's sneezing and coughing, came a high-pitched cry: *"Stanley!"*

The crowd turned back toward the top row of the bleachers and saw Doc Sprinkle burst into tears. "Stanley! Stanley!" he cried.

When Stanley heard Doc Sprinkle's voice, his eyes uncrossed and he froze in front of the water tower. The instant he caught sight of the old doctor, standing there next to Ben's father, his furry face lit up like Christmas morning. A rush of joy brought his limbs to life and he broke into his happy Irish jig. Holding his arms high in the air, he hopped back and forth from one foot to the other. He gave a grinning roar, then sneezed again.

"Stanley!" Doc Sprinkle cried, blubbering with relief. The people of Boony Point were swept up in the joyful moment. They laughed with delight at the heartwarming reunion between the doctor and his dancing bear.

"Stanley! Stanley!"

Stanley bounced on his bow-legs and beamed at the crowd.

Then the whole world flipped upside down.

Booming footsteps rocked the ground; a deafening roar ripped across the field, rattling every window on the town square. The sudden shock paralyzed us in our places.

Now the huge, hairy ogre of Crabapple Cliff thundered into view from behind the water tower, snatched up Stanley in its massive hand, and gobbled the grizzly bear right down, tutu and all.

"NOOO!" wailed Doc Sprinkle.

Of course, the crowd was horrified too, and erupted in crying and shrieking and shouting. But before anyone could flee—*BANG!*—Sheriff Silver fired a shot in the air. Smoke rose from the gold barrel of his gun.

The crowd froze and fell silent—except for Doc Sprinkle, who swooned onto Walter Boyd's shoulder and began to sob.

The ogre, for its part, probably had a mind to roar at the sound of the pistol; instead, it opened its mouth and out came a hearty burp.

"People of Boony Point, this is Sheriff Gold!" the sheriff yelled, trembling at the sight of the ogre, yet thrilled to find it still alive. "Remain calm! As a ten-time champion of the Boony Point Shootout—and soon the new record-holder with my eleventh title this fall—I will drop that monster with one shot to the head."

The crowd held its breath as the sheriff pointed his gleaming gun high over the antlers of the Marching Moose, still fixed on the field, their eyes bugging up at the ogre.

Ben saw the shredded earlobe, now dark and shriveled. He bit his lip, waiting for the shot.

Sheriff Silver aimed at the monster's gray eye. It was glaring down at the stage from its spot by the water tower. The sheriff smiled grimly, flashing his gold-capped tooth.

He would kill the creature with one shot, one bull's-eye to the head. He would be hailed as a hero and the whole town of Boony Point—no, the whole state—would finally call him Sheriff Gold.

The sheriff was set to squeeze the trigger when he suddenly frowned, his concentration shaken. "Doc Sprinkle!" he shouted, his eye still narrowed on the ogre. "Could you please sob more quietly for a moment! I'm trying to shoot this monster dead, if you don't mind!"

It's hard to blame Doc Sprinkle for being unable to contain himself. After all, he had just seen Stanley get eaten alive.

So Sheriff Silver could only shrug off the distraction by fixing on the new name that would soon be his...

He aimed. He fired.

And just as he pulled the trigger, Deputy Thunk keeled over like a ragbark oak. Spooked by the ogre's glaring eye—no doubt staring at its other eye, which was staring right back from Thunk's arms—the giant deputy came crashing down into Sheriff Silver. Their skulls cracked together, their hats flew from their heads. The pumpkin-sized eyeball went up in the air and plunged to the ground with a dusty *splat*.

BANG! went the gun, but the bullet streaked into the sky. Sheriff Silver squeezed out another shot as he fell, but that bullet sailed straight into the ground.

The sheriff then crashed into Mayor Sackbutt, their skulls knocking together too. The mayor's moose hat finally popped completely off his head, but the bone-baton stayed clenched in his hand as he toppled over.

The three men went down like dominoes, dropping unconscious to the stage.

Deputy Thunk's wad of Powermint gum fell from his mouth, hitting the floor with a quiet *plop*.

This time the ogre gave a proper roar at the gunshots and took a lumbering step toward the marching band. Its mouth hung open, the fat lower lip dripping with drool.

Voices in the crowd cried: "The monster's coming!" and "It's going to eat the Marching Moose!" and "Oh no, not again!" and "Run, children! Run for your life!"

If it had been anything other than a gigantic ogre bearing down on them, eager to gobble them up, the Marching Moose would have continued to wait faithfully for Mayor Sackbutt's whistle. Under the circumstances, though, I think they can be forgiven for finally breaking from their formation of the crippled cow and fleeing in wild-eyed terror. Pitching the bigger instruments to the ground, they screamed for their parents and ran toward the bleachers. But the bleachers were in a panic too, and people were falling all over each other trying to escape.

It was a moment where being an undertaker came in handy. Papa wasn't a big man, but he had big forearms from carrying all those caskets. As he cleared a path for us, Mama quickly followed and we made our way down from the center of the stands. By now your Grandpa Gristle was bawling so hard it's a wonder I didn't expel an internal organ or two.

The ogre's next step crushed a bass drum, a tom-tom, two snare drums, and Glimmer's glockenspiel. Another step, which brought it booming to the center of the field, flattened four trombones, three baritones, and a tenor saxophone. But this time when its foot fell, its little toe jammed the bell of Gusto's tuba. The ogre paused and stomped its foot on the ground— once, twice—but the tuba wouldn't be jarred loose.

The ogre grumbled and shook the ground even harder with a third stomp. The tuba now tumbled free, but as it did,

a scream cut through the clamor on Olympus Field.

"*Ben!*" his mother cried. "*Ben, no!*"

Ben turned briefly and saw his family, boxed in at the top of the bleachers. They were gazing down at him, their eyes round with fright.

Then he went on, limping toward the ogre and pounding on the bongos.

A Wisp of Smoke

BEN HEARD THEM SCREAMING HIS NAME, but he knew he couldn't turn back. He also knew he had to get as close to the ogre as he could: the uproar from the fleeing crowd was drowning out the sound of the drum.

The ogre loomed in the center of the field, eyeing Ben curiously as he approached. Finally, as Ben hobbled near, the monster smacked its lips and moved to grab the boy in its great hand...when it paused...and blinked. Then its eye fluttered shut and its arm swung back to its side. The ogre straightened up and began to sway, the rhythm of the bongos filling its bones.

All around Olympus Field, the people of Boony Point froze in their tracks. They stood dumb, their cries dying in the air, their eyes goggling wide at the hulking monster now quietly rocking in front of the small boy beating on the bongos. Even Ben's family and Doc Sprinkle were startled into silence.

Your Grandpa Gristle had made it to the front row of the bleachers by this time. And there we paused, as jarred as everyone else by the sight of Butterfingers Boyd bewitching that terrible brute.

But when the ogre's eye popped back open, the whole town flinched. The ogre, though, gave a graceful leap, and went dancing right across the field.

The crowd held its breath when the monster came prancing back toward Ben, but quickly discovered he was in no danger. As Ben already knew, the ogre was so light on its feet—even with a large mammal in its belly—that it could glide around anything in its path. Not only did it dodge Ben, but it skipped nimbly past every musical instrument still lying on the field.

The crowd looked on, astonished by the sight of the monster dancing gaily to the sound of Ben's ringing bongos. And as the ogre bounded back and forth, its eye shining silver in the sun, Mayor Sackbutt slowly sat up and rubbed his head. This ogre may have eaten Mayor Olympus, but when Mayor Sackbutt heard Ben playing the Giant Heart bongos, and saw the monster romping along to the boy's remarkable drumming, his eyes filled with tears of a different kind.

"Scrumptious," he whispered.

The dazzling duet taking place on Olympus Field had the whole town spellbound—well, except for Sheriff Silver and Deputy Thunk, who were still out cold on the stage floor. As for Doc Sprinkle, I suppose you could say he was only half-entranced, with one eye mesmerized and the other in mourning.

While the drumming and dancing went on, Walter Boyd slipped Doc Sprinkle's side and began threading his way down the stands.

It was then that a faint buzz came from the sky.

Ben glanced over his shoulder and saw a dark dot in the distance, heading straight for Olympus Field. The noise was building fast, so he hit the drum even harder. The ogre carried on, but the crowd now blinked. Of course, a dancing monster—and especially one dancing as divinely as that ogre—is not the sort of thing you'd normally turn from. But the dark dot buzzing our way was like a mosquito in the ear, and all eyes went squinting at the sky. Even your Grandpa Gristle had a little hand to the brow to see what was speeding toward us.

Moments later the dot became a roaring, ramshackle plane, with wild whoops heard rising in the air.

Strapped in the open cockpit of that plane was Old Man Fibber. He was sporting a ratty aviator's cap and goggles, his fiery red beard snapping in the wind. Carl was there too, sprawled happily across the old man's lap, his tongue hanging out like a hound.

And painted on the plane in big black letters (but missing the final "E") was this:

AIRBORN

The small plane was a homemade affair, like the junk monster, welded together with metal from tractors, trucks, cars, kitchen appliances, and bathroom fixtures, with a souped-up engine from a leaky fishing boat in the nose and a gas tank from a battered school bus in the tail. Old Man Fibber had cranked the propeller (made from dozens of steel cookie sheets) not ten minutes before and hardly had time to scramble back into the plane when it went barreling out of the barn. It was the first time he was flying it, in fact—he didn't want to stir speculation before the big day, of course—and his take-off through the hills of junk was a bit rougher than expected, particularly when one wing clipped a great mound of old toasters.

Still, he managed to nose it in the air then spend a few minutes circling his farm to get a feeling for the sky. And what a glorious feeling it was! It's true, he nearly crashed into the head of his junk monster, but besides that small moment of terror, he felt only wild bliss at finally being airborne again.

"*Airborne!*" he whooped, his face glowing like an infant under the oily black smudges. "*I'm Airborne!*"

The snapping turtle hissed with delight.

Old Man Fibber swooped around the farm one last time, whooping all the while. Then he checked his father's pocket

watch and yelled above the roar of the plane: "Carl, it's time! It's time to show those hogheaded dolts once and for all—*I'm Airborne!*"

Jerking the long throttle (made from a sawed-off shower pipe), he reeled the plane toward town.

Old Man Fibber was feeling happy as a hummingbird as he soared toward Olympus Field to at last reclaim his old nickname—well, at least until he closed in and caught clear sight of the ogre. When he saw the monster twirling about in the middle of the field, he suddenly flashed back to his terrifying encounter of long ago. And here he was, sixty-nine years later, making a beeline right for it. In fact, he was so frazzled he now froze there at the throttle as the plane streaked over the bleachers. He and Carl were aimed straight for the ogre's huge head.

When the town saw "AIRBORN" on the side of the plane, people knew right away it was Old Man Fibber. And there was a loud gasp as everyone realized Old Man Fibber hadn't really been a fibber after all and he was about to crash into the monster and never hear an apology for all those years his story was doubted.

Then a split second before the plane slammed into the ogre's head, Carl lunged for the throttle with his open jaws. He drove the lever to one side and held fast, his mouth clamped to the steel. The plane lurched, curving past the ogre, then started buzzing around its head like a pesky horsefly.

As Ben had feared, the roar of the plane was now drowning out the bongos. He groaned as the ogre came to a halt in front of him, its eye rolling back to gray. Then it howled at the circling plane and made a clumsy swipe for it.

Ben stood his ground, pounding on the bongos with all his might, desperate to get the ogre dancing again.

But now it wasn't only the noise of the plane he was battling. With the monster snarling and swatting at the air,

the town was back in a full-blown panic. People were running and screaming like their teeth were on fire. Mama hustled me away from the bleachers, hurrying after Papa as he and his forearms made their way toward the water tower. He was thinking we might hide behind one of its legs, like Old Man Fibber once did.

It's no surprise this new burst of bedlam finally roused Sheriff Silver and Deputy Thunk. The deputy pushed up first—then took one look at the ogre and fainted right back to the stage floor.

Sheriff Silver sat up with the golden gun still in his hand. Mayor Sackbutt helped him to his feet and the sheriff stood there on shaky legs, blinking at the sight of the ogre raging at the buzzing plane. Then he raised the gleaming pistol and aimed it at the ogre's head. He fired quickly: *BANG! BANG! BANG!*

But Old Man Fibber's plane had darted in front of the ogre and the bullets riddled the body of the plane instead. The first bullet hit the nose and blew the boat engine haywire; the second bullet tore through the side, turning "AIRBORN" into "AIPBORN"; and the third bullet pierced the tail and sparked a spitting fire.

The plane now bucked and bellowed like an angry bull. The throttle snapped clean off and Carl went clanging to the floor of the cockpit. Streaming black smoke, the plane broke from its buzzing around the ogre and began flying wildly above the field.

Old Man Fibber could be heard hollering the most colorful curses of his entire life. Carl finally let go of the shower pipe to hiss a blue streak right along with him.

With all this fresh turmoil, the town couldn't help pausing to gape toward the field. The sheriff tried firing another shot at the ogre, but the trigger only clicked—his six-shooter was out of bullets. So he went to his belt for more ammunition.

As the plane came barreling by in front of the ogre, the creature lunged and missed—but when it stepped forward, it nearly crushed Ben. Still gamely playing the drum, Ben staggered back. With the plane bawling off to the far end of the field, this might have been the moment the sound of the bongos could break through. But instead, Ben stumbled backward over Gusto's tuba and went crashing down onto Astro Gal's cymbals. The ogre's gray eye flashed toward the noise. Its left hand shot out and snatched him up. Its jaws roared open as it moved to stuff the boy and his bongos into its mouth.

"BEN!" he heard his mother scream as the foul breath burned his eyes, the dripping drool soaked his skin…

And then a shot rang out. The ogre blinked, a bewildered look on its face. It stood tall for a long moment, holding Ben above its open jaws. Then it teetered and fell over backward, its arms reaching high, as if the mighty Queen Tartelicious itself was toppling to the earth.

There was a titanic crash, and a crush of instruments, then quiet. The only sound now was Old Man Fibber's plane, droning in a death rattle as it went reeling back across the sky, the old man and his turtle still yowling speech so raw it made the ladies blush beet-red.

All heads turned from the field to the stage. Sheriff Silver was there, his gun raised, but like everyone else (except Deputy Thunk), his eyes were on Walter Boyd, standing next to him in his goofy new glasses. Walter Boyd was holding the Serenity 66, grabbed from the pickup truck. His finger, peeking from the cast on his arm, was still squeezed on the trigger. A wisp of smoke curled from the end of the barrel.

"Ben!" his mother cried. She was jostling down the bleachers, Grandma and Doc Sprinkle on her heels.

"Ben!" Grandma cried.

"Stanley!" Doc Sprinkle cried.

Their shouts were quickly followed by shrieks from the crowd: *"It's moving! The monster is moving!"*

The town gaped again at the field. The ogre was still sprawled on its back, its arms flung out, but the fingers of its left hand were now uncurling…

And then, as the crowd screamed and the plane roared and Old Man Fibber raved, Ben staggered out from the ogre's hand.

"Ben!" his whole family cried. Ben's father bolted from the stage, his rifle in his hand. Ben's mother and grandmother scrambled right behind.

"*Stanley!*" The old doctor scurried after with Agnes.

But before his family reached him, Ben was at the ogre's side, staring at a stream of dark red blood bubbling down from its chest. The shotgun blast had blown a hole right through its heart.

Ben raised his hands and struck the Giant Heart bongos—once, twice. As the sound rang in the air, the ogre's head rolled toward him. It gazed down at him and gave a soft grunt. Then its eye closed and never opened again.

Ben's hands sagged to the drum heads as his father and mother and grandmother swept up from behind. His parents wrapped their arms around him and fell into sobs. Sniffling back her own tears, Grandma reached out and fluffed Ben's curls.

Seconds later, a sudden *BOOM!* shook the sky. The flaming tail of Old Man Fibber's plane had finally engulfed the gas tank. The explosion now sent the plane rocketing across Olympus Field.

"DIRTY REEKIN' MUCK-ROLLIN' SLOP-SLURPIN' FILTH-FEEDIN' DUNG BEETLES!" wailed Old Man Fibber.

Heads jerked and saw chunks of the plane breaking off: white metal from a milk truck, red fenders from a tractor, tin sheets from old outhouses...

As the right wing snapped away, the plane spun upside down. Old Man Fibber was belted in tight, but Carl was still there on the floor and he dropped like a bomb. He might have even plunged down onto Ben's family, but Old Man Fibber managed to catch the big turtle as he fell.

Then the flaming plane, spewing black smoke and bits of ice cream truck, continued its beeline for the water tower and barreled upside down into the Marching Moose mascot. The spinning propeller tore through the painted metal and shattered the cookie sheets into ragged shards that went flying in all directions. The town's water supply poured out

the hole in a great gush, dousing the fiery plane to a smoking, sizzling steel husk.

Old Man Fibber sat there upside down in the cockpit, Carl hugged in his arms, and both of them blubbering for air in the flood of water—but they didn't have half a cat scratch between them.

Yet your Grandpa Gristle wasn't so lucky. I was there by the water tower when the plane hit, held tight in Mama's arms. And one of those shards of cookie sheet came flying right for my head.

Final Formation

Two months broiled by. Summer was now easing into fall—in fact, it was the last day of summer vacation.

The Marching Moose were back on Olympus Field, in full uniform, rehearsing for the performance looming the next day. It was the annual performance to mark the new school year and introduce the new members of the marching band. The whole town would be turning out again.

Mayor Sackbutt stood before the Marching Moose, fifty strong. He straightened his tall moose hat and smoothed his silver sideburns. "Let's march through the finale now," he boomed.

The mayor's new uniform gleamed in the late afternoon sunlight. The rip to the seat of his pants might have been sewn back together by Dandy, the Boony Point tailor, but the mayor had decided it was time to trade in the snug old uniform for a larger size.

But it still looked about two sizes too small.

And in his hand was the bone-baton, tenderly cleaned and polished. Mayor Sackbutt held up the shining white bone and beckoned to the small boy with the mop of crazy blond curls.

Benjamin Boyd was standing in the rear, among the drums and cymbals and triangles. He was lost there in the forest of taller children—and even lost in his own baggy brown uniform, which still needed tailoring by the overworked Dandy—but his face was beaming brighter than a supernova sunflower. The bad ankle now healed, he strutted quickly to the mayor's side, his hands tingling on the Giant Heart bongos.

"Ready?" whispered the mayor, grinning down at Ben. His teeth were clenched on the silver whistle.

Ben smiled and nodded.

Mayor Sackbutt blew two long blasts, then three short tweets, and the Marching Moose erupted in song. They went high-stepping down the field, sounding the big finale that the mayor himself had composed after the tryouts. It was a tribute to Mayor Olympus and his marching band.

It was called "Long Live the Moose!"

Now remember this: Grown-ups say you control your own fate in this world, and that may be true up to a point. But my ear and I happen to know that sometimes the simple difference in a destiny is just where you happen to be standing that day. And for Ben, if he had been a fraction to one side when the ogre stepped toward him, well, I don't imagine Mayor Sackbutt would have chosen him for the Marching Moose. Even a miracle worker like Doc Sprinkle couldn't have saved a single pinky.

Yet Doc Sprinkle did have a life to save that day. After retrieving his doctor's bag from his office (and leaving Agnes behind in the yard with her sweet potato), he scrambled up onto the monster's belly with his biggest scalpel. The moment he sliced through the hair and skin, poor Stanley popped right out, coughing and gasping for air.

Of course, the grizzly bear's fur was so badly matted by the ogre's goo that he had to be shaved from head to foot. But two months later, it was already growing back. And Stanley had even begun dancing again, in a new plum-colored tutu.

Ben's eyes flicked toward the bleachers as he marched past, thumping on his bongos alongside sweaty Mayor Sackbutt. The band had formed a picture of baby Norman, loping on three legs.

The stage was gone now, and the stands were empty—that is, except for one small person, sitting there in the front row: Grandma. Her hair still hadn't grown back, but the blond wig was on her head and the faded yellow ribbons were tied carefully in bows around the golden curls.

Next to her on the bench was a large red case with rusty brass trim. The case was open and empty...well, except for a copy of *King Grub*, with a bookmark peeking from it. (Reading had replaced those practical jokes—at least most of the time.)

And in Grandma's hands was a red accordion, shiny as a ripe crabapple. She was squeezing it happily, playing along with the marching band.

Grandma continued eating crabapple pie for almost a year, and Henry the Eighth and the herd now let her pass without so much as a dribble down their chins—but her hair never did grow back. Still, she seemed to find comfort in spending her afternoons sitting in the bleachers, pumping along during marching band practice.

Mayor Sackbutt even made her an honorary member of the Marching Moose.

Across the field from Grandma stood Boony Point's sparkling new water tower. Oh, Loudmouth had crowed that he could weld a patch across the old one, like he did before when Ben's father drilled it with the shotgun. But the hole from Old Man Fibber's plane was big as a barn door and the town wasn't fixed to wait six months to take a bath.

As it was, we waited six weeks for the new tower to be delivered from Bloat City. (The tower was in stock, but it took time to add a faithful reproduction of the mascot first painted by Mayor Olympus.) Still, everyone understood it was Old Man Fibber who deserved the apology for all the dishonor he had suffered over the years. And once he and Carl were safely back on the ground, he was never called Fibber again.

He was known, forever after, as Airborne.

The Marching Moose played on, now striding across the field in a long formation resembling the bone-baton. As the band headed toward the water tower, Ben's gaze fell on a wide spread of brown earth that stood out from the rest of the grassy-green field and stretched before the statue of Mayor Olympus. Ben noticed that the first sprouts of grass had begun to grow there.

Below that brown earth is where the ogre was buried, along with its eyeball.

A handful of folks—like Schemer, who owned the Olympus Gift Shop—had wanted to stuff the monster in a dancing pose to attract the tourists. But the rest of the town wasn't keen on tour buses rolling through Boony Point at all hours and alarming the children.

Walter Boyd, who once dreamed of flaunting the dead ogre far and wide, insisted the creature be laid to rest at Olympus Field.

He also came to feel differently about the new nickname the town honored him with: "Monster-Heart Bull's-Eye Blaster." He naturally preferred the sound of that to "Water Boy," but he took no pride in it. In fact, after he won that fall's Boony Point Shootout and claimed the record for most victories, he was able to get the town to drop "Monster-Heart

Bull's-Eye Blaster" (which was quite a mouthful, anyway) and start calling him "Wonder Boy" again.

The Marching Moose now swung into the finish, their long formation shifting as they advanced on the glowing bronze statue by the water tower. Mayor Sackbutt blew another shrill signal with his whistle and the band instantly drew up, just paces from the patch of brown earth. Facing the statue of Mayor Olympus and Norman, the Marching Moose stepped high and blared the final notes of "Long Live the Moose!" Mayor Sackbutt's eyes shimmered with tears as he pumped the bone-baton into the air alongside Ben.

The sound blazed above Olympus Field, then flamed out. Faces somber, the Marching Moose froze in their final formation: the biggest, bravest grin in the whole state. Over in the bleachers, Grandma froze too, her accordion drained of air.

When the echo had died to silence, Mayor Sackbutt made a soft toot on his whistle. But no one moved, except Ben. He marched out ahead by himself, taking three quiet strides to the very edge of the ogre's grave.

He stopped, waited. Mayor Sackbutt blew another toot and the Marching Moose bowed their heads. Grandma bowed her head too.

Then Ben raised his hands and brought them down on his bongos. He thumped the drum with all his might, all his heart, and the glorious sound of the Giant Heart bongos rang the highest heaven. He closed his eyes; he pictured the ogre dancing. And as he played, varying the rhythm, varying the speed, the ogre followed, full of grace, full of beauty, dancing on and on and on...

A tear rolled down Ben's cheek and he was done.

The tribute to Mayor Olympus and his Marching Moose—and the dancing ogre that had eaten them all—was over.

In the hush that now shrouded Olympus Field, Ben turned and marched back to Mayor Sackbutt's side. He bowed his head, like the others.

But the mayor stole a smile at Ben. "Scrumptious," he whispered from the corner of his mouth.

And then, on the heels of that praise came the nickname Ben would be known by for the next six years he played with the Marching Moose. In fact, it was the name he would be known by for the rest of his life, while captivating the whole state—the whole world, even—with his dazzling displays on the Giant Heart bongos.

Dragon Hands? Ben's heart soared at the thought.

"Simply scrumptious…Butterfingers."

A Shining Example

BUTTERFINGERS?

Ben's heart crashed. But moments later, he understood why Mayor Sackbutt thought the name still fit. After all, the mayor told him, what better nickname was there for a boy so scrumptious on the bongos, with hands churning out sounds as smooth and sweet as fresh butter?

I guess it all goes to show: In the end, it isn't you that needs changing, not really. You just grow into who you already are and change the way you eye yourself. You eye things in silver instead of gray.

Life will still have its boils, but all that beauty, all around at every thump of your little heart, will be far easier to see.

Put that in your piggybank.

As for your Grandpa Gristle, that ragged piece of cookie sheet came swooping at me like a tomahawk and cut my ear clean off.

Big and sharp as it was, I'm blessed it didn't lop off my whole head to boot.

I was just a baby, and I didn't even know how many ears I started with, really, but I was pretty sure I had lost one of them. So I let out my loudest, most woeful wail.

Mama took one look at me and started screaming too. It's not every day your newborn loses an ear, after all.

Discovering me earless, Papa dove to the grass. It was a big ear, for an infant, but Papa couldn't find it among the rubble of the plane.

At last, just as Stanley came popping out of the ogre's belly like a jack-in-the-box, Papa spotted it and hollered for

Doc Sprinkle.

Doc Sprinkle hurried over and laid me on the quilt. He took my ear from Papa and sewed it right back on.

I wore that ear for another week, but it slowly shriveled like a dried fig. Doc Sprinkle tried what may to save it, but finally he could only cut it free, leaving me with this handsome hunk of gristle.

I won't kid you, it's rough losing an ear, especially your favorite one. But growing up, armed with my teddy bear, I still made the most of who I am—and Butterfingers Boyd was my shining example. Maybe another night, when your dear mother is again occupied, your Grandpa Gristle can tell you more tales from times gone by.

But for now, sleep tight. This story is at an end.

And that, bedbugs, is how I lost my ear.

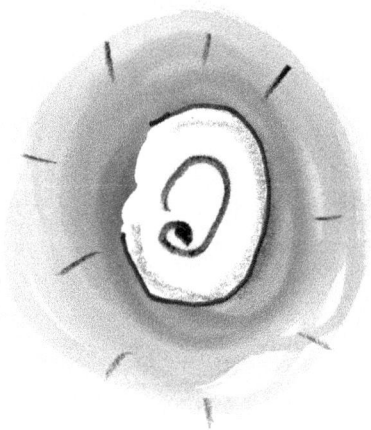

Adam BECK
author

Adam Beck is the author of the popular non-fiction book *Maximize Your Child's Bilingual Ability* and founder of the blog Bilingual Monkeys (http://bilingualmonkeys.com) and the forum The Bilingual Zoo (http://bilingualzoo.com). He lives in Hiroshima, Japan.

Simon FARROW
illustrator

Simon Farrow was educated at Loughborough College of Art and Design and has worked as a packaging designer and commercial illustrator for many years. He lives in Leicester, England.